Banner's Renegade

Banner's Series Book Three

Carole Ann Lee

Published by Rogue Phoenix Press, LLP
Copyright © 2020

ISBN: 978-1-62420-570-5

Credits
Cover Artist: Designs by Ms G
Editor: Christine Young

Dedication

To Rod, my very own noble rogue who so good naturedly pulled Clint Banner aside and taught him a few things.

I wish to thank Christine Young. Without your advice, encouragement and patience, Clint Banner's story might not have been told.

A special thank you also, to Genene Valleau for all your hard work in bringing Clint Banner to life on the cover.

And as always, thank you to Holly for your constant support, and for knowing when I could do better and not letting me get by with less. Also thank you, my friend, for that very special trailer hitch. You *know* which one.

PROLOGUE

2173
Earth–United States of America
Newtown, South Carolina

A vicious backhand sent her slamming against the wall where she slid to the floor like melted butter. For a few blinding seconds, Angela laid there numbly staring up into her husband's enraged face. Mason Cooper was furious, shouting obscenities, accusations and threats, none of which were making any sense. A lance of severe pain shot clear to her shoulder when he grabbed her by the wrist, violently yanking her to her feet for a fresh tide of punishment.

"You want a divorce? You got it, babe. And you have exactly six days to get yourself together and find somewhere else to stay." He slapped her. Hard—shoving her to the floor once again as he did so. "Just so you know," he snarled, looking down at her with sheer disgust, "I never did want to marry you in the first place." She could feel the hot imprint of Mason's heavy hand forming on her cheek. "You were never my type," he snarled, "but both of our fathers insisted that marriage to you would be good for business. And you know what? They were right. Because now that your daddy is out of the picture, and once I'm rid of you, I will be the sole owner of Southern Charm Development." Grabbing her by her hair, he jerked her once again to her feet, ignoring her resulting cry. "You see," he continued, his face mere inches from hers, "once I legally deny that brat you're carrying, there'll be no question of who gets the best end of the divorce."

"What are you talking about?" she cried. "*You're* the father,

Mason!"

"The hell I am."

"But a DNA test will prove—"

"Nothing. Absolutely nothing, Angela." He smiled and slowly shook his head "I've already arranged it. DNA will only prove that I'm not the father. You think I don't know about your Acacian lover? Believe me I made it a point to cover all the bases. You can take it as high as you want to take it and still you won't win." He smiled, "Ahhh, it's so nice having powerful friends in all the right places."

At her stunned expression, he added, "Plus, I've even got witnesses willing to testify of your infidelity."

It was a lie—all a horrible lie. There had never been anyone else, and he knew it. Angela tried getting up and failed when his expensive booted foot knocked her back down.

His laugh was without humor. "Here I've been working day and night, trying to give you a good life—to be a loving husband. And what do you do? You've been seeing your flyboy on the sly and got yourself knocked-up when I've been out of town on business. You're nothing but a whore. And that's exactly how the court will see you."

"You know that isn't true," she cried.

He ignored her. "Such a shame," he continued with mock disappointment. "You could have had it all, but instead you threw it all away.

"Oh, and one more thing. Take your damned dog with you. But you're not taking Piper." He laughed. "She's sold."

"No!" Angela cried, once again struggling to get up. And once again, he planted his boot on her shoulder and gave her another hard shove, sending her back to the tiled floor.

"The mare's mine! You can't sell her, Mason!"

"Wanna bet?"

He started to turn away but then stopped. "Oh, and one more little thing. I can't remember if I ever expressed my sympathy about your momma dying along with your daddy in that accident. She was an unforeseen victim. I always liked her. Unfortunately, there was no way

2

to predict who was going to be in the vehicle that day."

"What are you saying?"

He smiled down on her, and with a wink added, "You're a smart girl. You think about it."

Too numb to fully understand, too shocked to even think, let alone believe what he'd just implied, Angela remained on the floor as he turned and stormed out, slamming the door behind him.

She was a mess. Her face and eyes burned from being backhanded. Her nose was bleeding. She was sure a rib was cracked, and her shoulder throbbed as if it had been ripped from its socket.

As his fancy sports car screamed out of the drive, spraying gravel in its wake, Angela knew he wouldn't be back until sometime tomorrow afternoon. She had originally planned to leave him two weeks from now, but it seemed that her plans would have to change. For all she knew, Mason had a fatal accident planned for her. If she were to die, his problems would be over, leaving him the poor grieving husband.

If she left tonight, it would also mean she would have to get in touch with Rae Banner and change the previous arrangements for transportation. As it was, preparations had been made for Max Banner to rendezvous with her at the Pacific Northwest Intergalactic Spaceport. But now she was leaving earlier than planned.

With her arms gently enfolding her slightly rounded belly, Angela inhaled a painful breath and tried to rise to her feet. only to fall back onto the floor. She had to get up if she was going to escape tonight. There was too much to do.

She just prayed the baby was alright. Despite the pain and shock she had gone through, she had been ever mindful of the tiny life growing beneath her heart and had always tried her best to deflect any blows aimed at her stomach.

With her mind spinning, she struggled once more to get up and made it this time. She'd have to take one of the trucks and a horse trailer to haul Piper. As far as the vehicles were concerned, she'd leave them parked at the spaceport and let Mason figure out how to get them back.

~ * ~

Another rut in the highway grabbed the wheel, threatening to jerk it from her hands. Angela fought to get the rig under control. The way things were, there was no other option but to travel the old abandoned interstate system across the United States. Truth was, had she chosen to travel on the main interstate system, it would have saved her several days, yes, but Mason would have had his goons out looking for her and dragging her back before she'd even started.

Having been forced to leave earlier than planned, Angela had chosen the middle of the night to make her escape. Loading her mare into a trailer and her dog, Trixie, into one of the trucks, she made her escape and headed for the Pacific Northwest. If nothing else she would at least have a good head start on Mason's trackers.

There were a couple of ways she could have chosen to make the journey west. She almost headed north and followed the Canadian border west. As it was, to take the back roads instead of the main interstate seemed the safest way to go, especially hauling Piper. A truck pulling a horse trailer would have stood out like a beacon on a main interstate.

With the previous arrangements already made to rendezvous with Max Banner at the Pacific Northwest Intergalactic Spaceport, she wasn't sure what to do since she would now get there way too early, and what would she do with the animals while waiting? Hopefully it won't be too much trouble to bump up the rendezvous a week or two earlier.

She would love to be a fly on the wall when Mason finds out. She could just envision his fury. She could picture him, uncouth and foul-mouthed as he threatened his men to find her or else. Though her face hurt to grin, Angela couldn't help grinning at how smoothly she'd pulled it off. And knowing Mason, he'd figure she was just stupid enough to try to escape him on the new highway—at least Angela was counting on him thinking that. And the very fact that no one had discovered her yet, only confirmed her hopes that Mason was not checking the old Interstate for her. At least not yet.

Hopefully, he hadn't put security tracers on the work trucks.

Tracers were a theft defense that he had automatically installed on the other vehicles. Angela prayed that the work truck and horse trailer were not important enough to have a tracer on them. Again, she felt sure she would have been caught by now otherwise.

With a trailing cloud of dust in her wake and having maneuvered around literally dozens of "Abandoned Highway" blockades, she had just crossed over the Indiana border into Illinois. The first blush of dawn was beginning to brighten the eastern sky behind her. In the distance to the west, the city lights of Danberg were glowing as she approached on old I-74. Nearly thirty-six hours had passed since leaving South Carolina. And actually, she had made pretty good time, but she needed to find a place to pull over and rest—somewhere quiet and secluded where she could let Trixie out again, check on her mare, call Rae, and hopefully catch an hour's sleep before pulling back onto the road.

Her shoulder and arm were aching fiercely from when Mason roughly yanked her up off the floor by one arm. And it hadn't helped to be struggling with the steering wheel as the truck lurched down the old unimproved Interstate.

At last spying a good place to pull over, she steered the rig onto the shoulder of the abandon highway to park beneath a stand of tall timber. The trees grew close together and hung out over the highway enough so that they completely cloaked her truck and trailer from any eyes-in-the-sky. Eyes that Mason may have out searching for her.

The first thing she did was let Trixie out then she went back to check on Piper. If her entire body didn't hurt so badly, she would have gotten the mare out and walked her around a bit. But Angela just didn't have the strength to muscle a nervous mare. It was all she could do to force herself to freshen Piper's water, give her a handful of grain and a flake of hay.

"Now to call Rae," she murmured as she limped back to the truck and climbed in behind the wheel. Retrieving her personal *messenger* from her travel pack, she punched in Rae's code then settled back for the wait. Knowing from experience that it would be a long wait considering the call was traveling from Earth to Acacia, she leaned back, closed her eyes and waited.

Two hours and forty minutes later... "Hello? Angie? Are you there? ... Hello?"

Angela awoke with a start and scrambled for her *messenger*. "Hello? Rae, I'm here!"

"There you are. What's going on?"

Blinking back tears at the sound of Rae's voice, Angela was unable to speak past the lump in her throat. "Oh..." she finally managed in a tiny, strained voice. "Just Mason."

"What's he done now? Everything's still on, isn't it?"

"Well, that's what I'm calling about. Yes. Everything is still on, but I left Mason last night." Angela went on, telling what had happened, how Mason had become violent again, how he had said she couldn't have Piper, and that she had six days to get out.

"So, you left last night?"

"Yes. After he stormed out of the house."

"Does he know you left?"

"I would imagine he does by now." Angela said. "And that I've taken Piper with me."

"Where are you now?"

"I Just crossed over into Illinois. I'm not even half way across the states yet. I need time to heal up before I can make it much farther."

"He beat you again. Right?"

In answer Angela turned the camera on herself, "This is what *just* my face looks like. And the rest of me doesn't look much better. I have bruises on top of bruises."

She heard Rae's gasp upon seeing the picture. "What the hell did he do to you?"

"The usual. Only worse this time."

"That sonofa—"

"Plus... I think he was responsible, or at least involved in planning the accident that killed my parents. He basically admitted it." Angela blinked back more tears that were threatening to fall.

"Oh Angie, I am so sorry. I'm glad you're finally out of there.

Listen," Rae said fervently, "you need a safe place to rest up for at least three weeks if not four. And I think I might just know someone you can stay with. I'm hoping she won't be too far off course from where you are. She has horses and would be able to keep Piper for you while you recover. Tell me again, where exactly are you?"

"Just outside of Danberg, Illinois on old I-74."

"Okay, let me see how close you two are—or if this is even doable for you." Rae was silent for a moment as she quickly began skimming over a map she'd pulled up. "You say you're on the old highway? The one that's closed, right? Not the new one."

"Yes, the old one."

From there, Rae entered both her friend's address and Angela's location. More silence. Then... "Angie! Good news. She's about a hundred miles northwest of you! Basically, right on your way. What time is it there now?"

Angela glanced at the chronometer mounted in the truck's dash. "It's five forty in the morning."

"Okay. Tell me... are you safe where you are?"

"Yes, I think so."

"Good. Then stay put. I'm going to wait another half hour before I call Nora. It may take a while to get back to you, but I'll get back as soon as I can."

"Okay..." The tears started falling. "Rae, I don't know how to thank you," she said softly.

"Nonsense. You'd do the same for me. Now, you stay put and if you can, try to catch some sleep while you're waiting."

"I'll try."

~ * ~

Rae's friend, Nora, had proven to be a godsend. A throwback from the mid nineteen sixties, it was as if Nora was straight out of the hippie generation—best known back then for their peace marches and love-your-neighbor lifestyle.

7

Somewhere in her fifties and widowed, Nora was a beautiful woman, tall and slender with coppery skin, dark eyes and a ready smile. Long salt and pepper hair hung in a single thick braid to the small of her back with a black tipped eagle feather secured in it. Circling her head was a delicately braided leather crown band that spanned her forehead. Several turquoise beads were woven into the band, and on her feet were a pair of calf-high bleached leather moccasins with fringe and more turquoise beads to match the crown band. She wore a chambray blouse and a mid-length denim skirt that just barely met the top of her moccasins when she walked.

It was an unusual look, but Nora was an unusual woman that seemed very comfortable in her chosen style.

Rae had explained enough of Angela's predicament that Nora jumped at the chance to help out. She just so happened to have a fully furnished garage-apartment that had recently become vacant. With one bedroom, a large living room, kitchen and full bath, it was perfect. There was even room in the barn to hide Angela's truck and trailer from prying eyes.

Upon seeing for herself the condition Angela was in, Nora immediately told her not to worry about Piper or Trixie, promising that they would want for nothing. Later that next day, she shared with Angela that she was of Native American descent and that her great, great, great grandmother was a full-blooded Lakota Sioux Medicine Woman. Nora explained that much of her grandmother's knowledge had been passed down to her through the generations. "If it's alright," Nora asked kindly, "I would like very much to treat your worst injuries during your stay. I know I can speed the healing for you."

At Angela's consent, Nora quickly disappeared, returning with a colorful and intricately woven basket laden with a mug and a decanter containing some sort of tea. Also in the basket lay a small bowl with a white paste-like mixture that Nora said was a combination of freshly ground oak gall and the juice of milkweed.

She handed the tea mixture to Angela "Drink it all," she said, "it's white willow bark tea. And to answer any concerns you might have, it's a weak mixture and won't hurt you. But it will help with the pain." The tea was cool and felt like heaven to her dry mouth and throat, and despite its bitterness, she drank it all.

Nora then asked Angela to lie down on a nearby cot. From there she began a thorough examination, gently touching, poking and nudging every inch of Angela's battered body from head to foot until she was satisfied. By the time Nora was done, Angela's clothing had been embarrassingly reduced to simply her under things.

"Well, other than one fractured rib, at least you don't have any other broken bones, although I am afraid your shoulder will take more skill than I am able to offer. You will need to see a physician." She then reached for the bowl with the white paste and using her fingers she began gently smoothing the paste on all the areas of scraped and broken skin. And as she applied the paste, Nora murmured strange words in a soft, musical, chant-like dialect.

At last Nora straightened and began replacing her supplies back in the basket. "It's a miracle your baby is unharmed," she said as a matter of fact.

Angela's jaw dropped. "How di... How did you know I'm pregnant?"

Nora's knowing smile was subtle as she replied, "I knew you were with child the instant you drove onto the property."

~ * ~

What Angela thought might be as long as two weeks, had turned into four weeks and ready or not, it was time to head back onto the road.

Thanks to Nora's continued attentions, the worst of Angela's bruising and scrapes had faded to the point of being hardly noticeable. Her shoulder, however, was an entirely different story. It was just as painful as ever, and Nora, in a motherly fashion, cautioned Angela not to stress her shoulder any more than absolutely necessary. And once she got to the Banners, she should see a physician.

Promising she would, Angela offered to pay Nora for the use of the apartment as well as Nora's excellent care of herself and her animals, but Nora wouldn't have it, saying the apartment was empty anyway and that she had her own horses and dog to care for. What's one more? As for her care of Angela…she explained that she would not take payment for that. Healing was a gift bestowed upon her by her ancestors, to be used without restriction or payment. Still, Angela handed her a small clutch of credits that was more than enough to cover the feed and care she had given to Piper and Trixie.

What no one but Angela knew was that she had electronically cleared out Mason's bank account when she left him. So, she had plenty of credits to travel with and get settled once she found a place to live.

It wasn't long before she was slowly backing the truck and trailer out of the barn and loading up Piper. Once again, she thanked Nora for everything and with a hug and a wave goodbye, she turned out onto the road and headed for the old interstate to continue her trek west.

As the countryside whizzed by, Angela thought back to the very first time she had accompanied her father on one of his many business trips to Acacia to meet with Rae's father, Max Banner. She'd been almost twelve at the time, and she and Rae had formed a fast friendship. As time passed—even after her father no longer had business connections with Max—Angela would often make the trip alone to spend the entire *Solstice* on Acacia with Rae and her family. Early teens by then, the girls had always managed to find plenty of fun and giggles between sharing secrets, their love of horses, and their growing interest in boys.

And now she had been in touch with Rae almost daily over the past month. Since leaving Nora, arrangements had once again been made to rendezvous at the Pacific Northwest Intergalactic Spaceport. Only this time Rae had explained that her father would not be the one picking her up as originally planned. He had business obligations this time so her brother, Clint, would be the one meeting her at the spaceport. "You remember Clint, don't you?" Rae had asked innocently, to which Angela had responded by faking a foggy memory. "Clint. He's your oldest brother. Right?" Little did Rae know that even as an early teen, Angela had had a girlhood crush on Clint from the first day she had met him.

Clint... he always had a beautiful girl at his side back then and hardly knew Angela even existed.

By the time Angela was almost eighteen, she had returned for another six-week visit. The memory was still vivid as she thought back to that sultry evening. The Banner family had gathered at the main house for dinner. One of the few times when everyone was able to get together.

Angela had stepped out onto the back porch to find Clint standing at the porch rail, deep in thought as he gazed out over the landscape.

"I wondered where you'd disappeared to?" Angela said, stepping out to join him. "Aren't you going to have dessert?"

"Tell Delta I'll take it to go."

"You're not leaving already, are you?"

"'Fraid I have an early get-up in the morning."

Angela stepped closer. "Where are you heading off to this time, Clint?"

He straightened to his full height and turned to face her. "Terrace."

"Terrace? Doesn't it take a long time just to get there?"

"Nine weeks."

"Oh... then I imagine you'll still be gone by the time I head back home."

"Yeah, no doubt."

"Well, then I might as well say goodbye now." Feeling as if she were drawn into a trance, impulsively she raised up on tiptoe and timidly pressed her mouth to his cheek. Then, horrified by what she had just done, she quickly stepped back.

Clint grinned. "That was real nice, sunshine," he said, "but I think we can say goodbye, a little better than that." And before Angela knew what he was about, he had drawn her into his arms and kissed her full on the mouth.

A flash of heat streaked through her, making her heart throb. Her knees buckled, and only his arm about her waist kept her on her feet. Stunned, Angela found herself, for one passionate moment, kissing him back.

When he finally released his hold on her, she simply remained in his loose embrace, blushing feverishly as she looked up into his face. He was so tall, so handsome... and so—

"Well, Bro, I certainly hope we're not interrupting anything," Nick said as he and Zeke, with stupid grins on their faces, stepped out onto the porch.

With a squeal of distress, Angela tore herself out of Clint's arms. Brushing past Nick and Zeke, she disappeared into the house. She'd barely gotten out of sight before she heard a burst of male laughter as Nick razzed Clint about robbing the cradle.

~ * ~

It wasn't long after he returned from Terrace that Clint had applied for, and was accepted at the University of Texas for their Petroleum Geology program. His focus was on a BA degree. Once he had graduated, he had returned to Acacia and applied for off-campus schooling to earn his Masters.

And now, five years had passed since Angela had last seen Clint. It had been during the time when he was attending the University. She had initially invited him to come for Christmas, and that was the beginning of a friendship that grew to be more than simply friends. When graduation time came and Clint was preparing to return to Acacia, he'd asked Angela to return with him. By then things had gotten serious enough that they had discussed marriage. *Discussed,* however, was the key word. Angela was crazy about him—had been for years—would have married him in a heartbeat. Clint, although seemingly serious about her, had never officially asked her to marry him. He did, however, talk about needing to find a job while working on his Masters. Another thing that concerned Angela was that to her knowledge, Clint had never mentioned anything to his family about their relationship. If he had, Rae obviously would have known about it. In truth, Angela was never sure just where exactly she fit into Clint's life. Therefore, when her father asked her to stay at least six months until he could find a replacement for her in the accounting department of Southern Charm Development, she agreed. Southern Charm was a growing property development partnership between her father and Mason's father, George Cooper.

Clint reluctantly complied with her decision to stay back until they hired a replacement. However, after the first month or two, he quit contacting her—just stopped entirely. And no matter how many times she had sent messages off to him, he never responded. Consequently, she remained permanently in South Carolina and ended up seeing more and more of George's son, Mason, who'd been treating her like a queen. It was only inevitable that Mason would cast a shadow on her fascination with Clint. And when Mason asked her to marry him, she'd said yes.

With a sigh, Angela lifted her sights and gazed into the distance. Tranquil mountains lay miles ahead, reaching into the sky with their muted shades of purples and blues. Just another mountain range in a list of several she had yet to cross before arriving at SeaPort.

So, what would she say to Clint? What would *he* say? Did he know she'd gotten married and was now in the process of a divorce? And what about him? Was he married? Without a doubt, it was going to be awkward, and she steeled herself for their inevitable meeting when the time came.

CHAPTER ONE

Pacific Northwest Intergalactic Spaceport

Helluva way to break-in a new ship. Leaning back against the massive landing jack of the *Aris,* Clint Banner mulled over the lame excuse his family had trumped-up to talk him into this trip. *Hey, Clint, how'd ya like to take the Aris on her maiden voyage*? It was a trip that his dad had originally planned to make a few weeks back, but things had ended up being postponed until now. Normally, Clint would have jumped at the opportunity to take a new ship on her maiden voyage. Truth was, he had responsibilities at home that made it difficult to leave for the two-month round trip to Earth and back. Yet the temptation was just too irresistible to pass up. Despite the fact that the *consignment,* as they called it, was a horse, it was a birthday present for his sister and he would have done it anyway.

Some guy named Wayne would be accompanying the mare, so all he had to do was make the rendezvous on time and transport them back. Seemed simple enough.

With a compressed sigh he glanced down at his watch. Twenty-three hundred hours on the nose. Well, he'd kept his end of the deal, *over two hours ago to be exact,* and so far, no horse. Having arrived early, he'd managed to stay busy by grabbing a quick bite at one of the spaceport cafes. He'd also picked up a few special requests to bring back home from Earth. Then he ran a routine diagnostic on the ship's system and finally entered return trip coordinates into the NAVCOMP.

Thing was, at this rate it wouldn't be long before he'd have to extend the use of the landing pad, which would be a pain in the butt because you don't just do it electronically like most ports. Instead, you have to show up in person at the main terminal. So typical of Earth regulations. Why do it the easy way when there's a hard way?

Absently, he lifted his focus to the high-gloss underbelly of the ship as it reflected the glow of buoy lights circling the perimeter of the landing pad. The *Aris* was not only the newest addition to BANNER TRANSPORT INC., she was now the second ship in the Banner line that looked like a purebred sitting among the mutts. Clint thought she looked sleek and exotic with her shiny, black and iridescent exterior. To look at her one way, the hull was glossy black, but to look at her from a different angle, subtle iridescent ghost flames seemed to blow back across the sides of her shiny black hull. No doubt about it, she was flashy and gorgeous and unbelievably fast for a mid-sized freight vessel. Even her living quarters were extravagant. In a way, her fancy interior reminded Clint of the *Windstar*—a yacht his father had purchased a few years back. It didn't take long to discover the *Windstar* had been previously owned by a contraband runner who'd had it enhanced in every way imaginable. The discovery had become the source of much laughter as he and his brothers razzed their dad of going pirate.

A distant flash of lightning drew Clint's attention. According to the locals, the night was unusually warm and muggy—charged—as encroaching clouds slowly blotted the stars from the sky. It was brewing up one doozer of a storm. All the more reason to get the horse loaded and be on their way.

So typical of any busy spaceport, the air was inundated with the combined stench of exhaust and ozone. Out of nowhere a muggy breeze swept across Clint's heated skin, ruffling a spike of hair down across his forehead. It was the sort of night where idle thoughts drifted to tangled sheets, scented skin and sated needs. A few notable memories came to mind, making it impossible to relax. Leaning back against the column of the landing jack he braced the sole of his boot against the massive footing, folded his arms and waited.

Thunder rumbled on the horizon and again Clint lifted his eyes as another flash brightened the southern sky. It would be raining soon. His gaze slid to the surrounding spaceport. Even at this late hour, the place was abuzz with activity. He'd deliberately requested a landing pad at the far end of the spaceport, hoping for some semblance of isolation and less stress for the mare. Yet in spite of his good intentions, only four vacant landing pads separated him from the rest of the busy port.

So much for isolation.

Located between the merging cities of Seattle and Portland, the Pacific Northwest Intergalactic Spaceport—loosely dubbed *SeaPort*—serviced the entire Pacific Northwest and was the second largest spaceport on the west coast of the United States. As was common for many Earth-based spaceports, this one was designed with moorings both above as well as below ground. Clint had seen his share of underground moorings, his own home planet, Acacia, being one. The main idea was to compact the port. The lower level also provided a safe quarter for long-term moorage.

A robo-loader lumbered by with three cargo trailers in tow. Clint idly watched it disappear down the corridor and around a curve. As always with a bustling port, there's never a dull moment. Three bays down, a fight had broken out between a couple of workers. Watching the fight progress into a four-man brawl, Clint winced as a solid punch dropped one man to his knees. *Oh yeah, that one hurt.* With two younger brothers, Clint was no stranger himself to a good fight. Nick, his hot-headed middle brother always had a knack for settling things with his fists. Those days were gone now. Nick had changed since Tressa came into his life. And now that the baby was born, he'd even quit smoking, which was a miracle in itself.

Clint recalled the recent birth of Nick's son. Tressa had hoped for a girl. Nick wanted a son. They could have easily predestined the baby's gender but had chosen the old-fashioned way of leaving things to fate. Clint would never forget the first words out of Nick's mouth. *"She's a boy!"* he announced enthusiastically as he introduced newborn Braeden Maxwell Banner to the family. It was a sight to behold, and one Clint would remember—Nick standing there looking shell shocked while a tiny red-faced bundle voiced his opinion of the world from his father's ungainly arms.

Didn't seem possible that such a little package had the power to cast a life-altering spell on the entire Banner clan. Yet the baby had, and Clint was far from immune. In fact, he'd been doing a lot of soul searching lately. At thirty-four he couldn't help wondering where his life was headed. Running Solarblaze was satisfying and kept him busy, but he wanted more than just running a drilling operation for the rest of his life.

Feminine laughter broke into his thoughts as two attractive women made their way toward a nearby shuttle stop. Though they appeared a cut above the usual variety that hung about the ports, Clint had them pegged nonetheless.

The one with short-spiked dark hair noticed him first and stopped dead in her tracks. "HEL... LO... Oh baby, where have you been hiding? You're hotter than July fireworks."

The leggy blonde stepped forward. "Waiting all by yourself tonight, handsome?" she asked with a sultry smile.

"'Fraid so."

She sighed. "Not a good night to be kept waiting all by yourself."

He grinned. "I agree, but wait I must."

"Want some company?" the brunette asked, cocking a shapely hip. "Because I guarantee that all by myself, I can turn you upside down and inside out with my tongue alone." She licked her lips in expectation. "And if you're man enough to handle both of us at once... we can take you places that sexy ship of yours has never been. Together, we can suck the chrome off of—"

Before she had even finished, Clint broke out laughing. He couldn't help it. Up until now, he thought he'd heard it all. "I'm not sure I'd survive without my chrome," he said still laughing.

"We'd go easy on you. Promise. You won't regret it."

"So, what do you say, darlin'?" the blonde piped up, encroaching a little closer.

At last he stifled his laughter long enough to respond, "Not tonight," he said in a tone that brooked no argument.

With a collective moan of disappointment, and one last admiring backward glance, the two women turned and continued their trek toward a nearby shuttle stop.

Another flash of lightning spiked down from the sky, once again warning of the on-coming storm. The spaceport was beginning to get busy. The sound of an approaching open shuttle caught his attention. He watched as three women seated near the rear of the shuttle chatted among themselves. He figured them to be tourists on their way to somewhere special, excited and laughing over something one of them had said. There was an interesting age-gap between them and he idly wondered if they were friends or family. When the shuttle stopped across the causeway from him to pick up more passengers, the ladies suddenly turned quiet. That's when he heard, "Lord... have... mercy..." drifting across the tarmac. The older of the three was looking directly at him. Elbowing the others, and with a jerk of her head, she had all three of them gawking his direction. Clint casually glanced about to see what the hell they were craning their necks over.

As if on cue, another clap of thunder rumbled across the sky, and as the shuttle began pulling away, all three ladies continued staring. The youngest, who looked to be no more than a teenager, smiled shyly and waved at him with an index finger. With a cordial nod, he smiled back. The oldest of the three said something to her companions and with a bit of drama, frantically fanned her face with a splayed hand. The last woman simply stared until the shuttle disappeared around a curve. Like smoke in the wind, their chatter and peals of giggles drifted into the night air.

With a heavy sigh, Clint looked away. He used to soak up that sort of female admiration—thrived on it. Not so much anymore. As of late, he'd found himself needing more than the casual passage of women through his life. Plain and simple, he wanted what Nick and Zeke both had. The feeling wasn't new. This longing had been gnawing away at him for months. He'd had his share of gorgeous women over the years. It was past time he settled down. He needed a family to love, and to be loved in return. He wanted kids and a wife to come home to at the end of the day—a woman to share his life instead of a "trophy" hanging on his arm for all to see. Oh, it was fun back then—when he, Nick and Zeke were all in direct competition to see who could outdo the other when it came to beautiful women. But those days were gone. Times had changed.

For now, however, it was impossible to move forward with his life until he extricated himself from the one problem that was still hanging on. Shelbi, who couldn't, wouldn't accept that it was over between them and time to move on.

To be truthful, he actually found it surprising that right now he was drawing any female attention at all. He was sure he looked pretty rough, given the fact that he was not only windblown, but he hadn't shaved since he'd left Acacia two weeks ago. But judging from the unbidden attention he'd gotten so far, who knows, maybe Pacific Northwest women just happen to like their men unkempt. He silently laughed. For all he knew, *rough* might be the latest trend these days. If so, he was right in style.

CHAPTER TWO

A high-pitched whinny suddenly rose above the howling turbines of a nearby freighter. Clint turned to watch as a small man steadily led a nervous, crow-hopping horse toward the *Aris*. Every now and then a scruffy little black and white dog would come into view trailing behind the horse.

Still leaning against the column of the landing jack, Clint watched them advance. Something about the handler had his undivided attention. He watched through narrowed eyes as the trio advanced, moving in and out of the shadows. They were too far away to make a call, but there was something about the handler—he just didn't move like a guy for Clint's peace of mind. He'd seen slight-built men before, but this one didn't quite— Suddenly he caught a brief glimpse of cutoffs, shapely legs and ankle-high work boots before they disappeared into the darkness again. With a compressed exhale, he pulled away from the footing and turned to make his way toward the loading ramp.

The horse was flighty, skittish, the staccato of shod hooves on the tarmac becoming more pronounced the closer they got, yet the handler continued maintaining a calm control as they drew nearer.

It wasn't until they moved into full view that Clint's suspicions fully manifested themselves. Immediately his eyes slid to the shapely legs he'd only glimpsed earlier. And by the time the trio was drawing to a halt before him, his shocked eyes were fastened on... surprise, surprise, *Angela Wayne*.

Damn that Nick. Both he and Zeke had planned this all along. They knew Angela was the one accompanying the horse, and they'd led him to believe some guy named Wayne would be bringing the mare. There was no doubt but that Nick was behind it. Ever since that long-ago night when he and Zeke had intruded on him and Angela on the back porch, Nick never failed to remind Clint about robbing the cradle. Hell, they're probably still laughing at how he'd fallen for this latest prank. Dammit, it wasn't funny.

"Hello Clint." It had been a while, and she had definitely grown up since he'd last seen her. Still, had there been any question of who she was, her smoky contralto voice left no doubt.

"Angela," he replied with a curt nod. He idly studied her as she held the mare's lead rope in one hand. Removing a leather glove with her teeth, she fished for something in a hip pocket. Nearby lights glinted off wisps of her honey blonde hair. He suspected that at one point it had been pulled back into a pony tail and stuffed through the back of the ball cap. Escaping damp straggles now clung loosely about her face.

At last she handed over a folded document, and while he looked over the bill of sale, she spoke to the horse in gentle undertones. The dog lay at her feet, wary, unblinking eyes tracking Clint's every move.

"I trust you're all set up inside?" she asked.

"I hope so. Far as I know Rae had everything you asked for delivered, loaded and placed where you wanted them."

"Good. The sooner we get her on board, the better."

"I agree. Let's get it done." Withdrawing a remote from his pocket, Clint punched in a code. Overhead the bay door slid open and lights snapped to life, illuminating both the loading ramp as well as the inside of the cargo hold.

"Need help?" he asked.

"No thanks, I got it. Besides, she doesn't know you. You'd just complicate matters."

Well, far be it from him to complicate matters. Clint stepped back, folded his arms and watched as Angela tried coaxing the horse onto the ramp. He knew of one sure way to speed the process along, but he doubted his sister or Angela would approve. Even with the dog helping, it took over twenty-five minutes of gentle, low-voiced sweet-talk before the mare had all fours on the base of the ramp. He lost count of how many times the horse had backed off and Angela had to start all over again. Finally, with the dog growling and nipping wildly at the horse's heels, they made it up the ramp and into the cool interior of the ship's cargo bay.

A padded box stall had been erected in the right corner specifically for the trip. Feed sat to the left. A large pile of fresh shavings had been deposited along the aft wall as well as a sizable drop box for the used shavings. Everything was all set.

Completely absorbed in her work, Angela began preparing the mare for the voyage while the dog once again hugged the floor, chin resting between front paws, and attention equally divided between Angela and Clint.

Clint busied himself with meaningless tasks. Being sneaky was hardly his style, but for the time being it served a purpose—allowing him to satisfy his curiosity about the woman Angela had become.

As if suddenly sensing his attention, she looked up, their eyes locking. Clint, without missing a beat, smiled pleasantly and nodded to the safety harness she was fastening in place on the mare. "Quite a contraption you got there."

"I beg your pardon?"

With a soft huff of laughter, he clarified, "That harness."

"Oh. Yes," she replied, resuming her task of securing the horse. "It's necessary to keep her from becoming injured during takeoffs and landings."

"Ahh..." Clint continued studying her a moment longer, not bothering to explain that take-offs and landings were hardly noticeable with this particular ship. Well, holler if you change your mind about needing help."

No response.

Banking his thoughts for the moment, Clint turned for the exit, "Angela, if you need me, I'll be in the helm. When you're done here, come on forward."

"How long before we'll be leaving, do you think?"

"Just as soon as you're ready."

"I'm ready now."

"Then follow me, and let's put this baby into space."

Angela turned to the dog. "Trixie, stay." Making one final check on Piper, she followed Clint out of the hold, down a narrow corridor that led along the starboard side of the ship's luxurious living quarters and finally into the helm.

There she remained, anchored at the top of a short metal companionway that descended into a sunken command center. The complexity of the wrap-around helm was impressive with its multitude of switches, screens and tiny winking monitor lights. She watched Clint drop into the command seat and began waking up the onboard computer.

"It's okay. Come on down and grab a seat," he said without taking his eyes off the console.

The ship was beginning to come to life. Subtle vibrations played softly beneath Angela's feet as she made her way down the steps to settle into a leather seat to the right of Clint.

She turned to look out the starboard viewport. Outside, high intensity flood lights mounted beneath the belly of the ship snapped to life, engulfing the landing pad. Two small pulsing strobe lights danced on the tip of a swept-back wing, and in the distance beyond, another fork of lightning spiked downward out of the encroaching darkness.

"I realize this isn't your first trip off-planet," he said, still absorbed in the pre-lift tasks. "But the *Aris* is a hybrid," he continued. "She's a cross between a pleasure yacht and a mid-sized freighter." He turned to face her. "Hopefully, she'll help make this trip quick and as painless as possible."

Angela smiled. "Thank you." Wearily she cast her focus once again toward the viewport.

Clint opened the COMLINK, once again drawing Angela's attention as a row of small green monitor lights snapped to life on the console. "This is *Aris,* Delta, Beta, Eight-Six-Two-Niner, requesting clearance for departure."

"That's an affirmative *Aris.* You have vertical clearance to fifty thousand feet. Pacific Northwest Intergalactic Spaceport wishes you a safe trip and a soon return."

"Initiating ascent now," he replied, disengaging the COMLINK.

Clint turned to Angela. "All set?" Upon noticing that she was having a bit of trouble getting her safety harness fastened, he leaned over and deftly completed the task for her. "What do you say we get the hell outta here."

With a polite nod of acknowledgement, Angela pulled her gaze away. Judging from the surprised look on Clint's face when they initially met on the tarmac, she suspected he had no idea that she would be the one bringing Piper. And too, he wasn't happy. Didn't anyone tell him that she'd be coming along?

You knew the score when he quit replying to your messages. Without a doubt he had more than one woman just waiting for you to slip up. It was a stupid thing for you to allow your father to talk you into staying in South Carolina while Clint left without you. You have no one to blame but yourself.

It was true. Clint had returned to Acacia while Angela remained in South Carolina with the promise to follow him as soon as her father hired another bookkeeper to take her place. And indeed, she would have followed him, except Clint suddenly dropped all communication with her after he'd been gone only a month or so. She kept trying to reach him, sending off messages every day, but he never responded. Not once.

Ohhh... she didn't want to think about it. What good would it do? What was done was done.

She turned to watch Clint go through the lift-off procedures. One thing about it, five years had done nothing to distract from his good looks. If anything, the years had only enhanced his appeal. Even rough and unshaven as he was now, just looking at him still jangled her insides.

With a sigh she turned back to the viewport only to realize they were already airborne, and the spaceport was rapidly shrinking to a pin dot. That was a shocker she hadn't expected. She hadn't even felt the initial lift.

Leaving the Pacific Northwest Intergalactic Spaceport far behind,

Angela allowed herself no emotional backward glances of Earth, no regrets at having to sell Piper to Rachael or even having to make the arrangements to sell her parent's home—the only home she'd ever known until Mason had entered her life. Right now, however, the most important thing was to get away from Mason and to concentrate on the future for her and her unborn baby. From this point on, she had no past, only a future that she was determined to make the best of.

She had recently made arrangements with Rae so that when her parent's home sold, the proceeds would be deposited into a special account under Rae's name. Although it was pre-arranged, Rae would not know anything more than the fact that she was simply hiding the credits from Mason. In truth, Angela had planned that the funds would be specifically for her baby.

Clint swiveled the command chair around to face her. "You hungry?"

"Maybe just something cold to drink. Thank you."

He rose from the command seat. "Follow me. I'll show you to the galley." Leading the way, he escorted Angela back up the short set of stairs and down the corridor.

"Have a seat," he said upon entering the galley. He grabbed a frozen glass from the froster and began filling it with ice. "Water?" he asked, turning to face her. "Or something with a little more bite?"

"Just water please," she replied, making her way to a small booth along the exterior wall. With a weary groan she dropped onto the bench, extended her legs, crossed her booted ankles and blew several wisps of hair from her eyes.

"Water it is," he said having selected coffee for himself.

Angela's eyes were closed. She had an elbow propped on the table, her chin resting in her open palm. He set her frosty glass of water down on the table and took a seat across from her. "Been a long day?"

Tired green eyes slowly eased open. "That's an understatement. It's been a long four days," she replied, covering a deep yawn with her hand. Angela reached for the water, but instead of taking a drink, she lifted the cold glass to her temple and held it there. Innocent as it may have been, the gesture was sexy as hell. With a swallow, Clint looked away, unable to fathom how he could find a disheveled woman in boyish attire sexy. Angered all over again, he silently vowed to even the score with Nick and Zeke. Damn them.

His gaze returned to Angela as she took a long slow drink. With a deep sigh of fatigue, she leaned back against the seat and silently studied him with the most distant and unemotional perusal he'd ever been subjected to.

"Sure you're not hungry?" he asked.

"You know," she replied, "what I really want is sleep. Do you know if my travel packs made it onboard?"

"They did. I put them in a cabin for you."

Angela's expression turned hopeful as she sat forward. "A cabin? You mean I'm not sleeping in the hay tonight?"

Clint laughed. "Not unless you prefer it. Actually, you'll be staying in the best *Aris* has to offer."

"Really..." She looked intrigued.

He nodded. "Captain's quarters."

"Captain's quarters?" Once again leaning back in the seat, Angela simply stared at him in what could only be described as astonishment. "But I can't take your—"

"I insist."

Looking distressed, she scooted forward to face him head-on. "First of all, Clint, thank you for the offer, but no thanks." She looked away briefly as if selecting her next words. "Since there is just the two of us, maybe we should set down a few basic rules so that there is no misunderstanding between us."

Rules? a silent voice echoed.

"And the first one being," she continued, "I sleep alone."

Clint blinked. "Pardon me?" What the hell did she think he was offering? Besides, she was married, wasn't she? And even if he *was* interested, which he wasn't, he had a rule or two of his own. Number one, married women and virgins were nothing but trouble and had never, ever been an option.

Angela smiled. "I know you're very much aware of your good looks, Clint, and I bet you have no shortage of women fighting to share your bed."

By now, totally confused as to what the devil brought this on, Clint nodded, slowly crossed his arms and decided to play along. "Ahh, yes," he drawled, "all that fighting does get a bit tiresome."

"Without a doubt." Then as though to reinforce the rejection, she smiled sincerely. "The point being, you might have a never-ending supply of females at your beck and call, but considering our past failed relationship, I am no longer interested in being one of them. So, if the Captain's quarters come with a price tag, I'll just make a comfortable bed for myself elsewhere."

Clint stared at her. And perhaps for the first time in his hedonistic life, he found himself momentarily speechless with a woman.

Time to even the score.

He watched Angela's expression wilt as his gaze slowly traveled over her in a most thorough and insulting once-over—from her wilted hair, to her smudged face, to her mucky booted feet.

"Sunshine," he said with a lazy grin, "how long has it been since you last saw a mirror?"

"What?"

"Right now you look exactly like you did when you and Rae used to spend all day long with the horses."

Her mouth dropped.

"Point being," he added with a wink, "I have a rule or two of my own: no married women. *Ever*! And that's right at the top of my list. And even if you weren't married, I assure you that covered in all that sweat and grim you wouldn't exactly be number one on my beck and call list, as you put it."

He girded himself for the storm.

A long moment of silence passed before Angela's lips twitched. "Ohh..." she managed to get out before bursting into laughter.

Laughter. It was the last thing he'd expected. He'd braced himself for her fury, even tears, or a round of name calling. But laughter? He sure hadn't seen that one coming.

"I'm sorry, Clint" she managed to say before another bout of chuckles took over. "I can only imagine how awful I must look."

He merely raised a dark brow and regarded her quietly.

"Clint, I had no right to assume your intentions, and..." Rising from her seat, she met him toe to toe. "Oh, I'm just making a mess out of this. Could we please just start over again? To be perfectly honest, I'm beyond exhausted and I've said things I shouldn't have and..."

Clint folded his arms and struggled to keep a straight face while she attempted damage control.

"... so, if your kind offer is still open, I would love to accept it. In truth, right now I don't care where you put me. There's nothing I want more than a shower and a night's rest, hopefully in a real bed, but I'd gladly take a bed of hay in the cargo bay."

There was a suspended moment of silent eye contact between them before... "There now," he drawled with a slow grin, "you did real good this time, Angela. And yes, the offer still stands."

She looked genuinely relieved. "And you say there's a shower?"

"There is. This way and I'll show you to your cabin." He led the way out of the galley and down the narrow corridor. Having passed a line of storage lockers, he drew to a halt at the entrance to the second of three cabins. Clint touched a small pad on the wall and a door silently slid open revealing a small but comfortable appearing cabin. Angela's travel packs were sitting just inside the door. "I put your belongings in here earlier just to get them out of the way," he said. "Let me grab them."

"This cabin's is perfect, Clint. Really, I don't need the Captain's—"

"But you're not staying in this one. I've got other plans for it."

"Well, what about the first cabin that we passed. Is it about the same as this one?"

"Yes, but you can't stay in that one either." With the barest hint of a smile, he added, "I'm staying in that one."

"Oh."

He palmed the lock on the third cabin down. The door slid open, and the next thing Angela knew, they were entering a spacious chamber.

"Oh my..." she whispered as she remained transfixed at the threshold. A large viewport took up a good portion of the exterior wall. Indirect lighting snapped to life the instant they entered. Clint set her things down. "I guarantee you'll be more comfortable here."

The carpet and bedding, in shades of soft grays and inky blacks, glimmered beneath the low lighting that ran along the ceiling. "This is beautiful,"

"Yeah? It's a bit overdone for my tastes, but the cabin does have its creature comforts. And you'll be the first to stay in it."

Angela took a step back. "Oh, Clint I can't. It's too pretty."

"It's the only one with its own lav, Angela."

That did it. "Well, in that case, thank you."

"I need to get back up front. Just so you know, the lav's through that door," he added with a nod to his left. It's got that shower you asked about. And there's plenty of water, Angela, so don't hesitate to take a nice long one."

Angela couldn't help wonder if that was an implied slur, or simply a coincidence. Between Piper, Trixie and four long days on the road after leaving Nora's, she could only imagine how she looked and smelled. But if his long shower comment was on purpose, it probably suggested things were far worse than she realized.

He had just turned to leave when she asked, "Just how long of a trip is it to Acacia? I've forgotten."

A moment of silence passed before he looked back to answer. "Normally, it's a four-week run, but we'll be making it in two."

"Oh."

"Don't worry about the mare. I'll check on her before I turn in."

"Watch out for Trixie!" Angela called. "She doesn't like... men."

But the cabin door had already hissed shut, and Angela doubted Clint had heard her warning.

~ * ~

Max Banner always told his boys to never trust anyone who doesn't look you straight in the eye when they have something to say. And as far as Clint was concerned, Trixie was no exception. Gauging his every move out the corner of her eye, she'd been snarling at him from the moment he first entered the cargo bay to check on both her and the mare.

"Umm... nice teeth, girl." Rolling his back against the interior wall, Clint slid to the floor with the ease of warm syrup. "You and I," he continued. "we're going to have to work on a little truce. What do you say?"

The growling worsened.

"I bet your hungry, aren't you?" he said, withdrawing a half sandwich from a takeout container. Just in case the dog was hungry, he'd stopped by the galley long enough to grab the sandwich from the cooler—leftovers from the spaceport cafe earlier that evening.

The snarling eased up just a bit as Trixie's eyes shifted to the food that Clint held in his hand. "Thaata girl," he cooed softly. "You want it, don't you?" Breaking off a small chunk, he tossed it Trixie's direction and quietly waited. It had landed on the floor about two feet away from her. After several long moments of ignoring it, Trixie warily gave-in.

"When did you eat last?" he asked tossing a second and third bite her direction. They landed just a little closer to himself. Trixie guardedly crept forward amid softer growls and snarls to snatch them up then again backed away. A fourth chunk, however, Clint simply held out to her.

Trixie didn't move. The growling stopped, yet holding her ground, her focus slid from his face to the morsel in his hand.

"Ahhh," he murmured softly, "This is asking a just little more of you, isn't it, girl?" He waited patiently while the dog continued appraising the situation. "Come on, Trixie," he whispered. "I'm not going to hurt you. Besides," he added, "you know you want it."

He witnessed the very instant Trixie decided to take a chance, the very moment she made the choice to take that first step toward him. Edging closer, she cautiously snatched the bite from his hand then quickly retreated. "Good girl," he said softly. Slowly drawing his legs up, he draped his forearms over his knees and offered Trixie yet another bite to which she repeated the same guarded tactic. This time, however, after cautiously taking the bite from his hand, she held her ground instead of backing completely away.

Clint's mind absently wandered to Angela. If he'd passed her on a busy street, he never would have recognized her. In truth, she looked like hell. Beyond simply dusty and exhausted, she looked sick, hollow-eyed, and... thin. He didn't remember her being so thin. And although she'd been trying awfully hard not to show it, he'd noticed her favoring her left arm when bringing the mare onboard. What the devil happened to her?

A wet nose nudged Clint's hand, drawing him from his thoughts. Trixie was sitting directly in front of him, waiting expectantly. "What? You still hungry?"

Trixie's eyes brightened and her feathery tail wagged ever so slightly.

Rising to his feet, Clint turned for the exit. "Come on, girl. Let's go see what we can dig up for you."

Trixie's toenails clicked happily along the corridor as she followed Clint toward the galley. A truce had finally been reached.

~ * ~

Blinking sleep from her eyes, Angela glanced up to find herself focusing numbly on the star-studded viewport in the ceiling directly over the bed.

After a long, warm shower last night, she hardly remembered hitting the pillow. Glancing at the clock, she realized she'd overslept. Clint, no doubt, had been up long ago. Not that it mattered, but she had responsibilities with Piper and Trixie.

Shoving the covers aside, Angela scrambled out of bed, forgetting her injured shoulder until a bolt of pain sliced through her. Stifling a low moan, and not wanting to admit the injury might be serious as Nora had suggested, Angela tucked her arm tight against her body and reached for her clothes with her good hand.

CHAPTER THREE

Angela made her way down the corridor toward the galley, her pony tail bouncing behind her. "Good morning," she said smiling hesitantly.

Clint looked up from his computer to find her standing at the threshold. "Morning, Angela," he said, dropping his focus back to his work.

She remained where she was.

"Coffee's at the cook center along the back wall," he said without glancing up. "Help yourself."

"Thank you, but first I need to check on Piper."

"Piper's doing just fine. She's eating her breakfast right now."

"You fed her?"

"Hmmm."

"Thank you. I don't expect you to take care of the animals for me."

At that, he looked up from his work. "Never thought you did." He reached for his coffee. "Figured you could use the sleep though."

"Thank you."

"No problem." Once again, he returned his attention to his computer.

Despite the fact that he'd taken the time away from work to make this trip, he still had a business to run back on Acacia. Orders and off-planet assignments could not wait until he returned home. It meant grabbing every quiet moment to check-in with his foreman and to secure any permits necessary to satisfy the various interplanetary codes and regulations.

"I must ask though" she went on. "Then I promise to leave you to your work."

He stopped what he was doing to give her his full attention. "Yes?"

"How did you manage to make it past Trixie?"

"Trixie and I came to an easy understanding last night."

"Understanding?"

"She was hungry. I had leftovers."

"Ahh, you found her one weakness," Angela said lightheartedly. "Thank you, Clint, for feeding her."

"You're welcome. By the way," he said, changing the subject, "if you're hungry the locker is fully stocked. Help yourself anytime. Energy drinks are in the cooler. Breads, muffins and the like are in the sealed cabinet next to the cooler, and if you're looking for something hot, the meal selector has a complete inventory." Having said that, he again returned his attention to his work at the computer.

Angela remained in the doorway, carefully judging Clint's mood. Four and a half years of marriage to Mason had made her an expert on judging moods. Even though it appeared as though Clint had tried covering up his initial reaction, Angela was convinced that he was surprised to see her last night, and not happy by it. Oh, he'd been—and still was—politely attentive, asking if she was hungry, wondering if he could get her anything, making sure she had the best cabin on the ship, etc. And yet this morning she sensed that his mood wasn't much different than last night. It was awkward, and she wasn't about to stand around waiting for his mood to change, if it ever would. With her mind in a turmoil, Angela turned and headed for the cargo bay to check on Piper.

The instant she entered the hold, she knew something was amiss. Her first clue was the lingering acrid fumes of carbon exhaust and raw gasoline. A quick perusal located the offending source tethered against the aft wall. "A motorcycle," she murmured. Annoyed, she approached and greeted Piper. Reaching for a grooming brush, she began brushing the mare. "You smell that awful motorcycle too, don't you girl."

"It's not just a motorcycle," Clint's deep voice clarified as he wandered in. "It's an antique. A 1994 Harley Sportster."

"I don't remember that being here when I first came aboard. I'm sure I would have noticed."

"You're right. It wasn't." He huffed a soft laugh. "And had it been, I'm equally sure you would have noticed it then too. Actually, I made a stop after we left SeaPort. No doubt you were asleep at that time."

"But I can smell fumes."

"Yes. That's possible, but it's nothing more than left-over exhaust."

"Well, I just hope you weren't running that thing in here. I can only imag—"

"I wasn't." Clint backed off but continued watching her. She'd cleaned up nicely compared to last night, but as far as he was concerned, she still didn't look well. Plus, more than once he'd seen her grimace and clamp down on her lower lip while grooming the mare. He hadn't notice her protecting her arm to this extent last night. Sure, he'd noticed her favoring it, but assumed she'd pulled a muscle bringing a nervous horse across the landing field. But today it was obvious that it could be something more serious.

"What'd you do to your arm?" He asked as he came forward.

Angela looked up. "My arm?"

"Your left arm. What happened?"

"Oh that." She smiled. "It's nothing. I just sprained it getting Piper in the trailer."

"I see," he said, but he didn't buy it. He suspected it was more than just a sprain, and that Angela, for some reason, was covering up. Well, it didn't make any difference how it happened. If his hunch was correct, she needed to have her arm in a sling until a medic could take a look at it. "Well, just in case it's more serious than a sprain, it probably should be immobilized at least until a physician can see it."

"It's all right, Clint. It's just a sprain," she said as she replaced the curry comb.

"It's *your* arm."

"Really, I don't need a medic."

"Great. Looks like you've got it all under control then." He turned for the exit with Angela following him.

"Besides, I can keep it quiet by simply using my right arm instead."

"Sounds like a plan," he agreed, palming the touch pad to the door that led into the corridor.

He wore faded black denims, a dark blue shirt with sleeves rolled up to his elbows, and well-worn black work boots. Tagging along behind him, Angela couldn't help but notice the way his muscles flexed beneath his shirt as he walked, or the way his dark hair curled down over the back of his collar, or especially the way those denims clung to his backside. It irritated her to no end that he still sparked her interest. The least he could have done was let her know that he'd moved on, instead of leaving her to wonder what happened? If he had only cut her loose, maybe she could have met someone else and not even married Mason.

The thing that puzzled her was that he seemed equally irritated with her for some reason. He was the one who stopped answering her messages. He was the one who had dropped her and moved on without so much as a backward glance.

From the top of the steps, Angela watched him descend into the helm, drop into the command seat and wordlessly began monitoring the controls. Fine. Let him be all business. She could be aloof too. Two could play that game. She would mind her own business and let him mind his. Without a doubt the upcoming two weeks to Acacia were going to be two extremely long and unpleasant weeks.

~ * ~

Two weeks later. Three hours out from Acacia.

As promised, Clint had managed to cut the trip in half. The time on board ship with Angela had actually passed without incident. All communication and activities were on a strict no-nonsense, non-personal level the entire time, which suited him just fine. It worked best that way for both of them. The way he saw it, this trip was meant to bring the mare back for his sister, with or without Angela. He'd moved-on during the last five years, and the less said, the better.

Besides, even if they had gotten onto a more personal discussion, he wasn't interested in her excuses for dropping out of his life. He'd lost count of the times he'd tried contacting her without a response. He'd wracked his brain trying to figure out what, *if anything*, that he'd done wrong. Hell, he'd even made several separate trips to Earth only to learn that she'd moved out of her high-rise. And when he tracked her down at her parent's home, her father informed him at the door that she wasn't available but that he would give her a message. But when no response ever came, he's the one who got the message all right. Loud and clear.

CHAPTER FOUR

Angela had spent the last hour gathering what few belongings she had brought with her and preparing Piper for disembarking. The trip had actually gone faster than she ever remembered. Clint had been courteous the entire trip, but at the same time there was a constant undercurrent of coolness about him. She had no idea what he was so surly about. If anybody had a right to be, it was her. The least he could have done was explain himself. Oh well, she didn't want to hear it now anyway. She had wanted to hear it back then, when her heart was broken—when she ached to know why—had pleaded with him in her messages to tell her what had gone wrong.

Clint. Even now, her heart clenched at the realization of the damage that had been done by her foolish decision to stay at her father's bidding, for the promise she had made to remain for six more months. It would have given her father plenty of time to find a replacement bookkeeper. Naturally, her father was happy, and Clint had agreed to it, albeit reluctantly. But apparently six months was asking too much of him to wait. Obviously, someone else had taken her place.

To escape the pressure placed upon her by her father and Mason's father, she eventually married Mason. He wasn't her first choice. Clint was. But Clint was out of the picture, and in his stead, Mason had treated her like royalty. He had seemed to genuinely care for her, despite the subtle reservations she had about him—little things that she had noticed that concerned her. Yet her father and George both encouraged the marriage, something about combining the two families being good for business. Her momma had predicted she would regret it, and unfortunately, she had been right.

The first year was good. Even the second year started out well, but then little by little Mason began to change, and their marriage turned into a third year of hell.

Angela descended the steps into the helm where Clint was monitoring the controls. "How long, do you think, before we get there?" she asked.

"We're about two and a half hours out. I was just about to call you up front. Grab a seat. We'll be leaving hyperspace soon. And when we do, you'll feel a moment of dizziness."

"Yes, I remember that happening from when I used to come visit." She settled into one of the extra seats in the helm. Lately, she had been dealing with morning sickness, so dealing with the nausea of leaving hyperspace was no big deal.

It wasn't long before the onboard computer signaled their departure from hyperspace, and as Clint had promised, the wave of nausea came and went quickly.

"You okay?"

"I'm still alive if that's what you mean." Her halfhearted attempt at humor failed to get even so much as a smile from him. He remained stoically engrossed in piloting the ship. To be perfectly honest, over the past two weeks she'd truly had a belly full of *Mr. Cool and All Business*.

"In about forty minutes I'll be switching off the grav, and you'll experience a similar effect before we hit dirt."

Without comment, Angela chose to remain seated for the remaining leg of their approach to Acacia. Although the onboard computer had already transmitted the necessary information to the spaceport, Clint opened the COMLINK for a verbal reentry vector.

Fixing her gaze, she watched as the planet slowly became larger and larger until at last it completely filled the view screen. For Clint, it might be just an everyday event, but over the years she'd forgotten how spectacular the approach experience was.

The COMSET buzzed and a voice announced, "Please initiate your descent."

"Understood," Clint replied and assumed control from the ship's computer as the *Aris* began entering Acacia's uppermost atmosphere.

Plunging down through the multi-layers of a planet's firmament was a riveting experience. Transfixed, Angela watched in fascination as the tip and leading edge of the starboard wing began glowing like a fanned ember. Within seconds the entire wing was engulfed in flames that ended in long tongues of fire dancing off the back edge of the wing. More flames lapped across the exterior of the hull and viewport, casting an eerie glow within the cabin.

And although Clint may have long since become accustomed to the firestorm raging outside, for Angela, she had always found it both fearsome and exciting at the same time.

Gradually the darkness of space gave way to Acacia's luminous atmosphere. Glancing up at the overhead vid screen she saw a distinct line of demarcation between night and day tracking diagonally across the center of the planet. Presently, the ship was heading into the darkness. Ahead she could see small clusters of lights here and there dotting the dark surface of the planet—indications of colonized areas. One large spot of bright light stood out in particular.

"Is that bright spot up ahead, Imperial?" she asked.

"It is."

"So I take it then, it's nighttime there."

"Roughly 11:00 pm by standard hours."

Angela quietly watched Clint monitor the controls as the ship made its way down through the various layers of unsettled air. Despite the heartache of his desertion, the five years since she'd last seen him, and despite her resulting lack of interest in men in general, this man—and dear God, what a magnificent specimen of a man—still totally and completely rattled her.

Eventually he cut the speed; felt the response, booted the nose up and goosed the reverse thrusters to slow their descent. A vast dark ocean spread out beneath them, and soon they were skimming over a flat plain. A range of mountains stood beyond, and at regular intervals a soft chime sounded, signaling designated drops in elevation.

Angela lifted her attention to the master screen where the sparkle of city lights could be seen flickering in the darkness ahead. The city of Imperial looked so different at night. It had always been morning whenever she had arrived in the past. It seemed like such a long time ago, when she would come to visit Rae. And now... this time she wasn't just visiting. She was coming to find a new life for herself and her baby. And find it she would. There was nothing she wouldn't do for the baby's sake. She placed both hands protectively on her abdomen, curious if she could feel the baby at all.

Nothing. No movement yet. Her stomach was as flat as ever. One of these days, however, she would feel the fluttering. She recalled at the time of her marriage, asking her mother about pregnancy. She'd learned that the first signs of life would feel as if a tiny butterfly had been turned loose in her stomach. Angela could hardly wait. Her baby was the only good thing ever to come out of her miserable marriage to Mason.

Angela's attention was drawn back to the present as Clint began killing the ship's forward motion and once again firing the reverse thrusters. Next came a pulsing sound of the proximity alarm as the ground seemingly rose up to meet them. And with a gentle thump the *Aris* settled onto her landing jacks. Even from inside the ship, the whine of her powerful turbines could be heard slowly descending.

The COMSET chimed and Clint reached overhead to flick it on. "Clint Banner here."

"Well, well what a pleasant surprise, Clint. I ain't seen your pretty face here at the main spaceport in a long while." The voice and image belonged to Shara, a heavy-set middle-aged woman with brassy blonde hair and laugh lines framing her eyes.

"Shara. Good to see you too. By the way I've got live cargo to unload, so I'll be needing an above ground LZ, hopefully in a quiet spot at the far end of the spaceport."

"Hun, I've got just the landing zone you need and it's yours. Your father already hand-picked it and secured it for you. The robosphere should be pulling up in front of you any moment now. Then, darlin', whenever you can spare a moment, stop by the Outbounder. I haven't seen you in such a long time. Dinner's on me and you can tell me all that's been going on over these past few months."

"Sounds good." Clint cast his focus back to the exterior vid. As promised, a large robosphere had appeared and was waiting for them with the words "FOLLOW" flashing in bright neon. Clint fired the thrusters, lifted the ship inches off the scarred surface and slowly advanced toward the sphere. The robotic drone drifted left and the *Aris* trailed behind.

CHAPTER FIVE

Rachel Banner was gazing over a fence that separated the tarmac from Port Imperial's main terminal when suddenly a distant high-pitched whine drew her attention. "Look! I bet that's the *Aris* coming now!" The ship was about two miles out across the spaceport, it's landing lights bathing the tarmac in bright light. Even at a distance she was an impressive ship. Tiny lasers winked on the tip of each sweptback wing as she slowly taxied behind the robotic drone.

"Oh, Dad, I can't wait for you to see Piper. She's so beautiful."

"Shouldn't be long now, honey."

The closer the *Aris* got, the louder the scream of her turbines. "I wonder if we should at least get the truck and trailer and be ready to head out there to meet them?"

Max smiled at his daughter's excitement. "Just as soon as they get docked and shut down."

The *Aris* followed the robosphere down a long, wide corridor where at last they were led into a sizable pad of their own at the far end of the port. Clint killed the drives and once again eased the ship down onto her jacks.

As he depressed the keys to lower the loading ramp and release the lock on the exterior hatch to the cargo bay, he glanced up at the exterior vid-screen and watched the oncoming headlights of the ranch truck and horse trailer as it crossed the tarmac. It pulled to a stop about seventy-five feet from the LZ, and Clint watched as Rae hopped out of the truck and ran toward the ship.

Between Rae and Max helping to unload the horse, Clint was glad to know he wasn't needed. He had things to do and was anxious to get back on the job again.

Despite cutting the entire trip in half, he'd still been gone longer than he should have. And even now it will be at least another thirty to forty-five minutes before he could disembark. He still had to complete the ship's log, conclude the legalities of attaining the landing pad as well as secure the ship for overnight moorage.

Much to everyone's amusement, with Max leading the mare off the ship, Piper hesitated at the top of the ramp and with a snort, surveyed the area before loudly announcing to the world that she had arrived.

Once they had Piper off-loaded and secured in the trailer, Rae turned to Angela and the girls hugged. "It's so good to see you again, Angie." Rae stood back holding Angela at arm's length. "You certainly look better than that horrible picture you sent."

"I'm much better, thank you." Angela said. "And again, Nora was absolutely wonderful. She doted on me constantly."

Rae chuckled. "Yep. That sounds like Nora."

Nearly an hour had passed before Clint finally came off the ship. With his thumb hooking his jacket over one shoulder, he made his way across the tarmac to where the group was gathered. The easy masculine grace in which he carried himself was not lost on Angela.

"Sorry for the wait," he offered. "Apparently first-time authorizations take forever. I thought we got that all taken care of before I left."

Max spoke up. "We did. Most of it, that is. I forgot to tell you, with maiden voyages, the pilot needs to do the rest upon returning."

Clint turned to Angela first and perfunctorily wished her well and reminded her to see a medic about that shoulder. Then, after giving Trixie a friendly scratching, he turned to Rachael. "That's a real nice horse you got there, Rae."

"Isn't she a beauty? Thor's going to love her."

Clint grinned. "He sure will."

Before he had a chance to turn to Max, Rae addressed him again and nodded for him to step aside with her. "I must say, big brother," she began in a voice lowered for his ears only, "you look horrible. Did you do that on purpose?"

"I don't know what you're talking about."

Reaching up she touched his dark untrimmed beard. "Really, Clint, you couldn't look more disreputable if you'd tried." She softened her censure with a smile. "And I'm speaking as your little sister."

"Ahhh," He grinned. "I didn't know Piper cared whether I shaved or not." His teasing grin disappeared as his tone turned serious. "Someone should have warned me, Rae."

The double meaning went right over Rae's head. "Piper doesn't care, Clint," she said, "but maybe Angie might."

The instant she said it, his eyes narrowed. "That's a sore subject, Rachael. I suggest you stay out of it."

Without another word, he turned and made his way over to Max. "Bet you're wondering how I got back so fast?"

"You know I am. You cut the entire trip literally in half."

"Remember that power booster they were using as a big selling pitch when we placed the order? It works. I used it both ways, going and coming back."

"No kidding," Max said. "But what I want to know is, what sort of damage did it do to the fuel supply?"

"Not as bad as you might think. I'll figure out the numbers for you tomorrow." Clint cocked his head toward Angela and added in a lowered voice, "By the way, she needs to be seen by an orthopedic medic. She either has a wrenched shoulder muscle or worse. I suspect she'll fight you about it, and say it's nothing, that it's just a sprain. I say it should be professionally looked at."

"We'll see to it," Max assured him.

Clint started to turn away,] then stopped. "Oh, and will you give Nick and Zeke a little message for me?"

"Sure. What is it?"

"I left the cargo bay for them to clean out. And don't you go hiring anyone to do it for them."

"Nick and Zeke," Max repeated.

"Yes. They'll know why. And while I'm at it... did you know that Angela was the one bringing the horse? Not that I cared, but it would have been nice to have had a little heads-up."

Max frowned. "Yes. Why? Was there a problem?"

"Nothing I can't take care of. Just make sure Nick and Zeke get my message."

"And if they refuse? I'm not leaving a brand-new ship in a mess, Clint. I'll hire it done before I do that."

Clint grinned. "You won't have to. Just tell them to do it for Rae. I did my part for her birthday gift. Now it's their turn. It's the least they can do, especially since Rae volunteered to help Angela clean it tomorrow. And poor Angela with her bum shoulder and all. Oh yeah... they'll be mad as all hell, but they'll do it for the girls to save face. Oh, and another thing," he added, "tell them to leave the bike alone."

"Bike?"

"Yeah. I picked it up for Marc. We'll get it off tomorrow when I come to run the fuel figures for you."

Max simply stared in mute wonder as Clint turned, and with that free-flowing gait of his, headed toward the parking lot where he'd left his Ground Runner a month ago.

Rae couldn't help noticing Angela's intent gaze as she watched Clint disappear into the darkness. "So, Angie..." Rae asked, "was everything okay on the flight out here?"

As though the spell had suddenly been broken, Angela, blinked and quickly averted her eyes. "Oh yes... *Mr. Cool and All Business* hardly gave me the time of day. And, personally, I don't think he knew that I was the one he was meeting."

"Certainly he knew."

"I don't think so, Rae. Did you, by chance, tell him?"

"No, but...I saw the surprised look on his face the instant he recognized me. After that, I could tell he was irritated and basically, he seemed irritated the entire trip."

"At you?"

"I'm not sure, but I don't think he was irritated with me so much.

I'm just curious... who made the arrangements? Do you know?"

"I think it was Nick and Zeke."

"Would they have thought it funny to not tell him?"

"I don't think so." Rae frowned. "But I'll find out."

"No, Rae, please. Just let it ride. I'm sure Clint will get to the bottom of things just fine without our interference."

~ * ~

Two months had passed since Angela had arrived at the Banner home. She had hoped for maybe a two or three day stay before heading out. But that was not the case. They had insisted she stay and see a physician. Max and Delta had been the most insistent and hardest to convince otherwise.

As it had turned out, her worst fears were confirmed when the medtech informed her that she had a torn rotator cuff. Although she had stubbornly managed to convince the physician that she did not want an operation, she was then given orders to stay at the Banners for the next six weeks and to keep her arm quiet. He had insisted on placing her arm and shoulder in an orthopedic cast as well as a sling to make sure she kept it quiet at all times. Yesterday had been her last appointment, and the doctor had finally given his reluctant approval that she had healed enough to be on her way if she chose. But, he told her, no heavy lifting for at least another four weeks, and no guarantees the repair to her shoulder would last since she had refused to have an operation.

Angela was in the barn, sitting on a bale of hay visiting with Rae when Max entered. "I thought I'd find you two ladies in here." He turned his attention to Angela. "I hear you're planning on leaving us tomorrow. Is that correct?"

"Yes. I really should be on my way."

She extended her hand to Max. "I can't thank you enough for all that everyone has done for me."

"You are very welcome, Angela. May I ask what you're doing for transportation?"

Rae piped up, "Actually, I am going to take her into the city this afternoon to look for something suitable."

"Angela, would you mind if I jump in here and offer an option to consider?" Max asked.

"No, of course not. I'd be grateful for any advice."

At her consent, Max told her of a small Land Craft they had that was no longer being used. "It's not new, honey," he said, "but it's been kept-up and in good condition for its age. It's just sitting in our way right now, and if you're interested, you're welcome to it."

"A Land Craft?" she asked.

Max huffed a soft laugh. "I guess the last time you were here, you were more interested in horse power than vehicles." Both girls chuckled.

"Anyway," he went on, "A Land Craft, or LC as we call them, is more domesticated than a Ground Runner." When she still looked like she didn't have a clue, he added, "Come here, Angela, I'll show you what they are." She followed him to the yawning door of the barn, where it looked out into a parking area. "See that black vehicle parked over there by the workshop?"

"Yes."

"That's a Ground Runner."

"Oh, yes, of course. I know what that is. Besides, it looks like what we call a Jeep back home."

"Yes. Basically, it *is* a Jeep. Made by Jeep, and exported from Earth." Here, it's called a Ground Runner.

"And, see that red vehicle over there across the parking lot?" Rae added.

"Yes."

"That's my Land Craft. It's not as rugged as a Runner. It's more compact and rides much smoother."

"So, the Land Craft that I'm speaking of is very similar to Rae's," Max added.

"But I can't just… Seriously, you've all done way too much for me as it is."

He grinned. "Yes, you can. That vehicle is in our way, Angela.

48

Believe me, you'd be doing the workers around here a big favor by getting it out of here."

"I... I don't know what to say."

"All you have to do is say yes. Use it as a trade-in if you wish."

"Thank you. Again, thank you for everything."

"I'll have our mechanic check it out, get it cleaned up and running for you. It'll be ready for you tomorrow."

After Max left, the subject of Mason came up, and Angela ended up sharing a bit more of the hell she had gone through with him. She could tell Rae was horrified when she began unraveling the physical and mental abuse she had suffered under his iron control. Eventually, Piper came into the conversation, and when Rae had asked if Mason had any legal claim to Piper, Angela assured her that Piper was legally hers to sell and that the papers she had signed off on were original legal documents. In all the telling, however, Angela had chosen to leave out the part about being pregnant. By now she was almost four months pregnant and starting to feel the fluttering of a tiny life. It warmed her soul and made everything she had been through so worthwhile.

It wasn't that she didn't want to share the news with Rae. It was that once she left the Banners, she needed to completely break it—to disappear with no trails and to be absorbed into nothingness. She hated having it be that way, and she'd miss the Banners terribly, especially Rae. But knowing Rae, if she were to know about the baby, she would not let the subject drop. She would expect to be informed the instant the baby was born. Expect to come and visit the baby and have Angela bring the baby back for visits. It would never work. In this instance the less Rae knew, the better. Maybe later after sufficient time had passed, things could be different. But right now she didn't want any trails for Mason to track her down.

~ * ~

Angela had been on the road about ten hours. Roughly three more yet to go and she should be pulling into the small mountain town of

Aurora. She'd left the Banners shortly after dawn, saying her goodbyes and thanking them all again for everything. She chose to not say where exactly she was headed, for the obvious reasons—less chance for Mason and his hired thugs to find her. To most people, it wouldn't make any sense as to why he would track her down. He'd made it perfectly clear he wanted nothing to do with her or the baby. Having publicly denied being the father, he had even arranged for witnesses, if necessary, to testify of her unfaithfulness. And he'd taken it another step beyond the divorce and had papers drawn up that gave up any rights and any responsibility for the child. No, he wouldn't be hunting her down because of the baby and by now their divorce was final. But Angela knew in her heart that Mason would not give up the hunt until he found and punished her for the way she'd left him. That was it. It wasn't the fact that she'd left him. No, it was the *way* she'd left—a week early, in the middle of the night and especially for having taken Piper against his explicit orders. She'd out-smarted him and his pride was stung. Simple as that. He would no doubt track her down as far as the Banners, and hopefully the trail would grow cold from there.

The one thing that kept worrying her, however, was Mason's parents. He came from a wealthy family. Money was no object, and regardless whether Mason denied the baby or not, what if his mother were to insist she be the one to raise the child—in the same selfish and opulent lifestyle that Mason had been raised. There was little doubt but that his parents would follow her across the galaxy if necessary. Angela didn't even wonder what the outcome would be in a custody battle. What chance would she have if his parents, or if Mason, himself, were to suddenly decide to fight for the child? They could afford a legal battle. She couldn't. And there was little doubt but that they would fight dirty. She could just hear the argument their legal counselor would use against her, especially the fact that she was a single working mother living in a *sleazy* mining settlement. *Why what chance would the poor child have living among riff raff with no hope of a higher education or the luxuries the Cooper family could afford?*

With a heavy sigh, her mind drifted once again to the Banner family. In truth, her stay with the Banners had actually been an incredible reprieve. Rae was fortunate to have such a wonderful family. Max and Delta were amazing parents. She got to see Nick again and meet Tressa and their baby boy, Braeden. It was good to see Zeke again and also meet Kira who was heavily swollen with their first child. She also met Aylie, the three-year old little girl whom Zeke had rescued off of a slave ship not quite a year ago. As for Marc, unfortunately the youngest of the three Banner brothers was off-planet. For the time being, he'd managed to get involved in the family business of cargo hauling, a lucrative profession that not only took him away much of the time, but had Delta worrying over their youngest son.

But the one Angela had truly hoped to see one last time was Clint who never stopped by, not even once in the nearly two months she'd been there. Angela hid her disappointment. Rae had mentioned that he was making some off-planet delivery. Apparently, he'd left two days after he'd dropped Angela and Piper off. With a heavy sigh, Angela tried to convince herself that it was okay. But still, she wished she could have seen him just one more time.

~ * ~

Nine months had now passed since the day Angela had pulled into the little mining town of Aurora. Max's donated car had run like a dream the entire way. Back when she had been living at the Banners, she had borrowed Rae's computer, gone online and lined up a small miner's cabin to rent as well as looked for a job. With that done, she at least didn't have to wonder where she was going to live or work. And before the baby was even born, Emily, the young wife of one of the miners had offered to watch the baby for her while Angela was at work. Babies were a rare sight in a mining settlement, and quite frankly a novelty. Emily was beyond excited to be able to care for the baby. But to Emily's distress, and her own embarrassment, Angela burst into grateful tears when Emily excitedly agreed to watch the baby for whatever Angela could afford.

Things were going well, and although her home was small, a

woman's touch here and there had transformed a barren miner's cabin into a cozy and comfortable little cottage.

Turned out the job she had applied for was walking distance from home and entailed working in Accounts Receivable for a large mining enterprise. It was a position she was already good at. Bookkeeping is what she had been doing when she first met Mason, the *swamp rat*—back at a time when he had hidden his true self behind a charming façade.

Today was a day-off for Angela. Knowing she would be home today. she hadn't bothered with much more than the basics—a shower, brushing her teeth and whipping her hair into a careless ponytail. She loved it when she had days off like this. It gave her time to play with Lainie, her three-month old baby girl. It also allowed her time to take on projects like the one she was involved in today—repainting an old rocking chair that Emily had found in town at a second-hand store. It had originally been imported from Earth, which Angela liked the idea of.

While Lainie napped, Angela was sitting cross-legged in the middle of the living room floor, applying a second coat of white paint to the rocking chair. It was a good thing the floor was covered with a tarp, as splatters of white paint dotted the tarp. A few drips had even landed on her bare legs.

In spite of it all, it had been a labor of love, and the rocking chair was beautiful in its shiny white paint. She could hardly wait to rock Lainie to sleep in it. Maybe even tomorrow night, if it's dry.

Satisfied with her work, she set the paintbrush aside and rose to her feet and stretched. It was a gorgeous day. Emily had been telling her to get outside and take advantage of these beautiful days. Being in the mountains as they were, the weather would soon be turning much colder before long, far too cold to take Lainie out.

A knock at the door startled her from her thoughts. Who would be at her door? It couldn't possibly be Emily. Over the weeks since Lainie had been born, Emily had become accustomed to walking in with a simple "yoo hoo." There was no one else she could think of who would come visiting. Angela absently smoothed her hair and tried tugging her short, tattered cutoffs back into place. "Hello?" she said as she opened the door then went deathly still.

Clint Banner's sensual mouth slowly curved into an amused grin as he lazily took in, from head to toe, every delectable inch of Angela's disheveled appearance. "Hello, Angela."

CHAPTER SIX

Tendrils of shiny honey blond hair had worked their way loose from her ponytail to feather haphazardly about her cheeks and neck. And she looked, Clint thought, almost as disheveled as she did a year ago when she'd met him at the spaceport with Piper. Splatters of white paint now replaced the dust and grime she wore back then, and he pondered if she had any idea that there was even a smudge across her cheek. At least she no longer looked sickly.

He lazily wondered, too, if they were the same short cutoffs she'd worn a year ago. Today she had topped them with an equally shabby plaid shirt with rolled up sleeves and shirt tails tied in a knot beneath her breasts. Dear god, she was stunning.

His eyes were still twinkling with amusement when he finally asked politely, "May I come in?" At her flustered hesitation, he added, "Don't worry. I'm not in the habit of ravishing young ladies wearing white war paint." He sobered, gave her another once over then with a slight wag of his head he added softly, "Although, I must confess, with you in that outfit, I find it damned tempting."

Nearly groaning aloud, Angela glanced down at her scandalous attire and bare feet. She wanted to slam the door in his face and save herself additional humiliation. Instead, she mindlessly stepped aside, allowing him to enter.

Clint Banner, of all people. She had forgotten how tall and crazy handsome he was. His breathtaking presence nearly stole the oxygen from the room. Silently she took in his swarthy, bronzed features. He was very dark. Suntans like that weren't acquired by simply laying around in the sun. They were acquired by hours of working outside. The tiny squint lines that fanned from his eyes were just another indication of being outdoors. Petroleum geology? Wasn't that what he had gone to school for? She couldn't recall anything at the moment. It was as if her brain had been swept clean the instant he walked through the door.

"Nice little place you have here." he said, glancing around in appreciation.

She stood facing him with her hands on her hips. "How'd you find me, Clint, and why are you here?"

"How'd I find you?" One side of his mouth kicked up at the corner as he flicked hooded eyes over her once more. "Let's just say I find you... stunning and unforgettable." His tone was slow and seductive as he spoke, and Angela was drawn to the vertical slash of dimples on each side of his mouth as he smiled.

It was a sin for a man to have a smile like that, but she couldn't allow herself to focus on that now. "Please, Clint. I'm serious."

"You're right. I'm sorry. You weren't easy to find, Angela. You covered your tracks well. In fact, I was about to give up when Rae remembered you'd asked to borrow her computer to look for a job and a place to live. Even though you tried to erase your tracks, Rae managed to find where you had been searching up here in Aurora two weeks before taking off. She found both your application for this cabin as well as employment."

"But why are you here? Is everyone all right at home?"

"Everyone's fine, Angela." He sauntered over to the fireplace and inspected a small picture she had on the mantle. "Two weeks ago," he said, turning to face her," some guy came snooping around asking about you."

The announcement hit her like a horse kick, and she slumped against the door. "What did he look like?" she all but whispered.

"I have no idea. But from the questions Rae said he'd asked, I can only imagine he looked all business. Suit and the whole works."

Angela listened in a daze. Her world—the world she had worked so hard to build for herself and Lainie had suddenly begun spinning out of control. "What sort of questions?" she asked, her throat tight.

"That's why I'm here. And I have a few questions of my own."

"Clint, I tried not to involve your family in my problems. All I wanted was to start a new life for myself."

"Well, sunshine, guess what? We're involved. And the first thing I want to know is, are you, or are you *not* divorced from Mason Cooper?"

"Why?"

"Divorced?" he repeated. "Yes or no?"

"Yes. We're divorced."

"Alright. And another thing," he went on, "who owned Piper at the time you sold her to Rae?"

"I did. She was my horse. Why do you ask about Piper? Mason gave her to me shortly before we were married. You had to have seen my name on her papers when I gave them to you."

Clint slowly shook his head. "Thing is, Angela, once you married Mason, he automatically became half owner of everything that was yours, unless you had a pre-marital agreement that said the horse was off-limits. Why the hell does he want your horse anyway? Is he into horses?"

"That's just it. He doesn't want the horse. He wants to make me suffer, and that's his only reason. It's always given him pleasure to hurt me. He wanted nothing more than his freedom, and at the same time to strip me of what little happiness I had known."

Clint scowled, "What kind of sickness is that?"

"I suppose he's married to someone else now and blissfully happy. And, you know what? That is just fine with me. I don't ever care to see or hear from him again. Ever."

Suddenly there came a sound from somewhere in the back of the cottage as Trixie came rushing down the short hallway to greet him, whining, wiggling and wagging her tail with uncontrolled excitement at seeing Clint again.

"Hello, girl," he said, bending down from his tremendous height to give Trixie a belly rub.

It always amazed Angela how quickly Trixie had taken to Clint. Not just accepted him, but was genuinely happy to see him.

"Okay," he said at last, rising once again to his full height. "We'll worry about Piper later. Now, for why I'm really here. You can't stay here, Angela. Like I said you covered your tracks well, but the bottom line is, if I found you, so will they. Therefore, we need to leave right away. The sooner the better because there's a—"

"Leave? I can't just up and leave, Clint."

"Yes, you can. Did you hear what I said? If I found you, so will they."

"But I was on Rae's completely private server with security and—"

"And that's all true. But according to Rae, your asshole-ex comes from money. Is that correct?"

"Yes."

"Money unlocks a lot of doors, Angela."

"But—"

"But nothing. Besides, there's a powerful storm coming, and I intend to be down out of these mountains by the time it hits."

Another sound came from down the hall—completely different from the sound Trixie had made when she came running to greet him.

"What's that?" Clint's eyes narrowed and were drawn to the end of the short hallway.

The sound came again. This time louder, and he managed a low "What the... devil *is* that?"

It would do no good telling him that it was nothing. He was going to find out anyway. "It's Lainie," she said defensively.

"Lainie," he repeated with no inflection to his voice. "What's a Lainie?"

"My baby."

Silence. "You've got a *baby* here?"

"Yes."

"Whose baby?" he asked.

Angela wondered if he had suddenly gone deaf, especially since she had just told him Lainie was hers. "I told you. She's mine."

His eyes immediately shot to her breasts and then lowered to her bare stomach. Angela felt her face flush, wishing she hadn't tied the ends of her blouse under her breasts. For a long moment he simply stood there staring at her as if trying to decide what to do next.

"So, how old's the kid?"

"Lainie," she corrected.

"What?"

"Her name's Lainie, and she's three months. And to answer any further questions," she added, "I was pregnant when you met me at the spaceport."

He drove a handful of fingers through his thick black hair, only to have it fall back over his brow. "And Mason's the father I take it?"

"Yes."

"Does he know?"

"He knew I was pregnant, yes." Angela replied. "And he wanted nothing to do with me or our baby."

Clint scowled. "What do you mean he wanted nothing to do with you or the baby?"

"I mean, like trash, he threw us both away. He gave up all rights and financial responsibility for Lainie. I even have the signed papers to prove it."

Clint considered that for a moment, then, "In exchange for what, Angela?"

She had to hand it to him. He was quick, but it didn't surprise her. And considering all that she had just told him, it seemed pointless not to confirm his suspicions. "A lump-sum settlement."

Clint nodded. "One that was below what you might have gotten if you'd chosen to fight him?"

"Yes. Mason's family is rich and powerful, Clint. I couldn't fight them. Believe me, it was a good trade off." Despite feeling awkward standing there in bare feet and in what now seemed an extremely outrageous outfit, she met Clint's stare with as much composure as she could muster.

"You know that legally, he can't do that, don't you Angela? The law says he's financially responsible for his child."

Angela's laugh was without humor. "Yes, that may be true. But Mason bought off anyone and everyone who could probe that he was the father. According to him, I was unfaithful and Lainie isn't his. DNA won't even prove she's his. If anything, a DNA test would simply prove he isn't the father. All the right people with the right connections were bought off. He says he has proof—witnesses to my infidelity. And that's fine with me. Let them lie for him. I want him out of our lives forever and I willingly, joyfully take the blame for our failed marriage."

"Angela, all it would take is for you to go for a DNA test here on Acacia. I can assure you he didn't buy off everyone in the galaxy—"

"And why would I do that? I have no intentions of proving he's the father. And I know of no one else who cares. As I've said, I don't want him or his money. I want him to disappear from our lives forever."

"Well," Clint finally said on an exhale, "I want to disappear from these mountains before that storm hits, so you need to start packing whatever it is you 're taking for the baby and yourself. And make sure you pack warm things."

"I can't just up and leave, Clint. I have a job that—"

"Unless you want to deal with the hounds on your trail, Angela, you have no choice. I didn't come all the way up here to argue with you." Then he added, "And put something warmer on than what you're wearing. And same for the baby. Double layers, if you can. And what about food for the baby?"

"That won't be an issue."

"What do you mean, it won't be an issue?"

Angela never answered but went about quickly, albeit reluctantly, grabbing arm loads of warm clothing and handing them to him.

"I need your keys to open the back hatch of your vehicle," he said. "My Ground Runner is larger, but I had no way to bring it."

"Then how'd you get here?"

"Hired a minicab to bring me up from where I left the transport," he said as he put on his sunglasses.

~ * ~

They had been on the road about twenty minutes. Angela had packed everything warm that she could think of for Lainie and herself. At Clint's urging she packed a couple of extra warm coats and blankets as well. Trixie's dog bed sat on the floor behind Clint. Lainie's travel bed was secured on the back seat directly behind the passenger's seat, and so far, Lainie had been a perfect angel. But Angela knew it would only be a matter of time.

She felt sick at heart leaving without saying goodbye to Emily or giving notice to her job, her landlord, and others who might miss her. And what about the storm that Clint said was coming? Would they all be safe? "Are you sure there's a storm headed this way?" she asked, turning to face him.

"Yes."

"Well, then why is the sky still clear and the sun still shining."

"It's coming, Angela," he said without taking his eyes off the road.

As if on cue, suddenly, the blare of disaster sirens could be heard screaming in the distance behind them—Aurora warning its citizens of the coming storm and telling them to seek shelter.

Swiping at the tears she'd been trying to hold back ever since they'd left Aurora, Angela turned her head toward the side window and watched as the barren mountain landscape flew by in a blur.

"What will the people do?" she asked. "Where will they find safety?"

"I don't know, but I'll wager that mining company you worked for has a shelter all set up and ready to receive the entire town in a moment's notice."

She turned to face him. "But where? I don't know of anything big enough to hold everyone."

"A retired mine could easily be transformed into a shelter."

"It could?"

"Sure it could."

"Oh..."

By the time Lainie began fussing, Angela was already lowering the passenger seat as far back as it would go and climbing over it into the backseat next to the baby carrier. "Shhh. Mommy's right here, Love," she murmured softly, lifting the tiny pink bundle from the carrier. Lainie cried the entire time her diaper was being changed. Angela then placed Lainie against her shoulder while scooting sideways behind the driver's seat and adjusting her clothing. The sudden quiet was a sweet relief when she finally placed Lainie to her breast. They were traveling at breakneck speed as Angela laid her head against the back of the seat, closed her eyes and tried to relax while Lainie nursed.

After a while, Clint's deep voice broke the calm when he asked without looking back, "How long does that take?"

She knew what he was asking. "Not too much longer."

"So, she's about done then?"

"Soon," Angela replied as she kissed the soft downy top of Lainie's head.

"Reason I ask, the storm is moving-in fast. The wind is picking up and it's going to get rough. I want you and the baby both belted in."

Angela glanced out the back window. The sky had turned dark gray, blocking out the sun and blue sky that had been there only a short while ago. And by the gusts that were buffeting the Land Craft, she could tell the wind was indeed picking up. Placing Lainie to her shoulder, she gently rubbed the baby's back until she bubbled. She then quickly laid her back into the carrier and secured her before climbing back up front. All was quiet inside, while all hell was beginning to break loose on the outside.

"Damn. Here comes the snow," Clint said as the Land Craft suddenly moved into a massive curtain of snow and sleet. It was coming down so fast it was piling up on the road faster than they could move through it. "I was hoping we could make it down before the storm hit. The temperature's dropping rapidly. Is there anything back there you can use to stack against the windows for insulation? Blankets, coats, clothes of any kind?"

"Clint, most everything is packed in the back."

"Okay," he said, "We're going to have to stop and grab what we can and bring it up front."

The Land Craft had barely stopped when both Clint and Angela were wrenching on their warmest jackets and climbing out of the vehicle. Frozen shards of sleet and snow hit them in the face the instant they'd stepped outside. Bowing her head against the frigid wind and blowing snow, Angela made her way to the back of the Land Craft. Clint was already back there with the trunk lid open and looking as if he wasn't sure what to move first. Within seconds Angela had her hands on a couple of heavy coats and two blankets which he took from her and deposited in the front seat of the Land Craft.

With the help of the dim trunk light, they soon had their hands filled once again with more of the warmest articles of clothing that Angela had brought.

"Anything to eat back here?" he shouted over the howling wind.

Angela shook her head then turned to race back to the front of the vehicle.

When he joined her up front, she added, "I didn't even think to pack food."

"No worries. We'll manage. Once we get to the ship, we can weather it out for as long as we have to." He handed her an armful of clothing. "Stuff these against the back window and into any crevices along the back doors."

"How long do these storms last?" she asked as she wriggled her way over the front seat and into the back to cover windows and cracks.

"A Space-Vortex" can last anywhere from a couple of hours to as long as three weeks."

"Three weeks?"

Another frigid gust hit the Land Craft with a jarring jolt. "Honey, just keep doing what you're doing, and as soon as you're done get yourself back up here and belted in again. I'm going to put us back on the road before it gets any deeper. Hopefully, it won't be too much longer before we make it to the valley floor where I set the transport down."

Another twenty minutes passed before the Land Craft suddenly coughed to a dead stop. With a muttered curse Clint tried restarting the vehicle but to no avail. He released a compressed breath. "Damn. I wondered when this would happen." He turned to Angela. "Another reason I was hoping to beat the storm. Older Land Crafts like this one don't like sub-temps. Is this the vehicle you got from dad?"

"Yes, but it's never given me any trouble."

He nodded. "Like I say, it's the sub-temperatures."

Angela cast a quick glance at the gauges on the dash, "So what do we do now?"

"*We*... do nothing. You're going to wait right here while I see how far it is to the valley floor. I have no idea how long I'll be gone, but I need to know that you and Lainie will stay right here. Bundle up until I get back. And don't be opening the door for anything. It's too damn cold out there, and the vehicle's going to start getting cold now too."

"Would you at least switch on the temperature control?"

Growing quiet, Clint turned to look at her with a baffled expression and asked cautiously, "What the hell for?"

"Heat. So we can at least stay warm until you get back?"

Clint desperately wanted to laugh, but frankly was too stunned to do more than continue to stare at her. "Angela..." he began slowly, in a calm and soothing voice, "you won't get any heat out of this vehicle if it's not running."

"Yes, you will. Clint, there's lots of times I've driven into town when it's cold out. I've gone shopping and when I come back and start Bella, I don't have to wait for heat. The fan immediately starts blowing out heat without even being warmed up first or anything."

"*Bella?* You named your Land Craft *Bella*?"

"Yes. It means beautiful."

"Well... here's the reason you were still getting heat from Bella. It was because Bella wasn't waiting in the wind and subzero temperatures for you to return. I assure you that right now any residual heat is long gone, Angela."

"No it isn't. Just try it. You'll see. Please?"

"Look, I'm wasting time. I need to be on my way."

"Please?"

Clint released a heavy sigh. "Listen to me," he said slowly as if talking to a child, "if I flip on the heat, only the fan will come on. You understand? Just the fan. Nothing else. And very cold air will blow out of the vent—not even a little bit warm. And the cold air blowing out will be even colder than what's already in here, Angela. I'm telling you, it won't work."

Angela held his gaze. "Well, would you at least give it try anyway? Please?"

Without another word, he flipped it on. Not just cold air, but startling frigid air began blowing from the vents. Clearing her throat, she said softly, "I guess you're right."

"Now, bundle yourself and the baby up in anything and everything you can find to keep you both warm. And maybe throw something over Trixie to help hold in her body heat." With that he secured one of Angela's cardigan sweaters to become a makeshift facemask, he pulled on a pair of gloves and then slid the hood up on his jacket. Before opening the door, he turned one last time to Angela. "I'll be back as soon as I can," he said in a low, guarded tone through the draped veil of her cardigan sweater. "Okay?"

"Okay." Darkness was beginning to close in, and Angela watched as Clint quickly let himself out, slamming the door behind him. She continued watching him until he disappeared into the blowing snow and encroaching darkness.

Bowing his head against the wind and sleet, he trudged through deep snow, following what appeared to be the continuation of the road they were on. The only thing he could presume to be the road was to follow the wide swath between the trees.

Clint had heard talk from people who had been in these storms before. Once it starts, it only gets worse before it gets better. If there was any hope at all, he had to find the ship and he had to find it fast. It would be their only refuge. He couldn't just leave Angela waiting with no hope, no food, and nothing to drink. He could manage all right on his own—reach the valley floor, find the ship and hole up until the storm passes, but what about her? She and the baby would never make it. Besides, some of those gusts were strong enough to send the Land Craft sailing end over end, out of sight. Considering all the negatives facing them, Clint didn't want to think about Angela and the baby's fate.

CHAPTER SEVEN

Nearly an hour passed before he finally reached the valley floor, and there, roughly a hundred feet away, sat the blessed *Victorious*.

He reached for the remote, punched in a series of numbers, lowered the boarding ramp, and released the lock on the main hatch. Once inside, he cranked up the heat then grabbed anything that he thought might be helpful on their return trip. He took only the smallest amount of time to chase the chill away before setting back out. Hopefully, it wouldn't take as long to get back to the Land Craft as it had taken him to get here. For one, the wind would be at his back this time. His hope was, with a little luck he could make it back to Angela in maybe a half hour at the very most. By now it was fully dark, and Clint could tell that the darkness was only going to make matters worse on their return trip.

For Angela time dragged by in slow increments. First, she worried whether Clint would come back after her. Then she worried what if something were to happen to him? Now she was wondering what she would do if he didn't come back at all. Lainie had been good most of the time, but Angela knew she was on borrowed time. She also knew that there was no way she could brave it in that weather by herself. She had no choice but to wait. So, she waited, and while waiting she changed and fed Lainie, she played, sang, cooed, and babbled love words to her. And all the while time ticked on, a small knot of fear took root in her heart. *What if he doesn't come back?*

Feeling abandoned, cold and scared, Angela once again began worrying what would happen if Clint were lost or worse. What if he were injured and needed help? Almost two hours had gone by since he'd left.

Suddenly another gust of wind hit the Land Craft, this time with a force that literally lifted the front end up off the ground and slammed it back down. Even Trixie let out a whimper from her place on the floor. "It's alright, girl," Angela said as she rearranged the warm blanket that she'd placed earlier over the dog. "He'll be back soon." In truth, she wasn't so sure she could believe her own words.

Angela had about given up hope when suddenly the driver's door was wrenched open and a snow-laden figure dropped inside with a thud, jerking the door closed behind him. "Ho! Damn, it's cold!"

Clint had returned wearing a much heavier coat than the one he had left in. No doubt, something he had found in the ship. This one had a fur-lined hood, and though it was covered with snow, it looked like it had protected his head from the bitter cold. His breath rose in the air as Angela watched him from her cocoon of warmth. "I take it you found your transport?"

"Yeah." Off came the gloves, the hood and the jacket. And before she realized what he was about, he was in the backseat with her, crawling into the warm nest of blankets and heavy coats she'd made for herself and Lainie.

"It's sub-zero out there, babe," he said roughly as he pulled both her and Lainie into a close embrace.

Angela let out a small gasp. Her shock wasn't just the cold alone but the intimacy he was imposing upon her. She couldn't remember the last time she had been this close to a man without being afraid or repulsed. And instead of smelling of expensive cologne like her high-powered ex, Clint smelled of the cold outdoors—of snow, evergreens, and something so male she found herself curiously welcoming the strength she sensed lay beneath the chill of his body. And even though he burrowed intimately close, she oddly didn't feel smothered. Nor did she find it exactly unpleasant.

"You've got a warm little nest here, honey. Let me stay just a minute or two before we head back out." He took another shuddering breath against her neck before adding in a deep raspy voice. "Just another minute or two. That's all."

"It's Angela. Not honey," she said softly.

"What?"

"Angela," she repeated. "Remember? My name's Angela. Not babe, or honey, or anything else."

"Give me a few minutes to thaw out a bit, and its anything your sweet little heart desires."

She truly believed the intimacy he was imposing on her wasn't sexual as much as it was exactly as it appeared—a basic need for warmth. She owed him the time to recover from the cold. Despite the length of time it had taken him to get back to her, she suspected that he had chosen not to remain in his ship very long before heading back out to rescue her.

"How far is your ship from here?" she asked.

It took a minute for him to respond. "Roughly a couple of miles." He took a shaky breath. "But to get there, we'll have to buck a nasty headwind." He paused as a shudder passed through him. "With conditions the way they are, it may take us as long as an hour and a half just to reach the ship." He lifted his head enough to look up at her. "Think you can make it?"

"Are you suggesting I have an alternative?" she asked.

"I wish."

"Then, yes. I can make it," she said with conviction.

"Once we start, Angela, there's no stopping to change a diaper or feed Lainie. In other words, do whatever it is you have to do before we leave." His head was resting on her shoulder, his cold face pressed to the base of her neck as he curled into her warmth.

"Lainie's ready to go. I changed and fed her shortly before you got here. I just need to get her in a front pack," she said. "Other than that, I guess I'm ready whenever you are."

But when she started to disengage herself from him and move to the front, his arm caught her about the waist and drew her back. "Give me just a little longer," he said burrowing deeper into the warm shelter of blankets and Angela's welcoming body heat. He had begun shivering, and Angela recognized it for what it was—nature's way of pressing the panic button when the core body temperature has dropped too low. She quickly rearranged Lainie so that she could at least reach up and cup his frigid face and ears with both hands. Silent shock swept over her at how cold he felt to her touch. How was it possible to be that cold and still be alive?

Another gust slammed into the Land Craft, rousing Clint from his frozen lethargy. "We need to move," he growled, and yet he continued to remain where he was for just a bit longer. It felt too damn good absorbing the warmth of her body.

At last, reluctantly coiling up from Angela's warm envelope of blankets and body heat, he gingerly eased himself back into the front seat. "Okay, here's what I need you to do. I need you to strap Lainie in that front pack you brought. Then I want you to put on your warmest sweater, coat and anything else you can think of, as many layers as you can, at the very least, three. From the ship, I brought a pair of thermal pants and a heavy parka with a hood. Those will go on last. Also, these gloves."

Once they both were bundled up for the cold, Clint tied a line around her waist and attached it to himself. The length would allow them about eight feet of distance before growing taut.

"What about Trixie?" Angela asked. "We can't leave her, Clint."

"We won't. I'll carry her. Ready?" he asked as he wrenched open the door. Unfolding himself from the driver's seat, he stepped out into the storm and jerked open the back door. Reaching for Trixie, he tucked her inside his coat as best he could and wrapped a blanket about the parts of her that hung out. Then he picked up one of the packs from inside the Land Craft and shouldered it. "Let's go!" he shouted over the roar of the storm and extended a hand to assist Angela from the vehicle.

The wind continued to batter them. Snow and sleet piled up in deep drifts as Clint led the way toward the valley floor. Following the road on foot under normal conditions might have taken a half hour to forty-five minutes at the most to hike, but with the inches piling up and the headwind blowing sleet and snow in their faces, their forward motion was slow and agonizing.

Peeking through an opening in his jacket, Trixie lifted her head, burrowed it under his make-shift face mask, and gave Clint a quick kiss on his chin.

"You're welcome, girl."

At one point they came to a break in the landscape with a view of the valley floor. Below, a hazy blur of light emanated from a large silver object sitting in the midst of a snow-covered clearing. The *Victorious*. Tiny red strobe lights seemed to be dancing on the tips of her swept back wings. Clint had partially awakened the ship on his earlier trip, and she was ready and waiting for their return.

"How are you doing back there?" he hollered for what surely seemed the hundredth time since they'd started out.

"I'm good."

"Here, let me get that pack for you."

"No, I've got it. Besides, you already have your hands full." When he was about to insist, she quickly changed the subject, "Is that your ship sitting down there in the valley?"

"Yes. We're almost there."

She was tiring fast. He could hear it in her voice. He'd asked her a couple of times if she needed to stop and rest, and each time she'd turned him down, saying she wasn't going to rest until she got to his ship.

On they trudged. He'd slowed his pace to accommodate her. They probably would have been there by now otherwise. And then to slow their progress even further, limbs, brush and even trees, downed by the wind, were littering the road, many hidden by snow drifts, making it all the more difficult.

Suddenly the life-line between them stretched tight. Clint jerked around to find that Angela had stumbled on a downed limb buried in deep snow. The look on her face, as he helped her up, was so crestfallen he chose to stay by her side and help her along.

"You don't need to help me, Clint. I'm okay."

"No, you're not. Another fall and you could really hurt yourself... or Lainie."

If the sudden shock of pain in her once-bad left shoulder was any indication, she'd already hurt herself.

With Clint linking his arm through hers, they marched on as she mechanically placed one foot in front of the other.

"I don't feel so good," she moaned softly.

"I know. Hang in there, honey. Just a little longer. We're almost there."

Almost there. He wondered how many times he'd said that?

Fifteen minutes later he removed the ship's remote from his pocket and punched in a code. Additional embarking lights beneath the ship snapped to life, illuminating the boarding ramp as it slowly lowered to the snow-covered ground beneath.

Catching Angela by the elbow and with a steady hand at her back, Clint steered her up the ramp. And when the main hatch cycled open, he eased her inside where she leaned against the bulkhead in complete exhaustion. He immediately pressed a small touch pad on the inside wall, securing the airlock once again. It was dark inside the ship with the exception of a cluster of small monitor lights winking on the command console. He set Trixie down first then wrenching off his gloves, he turned for the helm and entered a sequence of keys. Soft lighting immediately came to life, illuminating the helm. Outside the storm raged, the wind howled, and gusts of sleet peppered the outer hull. Inside, life-support whispered warmth through the ventilation system, and soft chimes sounded from the helm as Clint made adjustments, taking control back from the onboard computer.

"Welcome back, Captain Banner. While you were gone..." came an electronic voice, updating Clint on the changes in weather, and a long list of info that ranged from minor damage to the outer hull, to the exterior temperature, the cabin temperature, the ship's manifest and water supply. At last came a warning to remain grounded during the storm—that the ship was not designed to take off or land in these conditions. Basically, it was an electronic version of *"Relax. Everything was under control while you were gone, but stay grounded until the weather clears".*

It hadn't quite yet registered with Angela that she was finally on Clint's ship. Her knees buckled, and she silently slid down the wall to the deck in a heap of coats, sweaters and a whimpering Lainie. Wordlessly, over the top of the heavy scarf covering half of her face, she kept her eyes fixed on Clint while he continued waking up the rest of the ship and taking control back.

His cold hands were making everything twice as hard. The thermal gloves he'd found earlier with the parkas had helped but not enough to do more than barely keep his fingers from frostbite. Reaching overhead, he flipped a toggle and watched an indicator respond. Then he kicked up the heat just a bit more. He'd already increased the temperature earlier before returning to rescue Angela, but as cold as he and Angela were, it still didn't seem warm enough.

Immediately he could feel the increase in heat and he lifted his hands in front of a nearby vent, rubbing them briskly. From there he knocked back the hood on his parka, undid Angela's cardigan that he'd borrowed to cover his face, and went at the snaps down the front of the parka. Once the jacket and multiple layers of clothing were removed, he dropped into a nearby seat and began pulling off his boots. At last, he glanced back at Angela to see how she was faring. Not only was she huddled on the floor, she was making no attempt to move. From across the helm, her lifeless stare was fixed on him. Swearing softly, Clint quickly crossed the cabin, dropping to his knees in front of her.

As though in a trance she continued wordlessly staring at him. The thing that alarmed him was that Lainie's soft muffled protests were coming from beneath multiple layers of bulky clothing. Clint wasn't sure that Angela was even hearing the baby. He suspected that normally she would have had Lainie unwrapped and in her arms by now. It was a sure sign of shock.

The first thing he did was pull Angela's wet gloves off. Then he shoved back the hood on her parka and removed the scarf covering her face. When he began easing her legs out from under her, he found himself tenaciously having to ignore her lethargic protests and moans of pain the effort was causing.

"I'm sorry, baby, but we need to get these wet things off."

Next, came her wet boots. Then he went for the parka, unsnapping the grippers and laying the parka wide open like a butterfly across her chest. A heavy coat beneath came next, and again he laid it back in the same manner he had the parka.

It wasn't until he'd finally opened the last of two bulky sweaters and was sliding his hands inside to work all the garments off her shoulders that she stirred with the realization of what he was doing. "Nooo... P-l-e-a-s-e..." she whispered pitifully. "It hurts."

"I know, honey, but they need to come off. Besides, I turned the heat up and you can sit in front of a vent now to warm up." Becoming more and more suspicious about her left arm, he carefully eased the garments off of her shoulders. At last beneath that final layer was Lainie in the front pack, plastered to Angela's chest—her downy hair sweaty and stuck to her head. Finally, with an ease that challenged and belied his own exhaustion and deprivation of strength, Clint lifted Angela into his arms, Lainie and all, and carried her to the other side of the helm, carefully setting her down in front of a heat vent. "I'll be right back."

Closing her eyes, Angela held out her hands to the vent and welcomed the warmth as sharp pins & needles began shooting through her thawing fingers. She should get Lainie out of the front pack and change her diaper. But Lainie had fallen asleep now that she was no longer suffocating beneath all the coats and sweaters. Angela didn't have the heart to wake her or the energy to undo the front pack for that matter. Besides, she told herself, Lainie had been so very good today, especially during the hellish trek in the storm, she deserved to sleep.

Clint returned, dragging a single mattress from a nearby bunk along the starboard wall. Having placed it on the deck next to Angela, he knelt behind her and lifted her up onto the mattress. "Before you get too sleepy," he said, "what do you say we extricate Lainie from the front pack first? Think she might appreciate that?"

Having hunkered down next to her, Clint watch as Angela began struggling with the clips on the front pack. He could tell her fingers weren't cooperating and she was getting frustrated.

"Here, let me help," His fingers weren't much better, but he managed to unfasten the clips for Angela. He would have gone on to help further by lifting Lainie out of the front pack, but in truth he had no idea how to even hold a baby, let alone extract one from a front pack. His luck would be that he'd end up doing everything wrong and have both Lainie and Angela mad at him.

As it turned out, once Clint had released the clips for her, Angela had the baby out of the front pack and was laying her down on the mattress.

"Do you know where her diapers are?" she asked, her voice no more than a raw whisper.

"Right here," he said bringing the pack with the diapers and depositing them next to her.

"I wish my hands weren't so cold."

"Here, let me get something to help warm them," he said as he rose to retrieve a small hand warmer that he'd activated earlier for her. "And while your changing the baby, I'll get us something hot to drink." He turned for the galley.

When he returned carrying two mugs of hot coffee, he found Angela curled up on the mattress. She'd fallen asleep with her arm around the newly diapered Lainie at her side. Setting both coffees down, he turned for the bunk, grabbed a folded blanket and came back to place it over Angela and Lainie. Although the ship was warm inside, as cold as he knew she had been, she could still use the extra warmth.

Clint had borrowed Nick's ship, the *Victorious,* for this particular errand. The *Victorious* was Nick's first cargo ship. Technically, she was a small mail boat that Clint felt would be more practical for landing in the valley than something larger. Retrieving his own mug of coffee, he made his way back to the helm where he dropped into the command seat. There was no use even thinking about trying to escape during the storm. The *Victorious* was a strong little ship, but she wasn't strong enough to even attempt trying to take off now. No, they were stuck and they'd have to wait until the storm passed. As if to emphasize the wisdom of that decision, another gust slammed into the ship with the force of a runaway freight sled.

He turned to see if Angela had been jarred awake. Apparently not, but from the squeak and tiny little fists circling the air above her head,

Lainie had obviously been awakened. Rising from the command seat, he slowly approached the mattress. It didn't surprise him that Angela had instantly fallen asleep. It had been a harrowing day.

He couldn't help feeling guilty. No doubt everything had been going just great for Angela until he showed up telling her that she needed to grab only what was important and leave her cozy little cottage and friends behind. He was well aware that she had silently wept as they left Aurora, but she never voiced a protest. Nor did she complain once about the snow and bitter cold when they'd staggered through knee-deep snow drifts and frigid high winds to get to the ship, nor when she fell. He could tell she was scared, but still she trudged on. He couldn't have asked more of her.

His eyes flicked once again to the tiny baby laying against Angela's side. Until now he hadn't had a chance to actually see Lainie. And now that she was no longer hidden beneath layers of clothing, he found her to be much smaller than he ever realized. She was dressed in some sort of pink one-piece thing. Her feet were covered, but her little hands were free and fluttering in the air. The two of them stared at one another in silence—Lainie, curiously staring at the ruffian looking down upon her, and Clint, awed by the fragile life who wasn't even aware of what her hands and feet were doing. He was surprised that she actually seemed to see him. Her eyes tracked his every move. It made him smile. As though spellbound, he listened to her cooing and watched her delicate hands circle the air above her. She was smaller than Braeden, Nick and Tressa's son. Clint had never seen such dainty little hands and fingers in his entire life. There was no question but that she was Angela's little girl. She definitely looked like her mother.

Suddenly, Lainie's face puckered up and for no apparent reason she began to fuss. Clint was tempted to do something to quiet the baby, but had no idea what to do, so he simply hunkered down out of her sight to see what would happen. Hopefully, she would stop crying, but unfortunately that didn't happen.

With a low moan, Angela reached for Lainie. "Shhh, shhh," she said as Lainie curled her fingers around Angela's pinkie, "Let mommy rest just a tiny bit longer." But again, that, too, wasn't in Lainie's plans and the crying intensified. Totally unaware of Clint's presence, Angela drew Lainie near, opened her blouse and exposed her breast to Lainie's ravenous mouth.

CHAPTER EIGHT

Clint eased back on his heels, hands splayed on his thighs, and in awed-silence watched the peaceful scene unfolding before him. He'd never watched a woman nurse a child before. Not like this anyway, and although he felt a small amount of guilt for watching, something so much stronger held him in complete rapture. What was it that held him prisoner? Was it the calm on Angela's face? The slender arm that held Lainie close? Maybe it was nothing more than the two of them, mother and child, light years away from here in a peaceful world of their own? Whatever it was, it was beautiful and it touched him.

But it also aroused less-noble instincts. Closing his eyes, he sucked in a deep breath and decided it was time to get up. With a low groan, he climbed to his feet. He was stiff—in the most literal sense of the word. What he needed now was a double shot. He had a pretty good idea where Nick kept it too. But he decided instead to settle for something to do, something productive to get his mind off of Angela and ivory breasts.

A year ago, after he had deposited Angela and Piper in his family's care, he'd deliberately stayed away during the entire time she had resided at his folk's place. He'd chosen to take on a four month off-planet delivery assignment which, technically, someone else could have handled. He should not have turned right around and taken more time away from his company, Solarblaze Energy, especially having already been gone a month as it was.

Angela was married, dammit, and he had hoped to clear her from his mind during that time. At least that was his intention, but by the time he returned and found her gone, he realized the voyage had only marginally erased her from his thoughts.

By now, he had been back home six months when just last week Rae told him of a man, who that very day, had shown up asking about Angela. Rae went on to tell Clint the things Angela had shared regarding her marriage to Mason, and even though she was divorced, Angela feared Mason would track her down. Clint found himself deeply troubled. Suddenly it made sense now how her shoulder had become injured and why she had looked so sickly back then.

But the thing that baffled him more than anything was when Rae told him that Angela couldn't understand why he had suddenly dropped all contact with her five years ago.

What the hell? Angela had that backwards. She was the one who had dropped all contact. Not him.

It had taken over a week of intense tracking before he and Rae had finally narrowed down Angela's location to Aurora, a small mining settlement high in Acacia's northern mountains. She'd covered her tracks well. He had to give her that, but truth was if he found her, so would Mason's goons. And now here they were stuck in the middle of a damned storm, unable to leave for who knows how long.

Making his way toward the galley, Clint decided to see what exactly there was to eat. While he was at it, he checked the water supply and surprisingly found it completely full, exactly as the onboard computer had reported.

The galley had been enlarged by several feet. A nice change, Clint decided, since the original galley was little more than pocket-size. Upon opening the cooler, he discovered that it was well stocked with everything imaginable. A far cry from what Nick used to store in the cooler before Tressa entered his life. Back then, they used to razz Nick that Echo Extra Dark was his mainstay—breakfast, lunch and dinner.

Water's good. Food's well stocked. Not bad, the place was clean and in order. There was no doubt but that Tressa was the one to thank for the nice accommodations, especially since the *Victorious* had been retired and transformed from a working mail boat to a private pleasure craft. It was easy to recognize Tressa's womanly touches here and there. Nick was lucky Tressa was in his life. Very lucky. Back when Nick had first met her, Tressa was too good for him, and everyone knew it, including Nick.

Selecting two commercially prepared meals from the froster, he placed them in the warmer and waited while they heated. Might as well go ahead and eat, since he was starving. But first, he checked on Angela and the baby one more time only to discover they were still both sleeping, in a world of their own, and he wasn't about to intrude on their peaceful solace. They'd both earned it.

Having refilled his mug of coffee, he grabbed the meals from the warmer when the chime sounded then turned for the booth. He had never been crazy about commercially prepared meals, but right now they were the quickest thing available. He debated about waking Angela to see if she was hungry. Who knows when she had last eaten, and after all she was eating for two. Nevertheless, he decided against it for now.

Outside the storm advanced. It seemed that every few minutes a forceful gust would slam into the ship. Not only was the *Victorious* heavy for her size, but Clint had decided when he first arrived to secure the ship even more with hydraulic anchors that bored into the ground for stabilization. At the time it was merely a precaution—just in case the storm hit before they returned. As a result, the *Victorious* was a safe ark. They had heat, food, water, and hopefully the storm would pass as quickly as it came. However, Clint wasn't holding his breath on that one.

As he ate, his mind wandered to the changes he'd already noticed in the ship. She was no longer the unadorned cargo ship that Nick had first owned. For one, the back wall that once separated a large cargo bay from sparse living quarters and the helm had been removed. He remembered when Nick had started the renovation, but until now Clint had never had the chance to see the end result.

At last rising from the booth, he scraped the entire contents from the second meal into a dish for Trixie who had been sitting at his feet, staring at him the whole time. "There you go, girl. Enjoy," he said as he filled a second bowl with water for her.

Stepping out of the galley, he glanced toward the front, wondering once again if Angela had awakened yet. Neither she nor Lainie had moved since he had last checked.

Turning toward the back of the ship he headed into the area that had once been a good-sized cargo hold. With new walls erected, most of the original cargo area had been transformed into a large master cabin with a king-sized bed that sat on a raised dais. Clint couldn't help but smile. Tressa, no doubt, was in charge of selecting the colors and décor. He had to admit it was beautiful, but he could hardly imagine Nick getting involved in selecting colors or furnishings. Braden's crib was positioned near the bed on one side, and a small cushioned kitty-bed sat on the floor near the front on the other side. Clint couldn't help grinning. Of course, TiMar would have a place onboard. TiMar was a Lyrin Desert Cat that Nick had rescued as a kitten several years back from a bunch of drunks at a port bar. The cat had become more of a pet than anything to both Nick and Tressa.

Adjoining the master bedroom was a large master bath with more coordinating colors. Indirect lighting glowed from a recessed ceiling in both rooms. Clint couldn't help but appreciate the transformation that had been made to the *Victorious* over the past year and a half. A far cry from the utilitarian mail boat that she used to be.

Following a small corridor that circumvented the master bedroom on the starboard side, Clint discovered the new cargo hold at the very back of the ship. Her once spacious hold had ultimately been reduced to an area approximately twelve by fifteen feet, much, much smaller than its original size, but still big enough to be usable. Using shavings that had been brought aboard specifically for Trixie, Clint arranged a small corner in the cargo area for Trixie's use.

He had just returned to the helm, trying to tune-out the constant barrage of ice shards peppering the outer hull when another heavy gust slammed into them with a quaking jolt.

Angela roused with that last gust. Lifting her head, she blinked, her eyes hazy with sleep and confusion. Her gaze rested on Lainie who was still sleeping through it all. Next her focus flicked toward the helm, finding Clint standing before the command console quietly monitoring the controls, studying a readout that he'd pulled up onscreen.

For a moment she simply lay there starring at his back as he leaned a forearm against the upper facia of the cockpit and continued analyzing the data in silence. Rising to a sitting position, she finally asked softly, "Is this your ship, Clint? Did we make it safely to your ship?"

He turned to face her. "Yes, we made it. You're safe, Angela."

Her eyes glanced about the compact living quarters of the ship. "Do you know if any of my personal packs came with us—from the Land Craft I mean?"

"All I remember is concentrating on anything warm, and baby stuff. It's possible one of your personal packs made it. I think I carried something back of yours, but I have no idea what was in it."

"It's okay."

"I set everything we brought with us on the lower bunk over there," he added, "just down from the airlock. From there you'll find the lav about ten feet down the passageway. Right across from the galley."

"Thank you." Angela gingerly stood up, turned to check on Lainie who continued sleeping, then quietly made her way to the lav.

By the time she came out, Clint was still standing at the controls. Leaning across the back of the command chair, he tried once again to pull up any information on the storm. "Damn," he growled, "that Vortex's doin' a great job of jamming communications. I not only can't get any updates, I can't touch base with anyone." He turned around to face her as she came forward. "So, how are you feeling?"

"A bit woozy."

He nodded. "You've gone through hell ever since we left Aurora and I'm damned sorry. I was hoping to make it down out of the mountains before the storm hit. We would have been back to Imperial hours ago," he said as he turned back to the controls.

Angela lowered herself onto the mattress, sitting next to where Lainie was sleeping. The feeling of deep weariness wasn't going away. She was more exhausted than she could ever remember being. At last she lifted her gaze and stared at Clint's back for a moment before finally saying, "Clint?"

"Yeah?" he said softly, his concentration still on the controls. When she didn't continue, he stopped and turned to face her. "Yes?"

Angela hesitated as big tears began forming.

Great. He hated tears. From his perspective, it had always been a phony ploy woman used to manipulate men.

"I just want to say..." The first big tear spilled over the dam to roll down her cheek, "Thank you," she added in a broken whisper.

Well, he hadn't expected that. Her tears were actually real. An emotional release, he supposed.

You owe her those tears, pal. The silent voice interjected. *She's gone through a hell of a lot in just a few short hours. Not many women you know would have silently gone along with you under the same circumstances. Can you picture Shelbi? Gathering up only what you said she can take and leaving her cozy little life and home behind? Tramping through deep snow in sub-temps? Ducking tree limbs sailing overhead in the dark? And all the while packing a three-month old baby? The women you know wouldn't have done it. And even if they had, you sure as hell wouldn't still be on speaking terms by now. And if you were, you'd be called every name in the book.*

Without a word, Clint stopped what he was doing at the controls, turned away from the command center and came to Angela. Dropping to his knees on the mattress, he put his arm around her and drew her back against him. He'd never felt more helpless in his entire life. He understood the tears, her need for an outlet. There was nothing he could say, so he simply held her, allowing her tears to provide the release he knew she needed. As much as he hated tears, she'd earned them—even to the point of tripping and falling down. And he was sure she'd reinjured her shoulder again. Yeah, he'd noticed her favoring it. He just hadn't asked her about it yet.

He drew her against his chest and held her while she cried about crazy things... the rocking chair she had just finished painting and would never get to use. The fact that she had walked out and left the oven going on the casserole she had just put in. The laundry that was in the washer.

She cried about leaving her cottage and her friends without so much as a goodbye, and wondered if they were safe? She even cried about Lainie being such a good baby during the worst of it.

Clint continued holding her for a long while until the tears slowly began ebbing. He sensed reality was finally beginning to set in when she eventually took a shaky breath and made a small move to ease away from him. Dropping his arms Clint shifted, watching her intently as she slid back down onto the mattress and drew Lainie close.

Her movements were slow and ungainly. He understood. He was feeling it too. For him, the trek to and from the ship and back again had been so demanding, every muscle in his entire body ached. Despite the fact that he considered himself physically in shape, the way he saw it, if *he* was hurting, then how much worse was it for her—especially having recently given birth? He idly wondered how long it takes for a woman to return to normal after childbirth.

A chime sounded from the onboard computer reminding him that he'd left in the middle of a directive that was still waiting for completion. There was plenty of things for him to do, the least of which right now was getting back to the helm. No sense expecting a miracle when he knew communications were down. So, for the moment, he remained where he was, sitting back on his heels and quietly observing Angela. She looked so young and pitiful lying there. Her honey blond hair was tousled about her face and shoulders, and beneath her eyes were blue bruise-like stains.

Gone was the sexy, vibrant young woman who had literally knocked him off his feet when she'd opened the door this morning. It wasn't only the scanty get-up that had his attention and kept her on his mind—although he had to confess, *that* was part of it. It was a combination of things: the pink flush of embarrassment when he told her he was tempted to change his mind about ravishing her. It was the way her ponytail swayed when she walked, the sparkle in her eyes when she held Lainie. He hadn't missed a thing and, in many ways, he was still reeling over the vision she had imprinted on him this morning.

At his advice before they'd left Aurora, she'd slipped into a pair of warmer jeans and an additional soft long-sleeve shirt. And now, as he watched her, Clint wondered if she was aware that she had mismatched the buttons on her shirt after she'd last fed Lainie. No doubt, another testimony to her exhaustion.

As she lay on her side next to Lainie with her slim legs bent at the knee, Clint noticed that the lower part of her pant legs were still damp— the ones she'd worn beneath the thermal snow pants he'd given her. Snow had obviously wicked in under the thermal pants. He thought she had changed them earlier, but maybe her personal things hadn't made it here after all. Regardless, she needed to get those damp things off, and he needed to figure out what, if anything, was around for her to change into.

Rising to his feet, Clint made his way to the galley to refill his coffee. In spite of the fact that the galley had been enlarged, it was still small by comparison to the galleys on the *Aris*, the *Solar Wind,* as well as the *Windstar*. Nevertheless, what this galley lacked in size, it made up for in an extensive selection of food. If they had to, he and Angela could hole up here for six months or more. Not that he wanted to be marooned for six months. Far from it. He was only supposed to be gone a day at the most. He had a business to get back to and the thing that annoyed him more than anything was the fact that communications were down. He couldn't even touch base with his foreman, and with weather conditions the way they were, God only knew when he'd finally get back.

Reaching for his mug, he refilled it with coffee then wandered into the master bedroom, hoping that possibly some of Tressa's clothes were hanging in the closet. Tressa and Angela looked to be about the same size, and just maybe he'd find something warm and dry for Angela to change into.

Within a few minutes he'd found something he thought would work—a warm pair of light blue sweatpants with a drawstring waist and matching pull-on top. Pleased with his find, he grabbed a pair of heavy socks then turned for the lav where he set the outfit on a small shelf. From there he crossed over the corridor into the galley again and wondered if he should just heat something up for her. She hadn't eaten or had anything to drink since they had arrived.

Lainie had started fussing again and was beginning to sound pretty serious. If he knew what to do, he'd do it and let Angela sleep a little longer. But since he knew absolutely nothing about babies and even if he did, he couldn't feed her anyway, it was time to add his voice to the mix. With that, he hunkered down at Angela's back and leaned over to speak softly in her ear.

"Hey, sleepyhead... I think Lainie wants something."

That brought Angela's eyes open with a jolt.

His amused masculine voice went on. "I don't know much about babies, but if you need me to help, I'm willing to learn." He watched as she slowly began stirring, blinking reality back into focus.

"But there's just one thing, sunshine," he drawled lazily, "I can't help you feed her. 'Fraid God didn't equip me for that particular job."

He waited, watching as Angela fought a smile. Next came a whisper-soft giggle as she rolled over to face him. "And thank God for that," she murmured.

"Why do you say that?" he asked, feigning a disheartened look. "You think I'd do it wrong?"

"Exactly." Angela said with a soft laugh as she reached for Lainie. Turning her attention to the baby, she asked, "Isn't that right, love? He'd just complicate matters, wouldn't he?" Listening to the familiar animated voice, Lainie instantly quieted and intently studied her mother's face as Angela reached for the new diaper Clint had just set down for her. At least he was beginning to understand that babies seem to need a fresh diaper every time they wake up.

"You are such a good little pumpkin. Mommy just loves you."

"Angela, when you're all done with Lainie, I got something I need you to do," he said as he turned for the short passageway that led toward the galley.

"Okay."

CHAPTER NINE

SOLARBLAZE ENERGY
Drilling and Production
East Flats, Acacia

Max Banner approached Clint's foreman as he entered the portable office building at Solarblaze's main drilling field. "Good morning, Dan. Anyone heard from Clint yet?"

"Not yet, Max. I'm thinking he's probably holed up somewhere until that damned space vortex passes. Tried getting through to him this morning, but communications are still down.".

Max nodded. "Yeah, I tried too. And from what I've heard, conditions aren't going to improve for possibly another week or so."

"What's going to take another week or so?" Chip asked as he came through the door. Chip was one of Solarblaze's six derrick operators. "Mornin' Mr. Banner. Any word yet on Clint?"

Max greeted Chip with a nod and mention of his name. "Not yet."

"So, tell me what's going to take another week?" Chip asked again as he grabbed a mug and began pouring coffee.

"That Vortex up in the northern mountains," Dan answered.

"Well, ain't that just great," Chip muttered. "The boss is gone. Communications are down so we can't get through to him, and it's going to be a week or more before that storm settles down." Chip tested his coffee and went on. "So, what are we supposed to do in the meantime? Shut things down and sit around waiting?"

"No," Max interjected sharply. "There'll be no shutting down. In fact, if you've shut anything down, I want crews put right back on today as well as tonight to make up for lost time. As of now, I'm filling-in for Clint and I expect everything progressing as usual.

"Dammit, I helped get Solarblaze into profit," he muttered beneath his breath. "I'd say I know a bit about running it until Clint returns." With that he said his goodbyes to Dan and Chip and turned for the door. "I'll be in at seven AM sharp, and I expect to see both drill rigs running when I get here."

"Yes sir, Mr. Banner," Dan replied. "I assure you, they'll be smokin'."

Max climbed back into his Ground Runner and turned for the long, dusty and rutted access that would bring him out onto the main road. He'd managed to deal with the problems at Solarblaze. The next hurdle is facing Delta when he gets home. He didn't look forward to having to tell her that nothing's changed—that Clint isn't back and communications are still down. Knowing the storm was coming, and that Clint was going to try to beat it back before it actually hit, Delta had been wringing her hands ever since he left.

Over the years, one by one, all three of the boys had moved out to be on their own. Yet as far as Delta was concerned, she was their mother and no matter how old they got, she still worried about them. Max had always felt that Delta would need to be hospitalized if she knew even half of what he knew about each one of his boys. There were plenty of things that were purposely never shared with her.

~ * ~

Angela had spent the last two hours feeding and playing with Lainie. She had just put her down for a nap and had made a trip to the lav. Noticing Clint in the galley when she came out, she crossed over the small corridor to join him.

Gusts continued pounding the ship as waves of sleet hammered the hull. "Isn't the storm ever going to let up?" she asked.

"I have a feeling we're in for the long haul on this one." His gaze flicked over her, and he noticed she wasn't wearing the outfit he'd placed in the lav earlier. Instead, she was still wearing the same shirt and jeans. Although the shirt had been properly secured this time, a slight frown creased his brow when he noticed that the fly on her jeans was only partially closed. "Something wrong with the things I set inside the lav for you?" he asked.

"I didn't know they were meant for me."

Who else would they have been for? he wanted to ask, but knew better. "Sorry, I should have said something."

Ignoring her half-buttoned jeans as best he could, he continued stirring the thick soup. The stove top was something Tressa had insisted on adding to the remodeled galley. Far as Clint was concerned, it beat the heck out of placing a commercial dinner tray in the warmer.

"You mentioned that there was something you wanted me to do?"

"Yes. I want you to get out of your wet clothes and change into that sweat outfit."

"I was wondering why my pants still feel damp. Shouldn't they be dry by now?"

"Probably. Vortex snow has a different chemical makeup. It's not the same as regular snow."

"But why after all this time do my pants still feel as if I just came in from outside?"

"I don't know Angela, but it wouldn't be a bad idea to change. I'm not sure it's a good thing to be laying against your skin like it is."

"Do you think it would it be okay if I were to take a quick shower?"

"Go for it," he said as he made his way out of the galley and turned for the helm.

She started to turn away when he asked in a low tone, "Angela, so other than feeling tired, how are you doing?" It bothered him that she had only managed to get her pants half way fastened. Something wasn't right. Did she know it and didn't care, or was she unable to get the buttons fastened?

As if reading his concern, she smiled. "I'm alright, Clint."

"Still cold?"

"Not so much now."

"Sore?"

"That's better too," she replied without looking at him.

Clint didn't miss the lack of eye contact, and Max's words quickly echoed in his mind about people not looking you in the eye. Something was wrong and she was refusing to admit it.

"Before I do anything, I want to pick up a bit around here," she said.

With a frown he watched as she bent down quickly picking up blankets, thermal outerwear, boots, gloves and whatever else was littering the floor. She was definitely working with one arm and favoring the other. He figured her shoulder again. Rae had told him that Angela had emphatically turned down the operation needed to repair her damaged rotator cuff.

"What's going on with your left arm?" he asked. He was leaning back against the command console, watching her. "You're protecting it like it hurts."

"No, it's nothing really. I think I just sprained it again when I fell."

He simply stared at her. She was back to that excuse again. It was more than just a sprain, and they both knew it."

Pulling away from the console, he started toward her. "Let me see it,"

Up came her good hand to stop him. "It's fine, Clint. Really. It's just a sprain."

He backed off but continued watching her as she went about tidying the ship. She was doing a grand job of playing the role, trying to impress him by using her injured arm as she worked. But she wasn't fooling him for an instant. It was obvious that most of the work was being done by her good arm.

"That's enough," he growled. He'd seen all he cared to see of her little performance, and he wasn't impressed.

"What?"

"I said, that's enough."

"I was only trying to tidy—"

"I know what you were doing. Go take your shower, Angela. I've got soup heating and it's almost ready."

"I'll hurry," she said as she disappeared in the lav, closing the door behind her.

Angela reached for the medal studs on her jeans, just now noticing and remembering she had left the top two undone. She could have fainted at the realization. There was little doubt but that Clint had noticed too. But thankfully he hadn't pointed it out.

Determined to hurry along, she began working on the next four studs that were still in tack. Somehow, she'd managed to undo them earlier when she'd used the facilities, but it seemed her arm was worse now, and the job was next to impossible to take on single handedly. With a soft whimper of pain and frustration, she tugged, pulled and pushed, until one stud finally slid out of the metal grommet. Now she only needed to do three more, but hopefully one more would allow her to wriggle out of her jeans as it had earlier.

With a low moan of pain, she started in on the next stud, using her left hand to hold the material still while she worked with the right to get it to slide through the grommet.

"Let me see your arm."

Angela jumped. He was behind her. The pocket-door to the lav was slid wide open and he stood infinitely framed in the open doorway. Angela dazedly wondered how he'd slid the door open without her hearing him but then decided it didn't make any difference how. Like it or not, he was there, invading her privacy.

"What are you doing?" she asked in a tiny voice.

"I didn't hear the shower. You're taking forever. I'm starving, and I got tired of waiting. Let me see your arm." He reached for her arm before she realized what he was doing. Pain shot from her shoulder down to her wrist as he gently drew her near. The only thing to ease the discomfort was to move right along with her arm until she was forced up against his body with her cheek pressed against his solid chest.

With careful probing Clint examined her wrist. "Hurt?"

"No."

He moved his tender assessment to her elbow. "How about here?"
She shook her head. "No."

But when he got to her shoulder, the story changed. Despite the fact that he was being as gentle as possible, Angela sucked in her breath when he probed a particularly suspicious area. He didn't need to ask if it hurt. It was painfully obvious it hurt like hell.

"You know what I'm going to say, don't you?"

Angela nodded. "That it needs to be immobilized?"

"Right. And the sooner the better."

"Clint," she pleaded, tipping her head back to look up into his face, "I have a baby to care for, and I can't do it with one arm bound."

"You can't do it without your arm bound either, Angela."

"But, I'm all Lainie's got. I won't be able to take care of her if you bind my arm," she countered in a tight voice on the edge of tears.

"Sure, you can. She's small. Besides, I'll help you. Simply tell me what to do."

"It's just sprained, Clint. Please, don't put it in a sling."

"Geezes, Angela, I'm only talking about immobilizing it. Not amputating it. And you'll only need to keep it in a sling until we reach civilization and a medic can look at it."

"But I don't want a medic looking at it."

He huffed a soft laugh. "Now *that* I can believe. Especially since you turned him down on the operation he wanted to do. That operation could have prevented this reoccurrence, you know."

"I had my reasons, Clint."

He chuckled. "Of course you did."

"Please... can't we just leave it alone for one more day and see if it gets better?"

"I'm telling you, Angela, leave it alone and it will only get worse," he said gently. "Look, I know about these things," he went on. "In my line of work, I've seen far too many broken bones and torn ligaments, and believe me procrastination isn't the answer. If it heals wrong, you're in big trouble. You may not have a broken bone as such, but I'm betting you've torn that rotator cuff again, which no doubt was a weak-mend in the first place. Leave it alone and you could find yourself living permanently with a bum shoulder." Inclining his head, he looked down at her and coaxed, "All I'm asking is that you let me immobilize it until we can get to civilization. What do you say?"

His voice was so deep and reassuring, his body so large, so warm and powerful. And although he still had an unyielding hold on her injured arm. he was gentle as he forced her to remain intimately close to him. She could almost hear the beat of his heart beneath her ear. Deep inside she wanted to say yes, wanted to tell him to do what he thought best, wanted to simply permit him to take the decision out of her hands. She hesitated for only a minute before whispering, "Let me think about it, okay?"

Without comment he released her, allowing her to straighten and ease away from the awkward confinement of his embrace. She could tell he was disappointed in her halfhearted answer.

"Let's eat. I'm starved." He turned for the galley to check on the soup. It was thick and loaded with meat and veggies. He'd set things on low at the time he'd left to check on Angela. The ordeal had taken longer than anticipated, and even on low, he figured they'd be lucky if the soup wasn't scorched on the bottom.

"Go ahead and have a seat," he said as he set down their bowls of soup and a container of crackers. "You want milk, tea or what?"

Angela came forward and took a seat. "Milk, if you have it."

Clint returned to the table with a large glass of ice-cold milk for Angela and a steaming mug of coffee for himself.

"Mmmm. It smells good, Clint."

"Yeah, we're just lucky it didn't get scorched," he said, taking a seat across from her.

They ate in silence with Clint getting up to refill their bowls with the last of the soup. And when they finished up, Angela helped, as best she could, to clean off the table and toss things into the recycler. And without a word he let her help, if that's what she wanted to do.

"Okay... now go take that shower you wanted. And then, after that what do you say we do something about your shoulder?"

When she turned for the lav, he added. "Are you going to be able to get those studs undone?"

"Yes, I can do it."

"Well, just don't overdo things trying to prove it. Okay?"

CHAPTER TEN

Clint watched her disappear into the lav and slide the door shut. This time he heard the snick of the lock being engaged.

Twenty minutes passed and still no sounds of the shower. Finally, he paced to the lav. "Angela? Open the door."

"I'm okay, Clint."

"Open–the–door!"

A long-drawn-out moment passed before he heard the lock being disengaged. "What?" she asked as she slid the door open only far enough to allow her face to be seen.

Clint wouldn't have it, and slid the door completely open, exposing Angela, still wearing the same things—the jeans no more open than when he last saw them.

Dropping to one knee, he went for her socks first. "Lift your foot for me."

"What are you doing?" she asked, her voice a bit higher pitched than normal. Placing a hand on his shoulder for balance, she lifted her foot.

"Dammit, I'm taking off your wet socks." The words were barely out when both socks were being cast off to the side and he was starting in on her jeans.

"Clint, I can do it." With her good arm, she reached down to stop him.

He pushed her hand away. "You already had your chance, sunshine. And why the devil are you wearing button-fly jeans? They went out of style decades ago."

"Maybe so, but it's called the retro look, and on Earth it's the latest style for women." she said, her tone nervous, yet defensive.

"Well, they're not in style for men. Not here, anyway. And even if they were, I sure as hell wouldn't be opening them one damned button at a time. I'd open them all at once with a single tug." With that, he grabbed the fly of her jeans in both hands and gave a strong yank, rapidly popping open all of the remaining studs in one action. "And you wanna know why, sweetcakes?" he asked baitingly, not waiting for her response. "Because when a man wants his pants open, he doesn't want to wait."

He didn't know why he was taunting her all of a sudden. In the long run he supposed it gave him and Angela something else to concentrate on besides the project at hand. He could tell he'd embarrassed her with that last smart-assed comment. Her face was flushed and she was no longer looking at him, let alone arguing with him. So, he guessed, there was a certain advantage to being an ogre after all.

"How the *hell* did you get them on in the first place?" he asked. "Wha'd' you do, spray 'em on?"

"I know, I'm still fat. Actually, I still have another few pounds to lose. I've been doing exercises every…" Her nervous prattle suddenly dropped off as he began adroitly working the jeans down her legs. She reached for his shoulder again. "Some women just don't have to work much to get back into shape," she chattered on, balancing first on one foot then the other. "But, unfortunately I'm not one of them."

Without comment, Clint tossed her jeans off to the side. He had another smart-assed comment on the tip of his tongue, but at the moment he couldn't recall what it was. His attention was presently focused on yet another surprising layer of clothing—the short cutoffs that she'd been wearing that morning. No wonder her jeans were so tight. "Why did you put your jeans on right over the top of your cutoffs?"

"You said to wear double layers."

Clint stifled his pleasure at seeing those sexy cutoffs once again as he began working on opening yet another button fly. It was like unwrapping a beautiful present, and this time around he took willful pleasure in opening up the cutoffs slowly—one button at a time. And she was worried about a few extra pounds? Maybe she knew where they were, but he sure couldn't see them. What he did see was a slim waist, sexy flared hips and a slightly rounded stomach, which in his opinion was more feminine than she could ever realize.

Once again Angela mechanically went through the process of balancing one hand on his shoulder as she lifted one foot, then the other. Having tossed the cutoffs aside with the jeans and socks, he discovered a pair of butter yellow bikini panties with gray lace that dipped in an open V beneath her gently curved belly.

Dear God... He had no idea. Angela was a vision of femininity in every sense of the word. With old feelings swiftly returning from five years ago, Clint's eyes lazily wandered down her shapely legs then back up again. Without even realizing what he was doing, he reached out to gently slide his cupped palm up the back of her leg, passed her calf and knee to settle on the back of her thigh. It was all he could do not to press his mouth against the open V of her panties.

Reality hit him when he noticed a stiffness in Angela's stance. Instantly, he stopped and glanced up at her, unsure what he would see when their eyes met. Pleasure? Anger? Hopefully permission? What he saw, however, wasn't pleasure or anger, but distress. Permission was denied by a subtle shake of her head.

It's a good thing one of them had the sense to put the brakes on. If she had been willing, neither of them would have been able to change the course of what would have followed.

Not trusting himself to keep his hands off of her, he rose to his feet and backed off. He needed to walk away and leave the rest for her to do. The main thing was to get the wet jeans and socks off, not seduce her.

He had to clear his throat before he could speak. "There..." he rasped, shoving the sweatpants into her hands, "the elastic waistband should be easier for you to manage."

"Clint, I can't wear this top," she said, her voice sounding equally strained.

"Why not?"

"It's too hard to get on with my shoulder the way it is. Plus," she added with a blush, "I need something that fastens down the front."

He didn't ask why. "You want me to see if I can find something else?"

"No, I'll just wear my same shirt."

"Whatever works."

If she only knew you've already seen her nurse Lainie.

It wasn't something he was exactly proud of, nor did he regret it either. It had all started out so innocent—or so he told himself. And it had touched him as he looked upon the peaceful bond between mother and baby, the serene look on Angela's face, but then...

But then it turned into more than that, didn't it, old man? It stirred you.

So...? I walked away, didn't I? Peeved at himself, and the whole situation in general, Clint turned and stocked toward the bow of the ship.

"I'll be in the helm," he snapped. "We'll do something with your shoulder later."

It was obvious nothing had changed outside the cocoon of the ship. As if to prove it, the wind was still howling. A large gust, in fact, had just slammed into the ship only a few minutes ago. Snow and sleet were still hammering the hull. It was also likely nothing had changed with communications, but at least being up in the helm gave him something else to concentrate on, to get his mind off of Angela and time to cool off.

Lagging back under the shower, Angela spent the time trying to figure out what had just happened. Her heart was racing, her face flaming. It started when he began undressing her. And then, when he touched her—her knees nearly buckled. His hand was hot, and she felt as though he'd branded her. The feeling was incredible. Scary, but incredible nonetheless. She wondered what Clint felt. In truth, he seemed to act as though it was no big deal to undress her, as if he undresses women all the time. Which she imagined he probably does.

Yes, a small voice agreed, *and when he does, you can rest assured that it's for an entirely different purpose than simply removing damp socks and jeans.*

Well, goodie for him, she thought sourly.

A full forty-five minutes passed before Angela finally emerged from the lav. Being mindful of the water supply, she'd taken a wonderfully warm shower, washed her hair and underthings, even dried and arranged her hair. Thank goodness, Tressa had placed a fresh bottle of shampoo and shower soap inside the lav for their use—just in case. She was also thankful that Clint had found something easier for her to put on than button-fly jeans.

Luckily Lainie had remained sleeping through it all. Embarrassed to face Clint, Angela's throat tightened as she ever so silently slid the bathroom door open and entered the short corridor. From there she padded quietly toward the helm where Lainie lay on the mattress only a few feet behind Clint as he sat at the controls. Lifting Lainie with her good arm, she quickly retreated back to the galley.

Where was that self-protective, independent person she'd been a year ago when she'd left Mason? As afraid of Mason as she had been, as mentally and physically broken as she had been, it still amazed her that she'd had the courage to take Piper, drain Mason's bank account and travel three thousand miles all by herself across the United States?

And now, how could she have simply remained standing there in complete submission, allowing Clint to remove her clothes and touch her as he had? Besides, once he got the damp socks and jeans off, there was no reason to continue removing anything else. Yet he did.

His purpose was two-fold, the silent voice argued. *First, to get the wet things off. Second, to make it easier for you to manage on your own. And that meant divesting you of button flies. Those cutoffs also had a button-fly too, remember?*

But, did he have to touch her like he did?

You allowed it. What healthy male is going to pass up that opportunity and stop on his own while you linger, trembling like a pagan sacrifice? You're lucky he stopped at all. Remember that, Angela, you're lucky he stopped–at–all.

Tired of arguing with herself on the subject, Angela sucked in a deep breath and turned her thoughts to Lainie who was quietly studying her mommy. "You are such a little princess," Angela whispered. "You've been such a good girl and mommy just loves you so much."

What had happened between her and Clint was over and it was time to move on. The question now was, how should she move on? Should she ignore what had happened, pretend it never occurred and just be her normal self? What was her normal self anyway?

At last she decided she would wait and let him set the pace.

Angela didn't have long to wait. Clint entered the galley with his usual easy stride that, just watching him, always seemed to set off a host of butterflies in her stomach. Placing his empty coffee mug down by the sink, he turned to her. "How's the shoulder?"

"Sore." she replied, remaining seated at the booth where Lainie was laying on a blanket kicking the air and smiling at her mommy.

Angela needed to gain control the way she had a year ago. They had been alone on the *Aris* a whole lot longer back then.

It was easier then, an inner voice reminded her. *Not only was the Aris a much bigger ship, Clint was the one setting the pace at the time. Not you. If you'll recall he couldn't get you back to Acacia fast enough. You had no control over the situation. What makes you think you can control it now?* The inner voice laughed.

It was true. She could never gain control of anything when he fascinated her so. Clint Banner was exceedingly virile. Everything about him smacked of man, and drew her like a magnet.

Bone tired, she gingerly picked up Lainie with her good arm, carried her out of the galley and over to the mattress where she began changing her diaper. She wanted desperately to keep Lainie with her. At the moment she needed to either hold Lainie or be held herself. She'd forgotten what it was like to be lovingly held. It was certainly something she had rarely known from Mason.

Knowing that it would be best for Lainie to be in the small crate that Clint had found and lined with blankets, Angela carefully laid her in the make-shift cradle. Then she went over to the bunks, removed a pillow and carried it back to the mattress. It was growing dark out, the end of a day unlike any other day she had ever known. She could only assume her cozy little home was gone. And what about her friends, Emily and the others? Were they safe? Would she ever see them again?

"So how are you feeling now?"

Angela jumped, not realizing he'd followed her out of the galley. "Better. Thank you."

"Then what do you say we get that arm in a sling?"

"Can we do that tomorrow?"

"It's *your* shoulder."

Without comment, Angela laid down in front of the heat vent, wrapped herself in a blanket, closed her eyes and listened to the wind howl. An hour later sleep was not forthcoming. Plain and simple, her shoulder hurt like the devil. If only she could find a comfortable position. She shifted from one side to the other, yet nothing was helping.

At last she sat up and tucked her arm against her body, hoping that would help. It didn't. The pain was relentless, a constant ache that was even worse than she remembered dealing with a year ago. And it wouldn't be silenced no matter what she did.

I'm telling you, Angela, leave it alone and it will only get worse.

It wasn't the first time Clint's warning had tramped through her painfilled mind. She knew he was right, and yet simply admitting it certainly did nothing to relieve the pain.

At last, she turned to see where Clint was. He was sitting up front, sprawled in the command seat. His legs were stretched out in front of him and crossed at the ankles. His hands were interlaced on his stomach and his head was resting against the back of the seat. It was nighttime and the inside of the ship was dark, the only lights were clusters of winking lights coming from the command console.

Angela thought he was asleep, until she saw a tiny glint of light flicker in his eyes. He was not only awake, he was stoically watching her.

Clearing her throat first, she asked in a small voice, "Is there something you can do, maybe?"

"...What do you mean?"

"My shoulder. I think it's getting worse."

"Yeah, that's to be expected with a sprain. You just have to let it run its course."

She didn't miss the implied challenge. "Clint, I should have listened to you. I'm sorry." She took a shaky breath and continued. "You've been right all along. I think that fall did more damage than I wanted to admit." She hesitated before going on. "It didn't hurt like this in the beginning, and I didn't want to believe it would get worse... but it has." She bit her lower lip and fought back tears of frustration. "I don't know how I'm going to take care of Lainie with only one arm, but... it really hurts. Is there anything you can do? Please?"

Before she was even finished, Clint was out of his seat, calling himself every name in the book for making her plead for his help. She didn't deserve it. From what Rae had told him, Angela had had a violent life over the last few years. Not only had she recently lost both of her parents, but she'd known nothing but abuse from her asshole husband.

It incensed him to think that Mason had been the one to damage her shoulder in the first place. Flipping on the overhead high intensity lighting, he directed her to sit in the command seat. "I'll be right back," he said as he headed down the corridor.

He was hardly gone a minute before he returned with what looked to be a bed sheet. Guessing at the length he would need, he took a knife from his back pocket, opened it and made a snip at the edge of the sheet. He then ripped off the length needed for a sling. Once that was done, he folded it into a triangle. "Okay," he said, "It's going to hurt when I start adjusting the tension. I'll try to be easy."

"Just do what you have to do," she said weakly.

CHAPTER ELEVEN

"Honey, twist the seat around to face me and scoot forward a bit." She did, and he dropped to his knees between her legs. As gently as possible Clint began positioning the impromptu sling. When he began setting the tension on the sling, she made no sound other than two or three muffled gasps and began leaning into him, pressing her face against his shoulder. Flicking a quick glance down at her, he noted that she had turned pale, yet she remained silent and unmoving until he finished securing the sling. This time, he strongly suspected the damage was even greater than it had been a year ago. Setting the tension was tricky. Too loose and it would do little good. Too tight and it could make things worse.

"All done," he finally murmured as he sat back on his heels to observe his handiwork. "You did good, Angela. I know it was painful."

She looked up at him and gave him a shaky smile. "I came awful close to slapping your hands away."

"I know you did," he replied sheepishly. "There was just no easy way to do it." He rose to his feet. "Stay put. I'm going to get an ice pack."

Angela slumped back into the seat, feeling weak and nauseous. In the silence, a soft chime sounded from the console drawing her attention as several lights winked out and others snapped to life.

Clint returned with an ice pack and hunkered down before her. "You need to keep this in place for at least a half hour. Your shoulder is very swollen, and it's important to get that swelling down as soon as possible. After twenty minutes or so we'll see how things are looking, but I suspect it will need at least another go or two of ice."

"How long do you think it will take for the pain to ease?"

"If I've done it right, it should ease up in a day or so."

"A day or so?" she whispered.

"If I know Tressa, there's a fully stocked first aid kit somewhere around here. I'll look to see if it's got something for the pain."

"No, Clint. I don't want any meds. Just knowing the pain is temporary, I can handle it."

"Okay, but if you change your mind—"

"I won't."

After a moment of silence, Angela straightened and started to get up. "I should let you get some sleep," she said. "I don't think you've slept at all since we arrived."

"I've catnapped. I'm all right. You're the one who needs sleep."

After several long moments, Clint rose to his feet and made his way over to a storage locker located along the corridor. He retrieved an extra pillow and a couple extra blankets and brought them back to where Angela was checking on Lainie.

Taking the pillow, he propped it on the floor against a short wall about two feet to the right of the heat vent. At last he sat down, leaned back against the pillow and stretched out his long legs. If she wasn't going to take any meds for the pain, then the least he could do is help her get comfortable and keep the ice pack in place. He could always catch up on sleep later. With that, he reached for Angela's pillow, placed it across his lap and patted it, motioning for her to lie down. "If you want to stretch out in front of the vent, do it on your right side and lay your head on the pillow."

She followed his instruction, except for laying her head down. Instead she propped herself up on her elbow.

"Relax, Angela. Lay your head down. It's okay."

"But what about my shoulder?"

"Let me worry about your shoulder."

Finally, she relaxed, allowing herself to fully ease down onto the mattress, this time laying her head in his lap as instructed.

"Better?" he asked.

"No, I think it hurts even worse."

"Okay," he said. "Then, let's try Plan B." Although her arm and painful shoulder were tucked firmly against her body, Clint proceeded to remove the sling.

"What are you doing?"

"For tonight, let's try something else and see if it's less painful."

"After all that work?"

"Yep. Just for tonight. Hopefully you can get some sleep. The sling will need to go back on tomorrow, I'm afraid."

Once the sling was off, ever so gently he lifted her arm away from her body and slowly ease it upward. With care, he coaxed her into bending her elbow so that her forearm rested across the top of her head. Then he stopped and surveyed the finished result. It was a gamble that he hoped would work for her. "How does that feel?"

At first Angela hesitated then with a hint of a smile, "Better, I think." As awkward and ridiculous as it looked, raising her arm had apparently eased the worst of the pain.

"Now," Clint began, "this is only a temporary reprieve, you understand. Something to help you get some sleep tonight."

Why hadn't he thought of this earlier? Only now did he remember that several years ago, his youngest brother, Marc, had suffered a rotator cuff injury. Although not nearly as serious as he suspected Angela's to be, Marc had discovered that it had helped to ease the pain if he raised his arm. It wasn't something the doctor had recommended or approved for that matter, but it had helped nevertheless.

Angela felt Clint place the ice pack in the hollow between her raised arm and her collarbone. With the pain gradually fading, she sighed. She couldn't help but revel in the warmth and closeness of falling asleep with her head in Clint's lap. Earlier she had turned down pain meds, but this was better than any meds he could have given her. Mason was the only other person Angela had to compare these uncharted feelings with, and in truth, there was no comparison. Shortly after one year into their marriage, Mason had begun showing her another side of himself—not just an unfaithful side, but one that included both physical and mental abuse. And now, the final blow was denying their child—a child who was never conceived out of love in the first place and consequently would never know her father. However, she would know nothing *but love* from her mother.

She felt Clint cover her with a blanket, and as she listened to the soft whisper of life-support and felt its warmth, she gloried in the tenderness of the man in whose lap she lay. Her last conscious thought as she slowly began drifting into a peaceful sleep was of a calloused hand smoothing a lock of hair from her cheek. One more thing to tuck away in that safe, secret little place of warm memories.

It was still dark out when Angela stirred. At some point she and Clint had migrated fully onto the mattress with Lainie still in her makeshift cradle. Gingerly, Angela tried to move her arm from off the top of her head only to feel the steely clamp of a hand holding her arm firmly in place. Again, she tried to lower her arm.

"Don't..." came a sleepy, masculine rumble near her ear.

That was when Angela's knew for sure that Clint was no longer sitting with his back against the wall, nor was she still laying with her head in his lap. They were laying together, and that thought alone cleared the mental fog in a hurry, bringing Angela fully awake.

With a sleepy groan he nuzzled her neck affectionately, and Angela's eyes widened at the realization that he wasn't simply behind her somewhere on the mattress. He had snuggled against her in spoon fashion, the physical differences unmistakable in their awakening bodies. Even his legs were entwined with hers. But what frightened her more than anything was the feeling of being trapped. With her arm caught in his unyielding grasp, her legs entangled with his, she was as ensnared as a Terran hare, and it felt too close to the sickening games Mason had forced on her. Fighting panic, Angela tried to remind herself. This was Clint. Not Mason.

As if sensing that her mother was awake, Lainie suddenly began fussing with soft little whimpers. It gave Angela the drive she needed to rise above the panic and try to ease away from the awkward closeness between her and Clint. The only problem was, he still had a hold on her arm. Unless she can get him to release her, escape was out of the question.

Normally Clint would have come fully awake at the first sound or movement, but being overly tired and having had virtually no sleep, not to mention lacking the advantage of maternal instincts, he was not aware of anything beyond the soft warmth cozied up against him in all the right places. The first he became aware of anything awry was when that pleasing warmth shifted and tried to edge away. Next came the feel of slender fingers attempting to pry his hand off of her arm.

That brought him instantly awake, and he released her, but not without a stern order issued in a rough voice that had yet to wake up... "Don't pick her up. I'll do it for you."

"I can do it with my other arm, Clint."

"I don't want you doing it. I'll do it. Just tell me what to do." He was up and coming around to hunker down before her and Lainie.

Angela took a long hard look at him and decided that if she had not already known Clint, she would have been running the other direction. Between the dark shadow of a beard, the shocks of black hair curling haphazardly over his brow, and a deep raspy morning voice, he appeared dangerous.

"What...?" he snapped, aware of her lengthy, silent perusal. He sounded impatient and a bit surly. Not surprising, since they both seemed to be on edge.

"Oh nothing. Just thinking."

He frowned at her. "I'm serious, Angela. I don't want you causing more damage to your shoulder."

"I know, but I have to lift her anyway to change her diaper and feed her."

"I told you, I'll do it. Just tell me what to do."

"What do you mean, you'll do it? You can't feed her, Clint."

He slid her a retiring look. "I know that, Angela."

Reaching across the mattress he snagged the sling that he'd tossed to the side last night. "And before we do anything, I want to get this back in place."

"I can tell you right now, Lainie's not going to wait for that, besides it's still the middle of the night. I need to feed her as soon as possible and get her back into her bed."

"Well, she'll just have to wait. There's good reason for you to wear a sling. I sure as hell didn't have fun adjusting the tension last night, and—"

"It's *still* last night. Come morning, I'll let you put it back on. Okay?"

With a curt nod he sat back. "But until we get back to civilization, let's at least give the damn thing a chance."

CHAPTER TWELVE

Meanwhile Lainie was working up a serious protest, and getting louder by the minute.

"I better get her, Clint."

"Stay put." He moved to squat down in front of the makeshift crib. With his hands poised, his look intense and all business, he faced Angela. "Okay, tell me what to do first."

Angela smiled. "You've never held a baby? Really?"

He scowled at her amusement. "Well, I've held Braeden," he said defensively.

Angela smiled and wanted to say, *but only after someone handed him over to you, I bet,* but she refrained from saying it. Instead she said, "Alright. Here's what I want you to do. First, slide one hand beneath her head and neck. The other hand beneath her bottom. Yes... like that. That's right. See? Now lift her. There. You've got her, and she's fine."

"No, she's not fine. She's screaming."

"She's hungry, and she's wet," Angela said calmly. "No doubt you'd be screaming too."

With heavy eyes and in need of a shave, Clint couldn't have looked more scandalous if he'd tried. The scene before her could have easily been entitled "The Baby and The Pirate," or better yet, "The Baby and The Pagan God." As heathen looking as he was, he fit either description. And there he was, hunkered down before her, holding Lainie as if she were a dangerous explosive about to detonate. The scene was priceless, and as badly as Angela wanted to laugh, she knew better.

"Now what?" he asked in all seriousness.

Angela held out her good arm. "I can take her now."

But Clint's attention was again drawn to the unhappy bundle in his hands. "I don't think she likes me holding her."

"She's fine, Clint. You're doing good." Angela appreciated his help and if he truly was going to be a help to her, she knew it was not only important that she *not* laugh, it was equally important that she calmly help him gain self-confidence. One slip-up on her part could have him backing out of the whole deal. And like it or not, she did welcome his help.

"She's still screaming, Angela."

"Clint..." Angela began softly, slowly, "I told you, she's hungry and she's wet. Besides, babies like being held in a way that makes them feel secure. Try to relax. You're very tense and Lainie senses it."

"I'm afraid I'll drop her."

"You're not going to drop her. I promise. Now relax." Angela waited until she saw him visibly attempt to relax.

"Good. Now, I want you to ease her around so that her head ends up tucked into the crook of your elbow and your forearm is supporting her back. Okay, now draw her in against you, so that she is supported by your body as well. "That's it. Perfect."

The crying instantly stopped as Lainie turned her head toward Clint's chest and began rooting around for breakfast. He didn't seem to realize what Lainie was up to, but Angela knew. And she also knew that it would only be a matter of time before Lainie realized breakfast wasn't coming, and the crying would begin all over again.

"This isn't so bad after all," he said, smiling as he made small lifting motions with his arm. "She doesn't weight much, does she?"

"No, she doesn't."

Twenty-four hours ago, Angela never would have allowed Lainie to be held by anyone other than herself or Emily, let alone someone who was practically a stranger. Well, maybe he wasn't exactly a stranger, but he was a stranger to Lainie and worse, he knew absolutely nothing about babies.

Come to think about it, maybe he was a stranger more than she wanted to admit. After all, it had been five years and she didn't know much about Clint's life now. She only knew bits and pieces that Rae had shared with her. As she understood it, he was working at some sort of drilling company. It's what he had gone to school for.

And she knew him to be loyal. If someone needed him, they could count on him. How else could she explain why he had made the trip to Aurora before Mason's goons found her, especially knowing there was a dangerous storm on the way. How else could she explain why, despite his own exhaustion, he had sat on the floor with her head in his lap, or the way he'd covered her with a blanket and held her as she fell asleep, or the way he kept her curled against him, even keeping her arm in place as he grabbed a bit of sleep himself. And now, the way he was holding Lainie, she could tell he still wasn't entirely at ease with it but wasn't quite ready yet to hand her back.

Odd, this time she'd barely been with him twenty-four hours and she felt she knew him better than she had years ago. Clint had a depth to him she doubted many men possessed.

Her focus dropped to Lainie who was looking up at Clint with unblinking eyes. Angela could only imagine what she was thinking as she stared at the man who held her in his arms. Unable to help herself, Angela's focus shifted back to the rugged face Lainie was studying. Despite the mussed hair and two-day stubble, Clint Banner was so heart stopping handsome that even in the dim lighting of the helm, he stole her breath.

His skin was dark. Again, she reminded herself that tans like that weren't acquired by limited exposure to the sun. And although Angela had no idea precisely what he did at Solarblaze, it was obvious he spent a good deal of time out of doors. The fine lines that fanned from the corners of his eyes were another indication of long hours in the sun. And his eyes... dear God, she could get lost in those eyes. One instant they were gentle and contemplative. The next instant they were smoldering with blue fire. Like they were doing right now. Angela blinked as a slow and ever so slight suggestive smile tugged at one corner of his mouth. It was a direct look that conveyed more than words ever could have. With just a look, it plainly said they shared something special tonight. Was it because he was holding Lainie? Or was it because they had slept together? Maybe it was both. She had never seen a look quite like that leveled on her. Mason had certainly never looked at her that way. The look alone had her breath tripping over itself.

With her eyes still focused on Clint, she whispered, "Maybe I'd better feed her. She quickly glanced at the clock on the command console, it's the middle of the night. She needs to get back to sleep."

Though he didn't say a word, Clint's gaze dropped to her breasts with one of those deep in thought looks she was beginning to recognize. The silence was intense as an unbidden tingling coiled downward from her breasts to settle low in her belly.

She hadn't known that feeling since Clint was in college and making regular trips out to see her. It was startling. It was completely unanticipated, and it was sexual. Other than when she was with Clint, Angela couldn't recall the last time she had felt sexy.

At last Clint raised his eyes to meet hers for one final, hot second before he began carefully reversing the steps he'd used earlier. Angela quickly began undoing her shirt, only to discover that she hadn't worn her bra since her earlier shower. Now it would mean exposing herself to Clint in the process of feeding Lainie.

By the time Clint was handing Lainie over, Angela had decided that the easiest way to handle the situation was to turn away from him. But when she began turning away, his voice came to her deep and smoky... "Angela. Don't turn away. Indulge me. Let me watch." His voice was soft and low. It was a plea more than just a request.

That low sexy male voice could still vibrate her heart. After all he'd done for her, how could she deny him this? Yes, it was embarrassing. Yes, it was inappropriate and yet it was such a simple request—or so she told herself as she slowly eased back the edge of her plaid blouse, exposing her breast to Lainie's ravenous mouth and Clint's hungry eyes.

Angela tried keeping her head down while Lainie nursed. She knew what she'd see if she looked at him. She'd already seen the heat in his eyes,] and felt the answering coil in her own body, and to her stunned amazement, it felt good.

For Clint, it was anything but a feel-good moment. Plain and simple, he was aroused and he had no one to blame but himself. The pressure behind his fly was getting tighter by the second. One minute he was holding Lainie, his thoughts focused on the baby, proud of himself for not dropping her. The next minute he's watching Angela nurse the child, and that's when trouble began. He was a goner for sure when he glanced up and found Angela watching him with a look that instantly turned him on.

What was it about Angela that drew him? He'd always been attracted to women who were tall, full busted, had long legs and long swirling dark hair that easily played peekaboo with a breast.

Angela was just the opposite of the women he usually sought out. And granted, her breasts might be large, but they were also filled with milk, which in itself should be a turnoff.

So... what was it that called to him? He guessed it was a whole lot of things.

Hell, this was Angela, his kid sister's friend. And yet he definitely felt something for her five years ago. And then he felt it again as he helped her out of her double layers of button-fly pants, especially when he touched her shapely legs, feeling the softness of her skin, and at last seeing her sexy panties that dipped into a V beneath the gentle curve of her stomach. He knew she'd been embarrassed, thinking she was still fat, but for the life of him, he couldn't see what she was concerned about. As far as he was concerned, she was sexy as hell.

No longer was she the giddy teen he once knew. Even back when she was in her teens, he'd noticed her beauty and recalled wishing she were older. Good lord, there were eight years between them. The age difference didn't seem such a stretch now, but back then when she was in her early teens and he was twenty-one, she was still just a kid. And yet, oddly, as time passed and Angela matured, like a metal spike caught in a magnetic field, he had found himself drawn to her. She sparked him as no other woman ever had. It really began during the years when he was in college and had made countless trips to visit her. It all started out with an invitation to come for Christmas. From there, it gradually grew into more, and as much as he wanted to make love to her, he just couldn't bring himself to take her innocence knowing he wasn't ready to commit to marriage just yet. And he also knew that Angela wasn't the type for casual sex.

Shortly before he'd graduated, they had talked of marriage. But talk was all it amounted to as far as he was concerned at the time. Regretfully, he never did ask her to marry him. Back then, he just wasn't sure he was ready. He'd been so anxious to return to Acacia and get on with his plans, anxious to put his schooling to use. He had asked Angela to come back with him, to give him a chance to get his life together before talking marriage. But it didn't happen the way he'd hoped. Instead, she'd given up on him. How many times had he cursed himself for not promising her marriage, for not begging her to come back with him? Hell, he should have just asked her to marry him right then and brought her back as his bride. Instead, he returned to Acacia, leaving them both to wonder where exactly they stood. Somehow, together they would have weathered the wrinkles of marriage and life in general while he got Solarblaze on its feet. But instead she ended up marrying Mason Cooper. The very thought of Cooper made him angry.

Anger was always a good outlet whenever he was aroused with no release in sight. And yet, in this case, he was still aroused. So why hadn't the damn thing settled back down, he wondered?

Because you're still watching, pal. You should be walking away. You're doing this to yourself. Get the hell up now and walk away.

Clint took a deep breath and released it slowly as his gaze drifted from Angela's bent head to her bare breast, to her suckling baby, to her slender hand lovingly stroking the top of Lainie's head. Yes, it was the source of his arousal.

He'd never had an innocent. Never wanted one. Not that he resorted to common whores, but the women he chose to seek out were far from innocent. They knew the game and didn't need pretty words or gentle sweet-talking.

Out of them all, Shelbi was the one who had managed to worm her way past his regret over Angela. Shelbi had been there for him, had willingly given of herself, taking from him without complaint, no matter what he demanded of her. It was not a good relationship, but at the time neither of them could see it or cared. She made him forget, and that's all that mattered. Basically, he got what he needed, and she got what she wanted... Him, worthless sonofabitch that he was. And for a while, the arrangement worked.

Aware that his body had finally given up hope and had begun to relax, he rose to his feet with a heavy sigh. He desperately wanted to apologize, to tell her how sorry he's been. Tell her how much he's missed her, how he has wished...

Wished what? That you had married her back then? The silent voice laughed. *A little late to tell her that now, wouldn't you say, sport?*

CHAPTER THIRTEEN

A half hour later Clint was in the command chair, studying the controls again, hoping for some change in communications, change in the weather, something, *anything*.

He pressed a key and brought forth the exterior camera on the viewscreen. It was still dark outside. Heavy snow continued blowing across the lens, illuminated by a couple of spot lights mounted on the ship's exterior hull.

Slowly, he became aware that Angela had laid the baby down to change her diaper. Rising to his feet, he left the command seat and came around. "Need help?"

"I got it. Besides, I don't think you're going to want to help me with this one, Clint."

"Oh..."

Angela laughed as she watched him turn away and cross over to stand before the viewport. Palms out, he'd slid his hands into his back pockets. His hands barely fit. In fact, squeezing them into his pockets as he was doing stretched the denim even more tightly across his lean hips. It wasn't until Lainie began fussing again that Angela suddenly remembered what she was supposed to be doing instead of gawking at Clint's backside of all things. Once she'd changed the diaper, she quickly placed Lainie back into her makeshift cradle.

"You done?"

"Yes."

With that, Clint turned off the overhead lights in the helm, leaving only the command console aglow with its myriad of tiny winking lights.

He then pulled the second mattress back to its original position against the wall. Realizing his intentions, Angela felt a pang of disappointment. She had so enjoyed the warmth of his body snuggled up next to her.

Lowering himself back down with his back against the wall, he laid the extra pillow once again upon his lap and encouraged Angela to lay back down with her head on the pillow. "Sorry about crowding you on the mattress earlier. I guess I fell asleep," he said as he covered her with the extra blanket. "Lay your head down, honey, like you did before."

Slowly she laid her head down on the pillow. "You had a right to fall asleep," she said. "I don't need you to stay awake to hold my arm in place. You need your sleep too. I can—"

"Give me your hand," he asked, cutting off her protest. At her reluctant submission, he ever so carefully drew her arm up to rest once again, palm-up upon her head. Gently he held it in place. In spite of the fact that she had enjoyed the shared intimacy of Clint's body-heat spooned against her backside, Angela supposed this was the next best thing. "I have to say," she murmured, "it does ease the pain when my arm is raised like this."

"Good. But, tomorrow it's back to the sling."

"I know."

She recalled with vivid clarity the heat that had flashed between them upon waking. Although the lure had cooled since then, she knew exactly what she felt, and she also knew what she had seen in Clint's eyes. It wouldn't take much for things to burst into flame again. So, under the circumstances, it was probably best after all that he wasn't stretched out next to her.

With her head once again resting in Clint's lap and the pain in her shoulder not nearly as sharp as it had been, Angela quickly drifted back to sleep. And almost as if she sensed her mother's need for sleep, Lainie also settled down, sleeping for nearly five hours.

It was going on nine-thirty in the morning when Lainie's soft whimpers woke Angela from a sound sleep. Instantly, she became aware of a pleasant warmth around her feet. At first, she thought it was Trixie, especially since at home Trixie was always curling up on the foot of her bed. But the more aware she became, the more she realized that the warmth wasn't coming from Trixie at all. Instead, her feet were entangled with Clint's once again, and for a moment she didn't move... didn't breathe. The feeling was too good, and Angela wasn't quite ready to lose it just yet. For a moment longer she listened to the storm still howling outside and concentrated on the soft whispering of life-support as it maintained the fixed warmth inside the ship.

Unfortunately, Lainie didn't care about the storm. She had other ideas for her mother, and with a sigh Angela started to sit up.

"Stay put. I'll get her," came a deep sleepy voice that contradicted the speed at which he scrambled over her. Angela didn't miss the new found ease at which he picked Lainie up this time. Instantly, the baby stopped crying. "Hey you," he frowned at her. "What was all that fussing about? I thought you were hungry, or wanting your diaper changed or something."

Angela laughed. "I think she just wanted to be picked up. But it won't be long and she will be fussing about both her diaper and being hungry."

Clint continued frowning and slowly shook his head. "They learn too fast."

"Yes, they do. But then I'm afraid I'm to blame. Being my first and only child, I'm guilty of jumping to her every whim. I've spoiled her. Lainie has only me and I have only her."

"What about grandparents?"

"Didn't Rae tell you?"

"Tell me what?" he asked, gently laying Lainie down on the mattress next to Angela.

"Both of my parents were killed in an accident a little over a year ago," Angela said as she began undressing Lainie for a diaper change.

"I'm very sorry, Angela. No, I didn't know."

"And as far as Mason's parents?" she went on, "I'm sure by now they know about the baby, but to hear Mason tell it, since he denied Lainie from the very beginning, they have no desire to even see her." With a sudden look of panic, she glanced up at Clint. "But what if they do want to see her?" she asked. "What if they try to take her away from me, Clint?"

"Angela... let's deal with that if and when it happens. Right now you and Lainie are out of Aurora and safe. They're not going to find you. I promise."

"But... where am I going to go? I have nothing. It's just me and Lainie. And that's it."

"Let me worry about that. Okay? Right now I need coffee." Rising to his feet, he turned and headed for the galley. Although it was subtle, he hadn't missed the hardening of Angela's tone when Mason's name came up. From what Rae had told him, Angela's marriage had been hell on Earth, both physically and mentally. Rae had showed him the picture of Angela's bruised face, the picture that Angela had sent to her the day after she'd left Mason. Clint cursed the memory of seeing those horrific injuries and silently avowed all over again that if Mason were to ever come after Angela or Lainie, he'd kill him.

By the time an hour had passed, Angela had fed Lainie and Clint had restored the sling on her arm before he headed for the shower. Whatever he'd done last night, her shoulder was feeling better this morning—not normal, but definitely less painful and for now that was enough.

She had just placed a well-fed and diapered Lainie onto a blanket and was nursing a mug of coffee when Clint came out of the lav, stripped to the waist, top button of his black pants undone, a towel draped about his neck, and his damp hair slicked back.

Trying her best to ignore the pleasant sight before her, Angela scooped up Lainie, rose to her feet and made her way out of the galley where she placed Lainie in her make-shift crib and began sorting out baby things to be washed.

"Clint, did you say there's a clothes washer on board?" she asked as she neared the galley with her good arm loaded with laundry.

He was carrying a bowl of hot water and a clean towel over to the table. "Yes, it's along the aft wall just inside the lav."

Once Angela got the clothes loaded and the washer going, she started to head back to the helm when suddenly at the entrance to the galley she stopped and went still. Clint was still stripped to the waist, sitting at the table with his back to her. Shaving.

A round mirror was set before him, and the bowl of hot water was sitting within easy reach. Presently, he was shaving his neck with some sort of old- fashioned type of manual razor, the likes of which she had never seen before. Stroking the blade upward, he continued making repeated channels in the lather as he progressed. He shot a quick glance at her in the mirror. "A bit old-timey, I know," he said, "but it's the only thing I could find. Why Nick had this relic onboard, I'll never know. Must have been a joke. I can't imagine him using it."

But it wasn't the shaver that had her rapt attention. It was the breadth of his sun-bronzed back and the muscles that rippled with each stroke of the blade. Transfixed, Angela remained frozen in place at the entrance to the galley, her eyes drawn to the scene before her. She remembered that he'd always looked fit, although she never realized just how fit. It wasn't until she had opened the door and let him into her small cottage yesterday morning that Angela remembered the raw power of his presence. But what she hadn't anticipated, was the effect he would have on her, seeing him as he was now. Angela swallowed hard, catching her lower lip between her teeth. She knew she should turn and leave, walk away from the visual banquet before her, but her feet refused to move, and her mind refused to order them to do so.

With her heart pounding, Angela remained rooted to the deck unable to take her eyes off Clint, noticing every glorious feature there was to notice. She noticed how damp spikes of dark hair fell over his nape. She also noted how the muscles of his shoulders bunched with each stroke of the blade. Traveling downward, there was an odd looking tattoo on his left side, and directly below that an irregular scar that disappeared below the waistband of his pants. From what she could see, the skin below his beltline was at least two shades lighter than his broad, coppery back.

Her gaze followed his spine back up to his shoulder blades then dropped again to his low-riding waistband. Dear lord, he was breathtaking, literally. Despite all the ugly things Mason had done to her, Angela was suddenly driven to visually acquaint herself with Clint's buff body. She wanted to reach out and touch him, to run her fingers through his silky black hair. He was more magnificent than she ever remembered, and the sight of him, half dressed, was doing strange and wicked things to her insides.

"Angela..."

She blinked as if coming out of a spell. He'd not only stopped shaving, with one brow arched he was looking at her reflection in the mirror.

"What are you doin'?" he asked low and soft.

"Nothing." Her mouth was dry, and her voice sounded as parched as it felt.

"Is that right?" He turned around to face her. His eyes narrowed, challenging her to level with him. "Sure looked like something to me."

At last Angela lifted her chin. "For your information," she snapped, "I came in to get a simple cup of coffee, and there you sit with your shirt off and taking up the entire table with your shaving things. What do you expect?"

"I guess I didn't expect you to stand there staring like you were," he said softly. "You've been married. I'm sure you've seen a man without his shirt before."

"Yes, I know, but—"

"And it isn't like you haven't seen a man shave before."

"Okay, but—"

He went on, "Maybe it's that you haven't seen a man shave the old-fashioned way as I'm having to do now? Maybe that's it? Except for one little thing, Angel... you weren't watching me shave. Were you?"

Angela stared at him, not knowing what to say.

"Maybe it's just that it's been a while, and you're hungry? Is that it?"

"What? No! I don't ever want another man in my life. Ever! And furthermore, sex is the very last thing on my mind."

A brief moment of silence passed before he spoke in that same soft, low-toned voice. "I saw the look, Angel. It was written in your eyes."

"Fine! And you can blame yourself for it, Clint." Dropping her voice to a low mutter, she continued, "Flaunting yourself in front of me like that, half naked with your dark suntanned body, your pants half undone and riding low on your hips and... and... Ohhh..." Her voice raised as she turned to storm from the galley, "I don't know what you expected, but you got exactly what you asked for, Clint!"

"What I expected?" He'd bounded to his feet to trail right behind her. "I expected you to have some self-discipline. That's what I expected. Don't look to me for it, Angela. We're going on three days now in these tight quarters, and believe me, baby, I'm fresh out of will power."

At that she laughed and turned to face him. "What do *you* need willpower for? I'm not one of your stunningly gorgeous women that you're used to having on your arm. And I'm certainly not sexy. And furthermore, my name is not baby. It's Angela."

He held her gaze before softly asking, "Mason tell you that you weren't sexy?"

She turned her back to him. "Yes, but I already knew it. And you know it, too, Clint. Don't deny it. I've seen the beautiful women you're usually with. And since I've now had a baby, I'm about as sexy as a *pakagodian*."

He came up behind her. "I disagree."

"You wouldn't say that if we weren't stranded onboard this ship in the middle of a storm."

"But we *are* stranded, darlin," he said in a lazy, velvet voice, "and when you look at me the way you just did, I get ideas."

He'd stepped even closer and she could feel the heat of his body merging with the memory and images of his muscled bareness. Once again her insides trembled, and a breathy "Ohhh..." was all she could manage.

She could smell the clean, woodsy scent of the shower soap he'd used, and when he moved closer yet, the contact at her back became all the more intimate—a track of scorching heat seared its way from the backs of her knees, up her spine to her shoulders.

"I'm not going to sweet-talk it, Angel. Plain and simple, I want you. I want to make love to you. Now."

Unable to speak, Angela silently shook her head in denial.

"Don't believe me?" Lowering his head, he placed his lips to the sensitive flesh beneath her ear while pressing another part of his body intimately against her backside. "Can you feel it?" he whispered lazily.

Angela swallowed and frantically nodded.

"Good. Then allow me to make a little suggestion," he added softly with slow resolve, "that you buck-up and make very sure you don't give me the wrong impression. Should you reveal in any way that you feel the same, baby... I can't guarantee I won't take you."

Moving his mouth down from her ear, he pressed his lips against the silkiness of her neck, punctuating his arrogant statement with a drawn-out, imprinting kiss that made Angela's toes curl.

It took a minute, after he'd withdrawn, for reality to surface. Angela lifted her hand to the spot on her neck that still burned as though she'd been branded. Immediately she turned to face him. "You! You put a hookie there, didn't you?"

"A what?"

"A hookie. You gave me a hookie!"

"You mean a hickey?"

"Yes! Whatever it's called."

"Not this time, Angel," came his soft and very promising reply. Then with a curt nod, he turned and strolled back into the galley.

"For your information, Clint Banner, there won't be another time," she called out before he disappeared around the corner.

"Five years ago you left me without so much as a backward glance," she muttered more to herself, yet loud enough for him to hear.

Dead silence from the galley.

CHAPTER FOURTEEN

With her mind in chaos, Angela made her way to the mattress next to Lainie's crate and laid down beside her. Outside the storm continued, matching her unsettled mood perfectly as she lay there, trying to make sense of what all had just happened.

It was then she slowly became aware of a lingering pleasant fragrance. Although it was masculine, it was different. It wasn't the masculine shower soap she'd noticed earlier, nor was it the musky, male scent she recognized to be Clint. With a frown she reached up to touch the place on her neck where he'd kissed her. This time when she withdrew her hand, it was smeared with the remnants of shaving lather. Shaving lather! There was even a smattering of it on her cheek as well as in her hair.

The realization made her squirm as she rose to her feet. Actually, she was tempted to stomp her feet and scream at the top of her lungs. As if it would have done any good. In truth, what she needed was self-discipline. What she didn't need was another altercation with Clint. With several fortifying breaths she sat up and reached for a small cloth from Lainie's bag and began wiping the lather from her neck, face and hair.

Clint quickly finished shaving and wiped any remaining remnants of lather from his face with the towel he'd been using. At last he pulled a clean black T-shirt over his head, fastened the top button of his pants and briefly finger-combed his damp hair before turning for the helm and Angela. They had some unfinished business to take care of.

"We need to talk. Now." His tone was grim.

She was lying on the mattress with her eyes closed. Only after a long drawn out moment of silence did she finally sit up and reply purposefully, "I agree."

He glanced down at Lainie. "As long as she's sleeping, let's take it back into the galley. Just in case it gets loud."

"I cleared the table, so have a seat," he said, turning for the cook center.

She took a seat and when he returned, he was carrying two mugs of coffee. "Okay..." he said as he slid one of the mugs her direction and dropped into the bench across from her. "Now, you want to tell me how I left you without so much as a backward glance?"

"That's exactly what you did, Clint."

"You're the one who chose to stay, Angela. Remember?"

"Yes, but you just suddenly stopped all communication. You stopped responding to my messages." She gave a brittle laugh. "Can you believe I still have the last missive you sent? It was so sweet and loving, and filled with promises." Her voice dropped. "It was also the last message I ever received from you. I sent you a message every day. Every day, Clint," she repeated, "but you never responded after that. Not once. The least you could have done was cut me loose. You couldn't even wait six months, could you? What happened? Did you find someone else in the long lineup of gorgeous females just waiting for you to come back home?"

He simply listened until she was finished. "You done?"

"I was *done* a long time ago," he snapped.

"First of all," he began in a low voice, "you say you messaged me every day?"

"Every single day for at least a month and a half," she bit out.

"Angela, I never re—"

"And not a word from you, Clint. Not one word."

"I'm telling you I never received another message from you after the first four or five. And not only did I message you many times, I made several trips to Earth just to see you. And each time I was turned away."

A soft gasp escaped her. "Turned away?"

He nodded slowly.

"Who turned you away? What did they say?"

"Your father was the one who told me you were unavailable, yet he assured me that he'd let you know I came by. He never told you, though, did he?"

Angela swallowed and sat stock still as she lifted her eyes to meet Clint's. The cabin was charged with a silence that not even the on-going storm could fill. "I... never knew," she whispered.

He went on, "By the fifth time I was turned away, I got the picture."

"I never got any of your messages, Clint. They just suddenly stopped."

Clint nodded. "Nor I yours." After a moment of profound silence, Clint asked, "Angela, could your father have—"

"No! He wouldn't do such a thing. Besides, he always liked you, Clint."

"Then, how do you explain what—"

"I don't know."

During the tense silence, he wordlessly stared into his mug of coffee. "I always got along well with your dad," he said. "At least... I thought I did."

Lifting his gaze, seconds ticked by before he asked. "What about your father's partner?"

"George? Why would he do such a thing?"

"You married his son, didn't you?"

Silence.

Angela swallowed. "But he wouldn't have done anything like that."

"I'm not saying he did anything. But am I not ruling it out either. I believe there was a plan involved. Someone not only intercepted our messages, Angela, someone saw to it that you never even knew I came to see you. I can't help but believe the purpose was for you to marry Mason for some reason."

"No... No one influenced us to marry. I just can't believe that my father or George were involved in something so deceitful."

After a long moment of thought-filled silence, he asked, "What kind of man is George?"

"What do you mean?"

"I mean, what is he like? What sort of relationship did he have with your father... and just as important, with his son?"

"Dad and George were partners, Clint. They got along well."

"Equal partners?"

"No. I think it was sixty/forty, with George in control."

"So, with your father now gone, what happens to the forty?"

She merely stared at him. "What do you mean?"

"I'm asking, what happens to the forty percent that your father had? Do you know? In other words, does it revert to George or go to you?"

Angela swallowed hard, lifted her chin and boldly met his gaze. "Clint, I don't like where this is going."

"Neither do I," his tone apologetic. "But if we're going try to make some sense out of this, it's necessary, and if my hunch is correct, you've got your father's forty percent, unless Mason managed to get his hands on that too. You never signed anything over to Mason, did you?"

"No."

Angela bit down on her lower lip then with a heavy sigh replied, "George is a decent guy, Clint, he wouldn't—"

"Then who owns the forty percent, Angela?" he asked very slowly this time. "Do you know?"

She hesitated then, "No. And I don't care either."

His eyes met hers disparagingly. "Well, you should care. The answer just might clear up a lot of questions."

"Lainie and I want nothing to do with Mason or George Cooper or Southern Charm Development for that matter."

"I have another question then we'll lay it to rest for a while."

"I don't want any more questions, Clint."

Ignoring her protest, he went on, "I don't know the whole story, but I know enough to make me wonder why you married that sonofabitch. Just from what you've told me, I believe it was an arranged marriage—unbeknown to you."

"No..."

"Did you love him, Angela?"

A momentary look of discomfort crossed her face before she answered. "At the time, yes... or, at least I thought I did." Angela rose from her seat, crossed over to the viewport and stared out at the blowing snow. "And I believed that he loved me. But by the time we'd been married less than six months, the glow was wearing off fast, and I began seeing disturbing changes in him."

Giving her space, Clint remained seated at the table. "Changes? In what way?"

She turned to look at him. "In every way. At first it was verbal— nasty, but verbal. Eventually it became physical."

"Plus, there were always other women in his life," she added. "He told me he never wanted to marry me in the first place, that I was never his type. He criticized me constantly. Everything I did seemed to be wrong, no matter what it was. The harder I tried, the worse he got."

That bit of news confirmed Clint's suspicions. He felt certain that unbeknown to Angela, it was an arranged marriage alright. One that Mason obviously was pressured into and wasn't happy about. No doubt unbeknown to Angela's father, the plan was to get rid of both him and Angela and keep the full one hundred percent of the business in the family. Clint couldn't imagine what they might have used to convince her father into going along with the deceit.

"I knew he was seeing other women," she continued, "but I was afraid to say anything. It wasn't until I became pregnant that the violence became even worse.

Clint cursed softly. "He was angry because you were pregnant?"

"That, and more recently, the fact that I had already filed for divorce."

His brows drew together. "You lost me. Didn't he want a divorce?"

"Yes, but *he* wanted to be the one filing for it. Not the other way around. It was a pride thing.

"Plus, he wanted it fast. He had apparently laid the ground work for speeding the process along. But since I filed first, it made more trouble for him to push the divorce through in a hurry."

"With you not wanting anything out of the marriage, who cares who filed first? And why the big hurry?"

"The hurry was because his latest lover was pregnant. But that's not the worst, Clint. Mason as good as said that he'd had a hand in the deaths of my parents."

Clint sat forward. "He admitted that?"

"No, but he eluded to it, and I knew if I had stuck around, it wouldn't have been long before I would be next. Besides, I'd already miscarried one baby because of his physical abuse. If I didn't leave that night, I knew I would end up losing, if not my own life, a second baby's life for sure."

"You were pregnant once before?"

She nodded, "Barely three months along."

Clint winced and shook his head. "What the hell..."

"All I know is I couldn't live with him any longer, Clint. I never wanted his money, nor did I want anything out of the divorce other than what I've put away for Lainie. I simply wanted out." Angela's chin lifted in defiance. "The night I left him was the last night he will ever lay a hand on me." Unshed tears glittered in her eyes. "All I ever really wanted," she whispered brokenly, "was to be a good wife and mother of his child." She tried blinking back the tears, but they spilled over regardless. "What was so wrong with that?" she whispered.

Rising from his seat, Clint came to her, enfolding her in his arms. "Nothing," he murmured. A shudder racked her body as she sank against him, her good arm stealing about his waist for support. "Not a damn thing, honey," he said softly as he tucked the top of her head beneath his chin and simply held her.

Angela desperately needed him at that moment, needed his strength, needed him to hold her. She had been both physically and mentally beaten down for so long—she'd been alone, dealing with her worst fears and uncertainties while trying to take the best care she could of Lainie. And for now, right this very moment, she needed someone to hold and protect her. She needed Clint. She felt so fragile and safe enveloped in his embrace. With her cheek pressed against his chest, she listened to his heart beat and inhaled slowly. Unlike Mason, who never failed to overdo his expensive cologne, Clint smelled good in an unpretentious way—a heady combination of lingering shower soap, a brisk scent of shaving lather and the musky male scent that belonged only to him.

Clint drew back to look down into her face. His eyes held an intensity that Angela easily deciphered. Her mouth softened. Her heart raced. She knew what was coming when his head lowered, and right now she wanted the kiss as much as he did.

CHAPTER FIFTEEN

His mouth touched hers, soft and tentative at first, a gentle testing and reacquainting that quickly called for another. The second kiss was much the same, gentle enough to be sweet and yet firm enough to offer a sense of safety and comfort.

At least that's what Clint had convinced himself he was doing. The real question was, for whom was he doing it? The thin line between comfort and desire could easily blur without warning.

He sucked in a deep breath and let it out slowly. He might not know exactly what it was that had Angela melting against him, but he knew he was doing something right. Her lips had softened beneath his. And when he gently eased her body to fit more intimately against his, she didn't resist and instead became pliable and molded easily with his subtle guidance.

Clint, however, didn't feel exactly pliable at this moment. His body was becoming more rigid by the second. His loins ached as he held her firmly, longing beyond reason to become physically one with her.

"Clint," she whispered softly.

"I know, Angel," he murmured, holding her close. "It's been awhile. Time to get reacquainted?"

"But slowly," she cautioned, her voice muffled against his chest.

"Slowly," he repeated dutifully.

You're fooling only yourself. Taking it slow is the farthest thing from your mind, pal. And now that you've said it, think you can follow through?

Miraculously receptive to the silent voice of reason, he pulled back and looked down at her. "We'll take it as slow as you want, Angel." And with utmost tenderness, he cupped her face with both hands, bent his head and captured her mouth in a cherishing kiss. "Then we'll see where it goes from there."

Angela swallowed hard, unable to look away. His gaze was doing odd things to her insides, causing a sudden fire to ignite low in her belly. She watched his eyes become hooded as a slow smile kicked up one side of his handsome face. Why did he have to be so damnably handsome? And why did her insides feel so strange when he was near? She didn't want a man in her life. Mason was enough to cure her for two lifetimes. Her world revolved around Lainie now. She didn't need anyone else.

Or did she? This was Clint, she reminded herself. Not Mason. Recognizing the desire in his eyes with instinctive clarity, Angela felt weakened, yet unmistakably alive. And at the moment there was nothing she could do about it. Nothing she wanted to do about it.

"Clint..." she whispered as she placed her free arm about his neck, running her fingers through the silky dark hair that curled at his nape, and pulling him down to her for yet another passionate kiss.

His gaze dropped to her lips and lingered there. "You taste so damned good, Angel," he murmured softly. And in an attempt to gain a firm reign on his emotions, he drew her close and raised his head above hers to suck in a couple of calming breaths. If he was going to keep his promise to take it slow, he needed to gain and hold the control. But the problem was, he didn't want to take it slow. He wanted her, and wanted her now.

At last, he lowered his head. "Angela..." he whispered. "I want to make love to you."

Angela looked down at the floor. "Clint... I know I'm not sexy. Not like the girls you're used to being with." She looked back up at him with a shy smile. "It's because we're locked up in this ship isn't it? And I'm the only woman around."

It was like splash of ice water. "Is that what you think? That you're not sexy and the only reason I want you is because we're stranded and you're the only one available?" He hesitated, measuring her for a moment before his forefinger lifted her chin. Once he had her attention and their eyes met, he began. "First of all, we need to get a few things straight here and now. Number one: If I get horny, I guarantee it's not because it's been awhile. It's because the woman I'm with turns me on. Two: I don't seek out just any woman, Angela. Three: I don't pay for it. Never have. Never will. So, if I've gone without a woman for a while it's because of my own choosing. And darlin', when I say I want you, you damn well better believe it's *you I want* and not because we're marooned out here in the middle of a damned storm and there's no one else around... or because I've confused you with someone else." He released her chin, and with a sniff, shot a glance at the ceiling before leveling his eyes on her again. "Besides, there is not one thing about you that reminds me of any other woman I've ever known. You're different from the others, in every way.

"And furthermore," he continued, "there's absolutely nothing sexy about being marooned in this ship when I have a crew wondering where the *hell* I'm at, speculating if and when I'm returning. Besides, at thirty-four, I'm used to my creature comforts, and sleeping on the floor doesn't cut it.

"I'll admit I've roughed it plenty when I was younger." Taking it even further, Clint continued, "There were times back then when it made no difference to me whether we were *doin' it* in the barn on a soft bed of hay, or the hard surface of a floor, or for that matter, up against a cold wall. And furthermore..." With a frown, he stopped mid-sentence, suddenly mesmerized by the drop-jawed, wide-eyed expression on Angela's stunned face. She was so damned innocent, in spite of the hell Mason had put her through. Nevertheless, he had one more thing to clear up between them. "And furthermore," he continued, "while we're setting records straight, I've noticed you've taken a dislike to pet names. Mason do that to you too?"

At first she remained silent. Then... "From the time we first met, Mason never, ever used my name, she said defensively. "It was always sweetheart, or babe, or whatever. It's such a lazy way for not having to remember the name of the person you're with. You can simply say honey, or baby and never have to worry about accidently blurting out the wrong name. It's insulting."

"I see... Well, I won't pretend to know Mason's reasons for not using your name, but when I use something other than your name, it sure as hell isn't because I can't remember it. When I call you darlin' or sunshine or anything else, it's an endearment. Not an insult. If I want to insult someone, I have a whole different vocabulary for that."

His eyes never left her face. "They reflect my mood, Angela, and what I'm feeling at the time. Mostly they express affection, sometimes to get a point across, or even on occasion to express anger. But never, *ever* because I've forgotten a name. Besides, you use those same little pet names yourself when talking to Lainie. I've heard you, and I can't imagine you forgetting her name."

Angela opened her mouth as if to say something then clamped it shut again.

Satisfied that she was speechless, he turned to stock from the galley. "By the way," he muttered over his shoulder, "the buzzer's going off. Your laundry's done."

For several long minutes, the buzzer continued squawking while Angela silently remained where he'd left her. Lainie. She needed Lainie right now, but first she needed to shut off the buzzer and get the laundry.

Angela made her way back toward the helm, laundry in hand. What she needed right now was a nap.

Clint, who had once again busied himself at the helm, never turned around at her approach. There was little doubt but that she'd pissed him off. Oh well... at least Trixie was delighted to see her and came bounding up to greet her. Angela scratched Trixie behind her ears and accepted her doggy kisses then with a heavy sigh she curled up on the mattress. Trixie made three tight circles before finally dropping down to snuggle against Angela's back.

With a soft oath, Clint reflected on how things had suddenly gone south between him and Angela. Cabin fever was beginning to get to them both. Irritations were rising and tempers were short. And over the past hour he'd been feeling guilty as sin. He shouldn't have lectured her the way he had. He knew she was simply suffering from a lack of self-confidence—thanks to her asshole ex.

And what had *he* done? He'd gotten angry, that's what. Even though his anger was directed at Mason, he took it out on Angela by lecturing her on his sex life. *Hell, his sex life, for godsake!*

And what did she do? She stood there taking it all in with unshed tears glistening in her wide eyes. Yeah, he saw the tears, but did he stop? Hell, no. He went right on to defend his use of pet names, knowing that in her mind, *thanks once again to asshole*, pet names were a cheap label—more of an insult than anything. But dammit, he'd never once labeled a woman in a demeaning way, let alone because he'd forgotten her damned name.

Two hours had passed by the time Clint heard the baby stir. Angela had fallen asleep nestled next to Lainie's cradle. If he thought his help would be welcomed, he would gladly offer to help Angela get Lainie into her arms. But maybe it was best this way. Afterall, the real purpose of this trip was to get Angela out of Aurora and out of Mason's reach. Had it not been for the storm, he would have had her safely back to Imperial long ago. Instead, here they were, marooned onboard the *Victorious* until the storm passed. And how long had it been so far? Going on a week? It seemed like years and he wasn't sure how much longer he could last.

He heard her quiet voice whispering to Lainie, heard soft rustling as he envisioned her lifting Lainie from the cradle. He felt like a damn heel offering no help, knowing she was, no doubt, using both hands. Yet he had convinced himself that there was no use offering to help. She'd just turn him down anyway. Still, he should ask. What the devil was he afraid of? Afraid of giving her the chance to turn him down? Afraid she'd make him feel even more of an idiot than he already felt?

"Angela... "

Clint came around from the cockpit and hunkered down before her. She'd been laying there watching Lainie happily batting the air. Lifting her gaze upward, she stopped when she reached Clint's concerned regard. She could feel the change in her breathing and heartbeat just from looking at him. Did he know that she loved him? Always had. Always will.

"Are you okay?"

No! she wanted to scream. *No, I'm not okay. I'm crazy in love with you, you big jerk, and there isn't a thing I can do about it.*

But instead she said, "I'm fine, Clint." She rose to her feet and reached down to pick up the baby. "I need to give Lainie a bath."

Instantly, he was on his feet. "Here, let me get her for you."

"I can do it."

Clint looked taken aback. "Angela... Let me lift her for you. I don't want your shoulder getting worse. And why is your sling off?"

"Because I removed it when I took a shower and didn't get around to getting it back on."

"We can put it on later. But for now, let me help you get Lainie."

"No," she said, trying to sound calm. "I can do it. Besides, I need to learn. It's not like I'm going to have you around all the time to help me." Her voice was as cool and calm as the eye of a storm.

Silence.

"Excuse me," she said, brushing passed him with Lainie.

Looking like a scolded puppy, Clint followed her into the galley, watching helplessly as she held Lainie with one arm while running warm water into the sink.

"Angela."

No response.

"Look... I'm sorry."

"There's nothing to be sorry for, Clint," she said without even turning to face him, her tone impassive. "At least now we know where we both stand, don't we?"

"Dammit, Angela. Let's not argue about this. Okay?"

"I agree because I don't want to talk about it anymore," she said as she eased Lainie into her warm bath. "There you go, sweetheart. You like that, don't you?" Lainie cooed happily. "You are such a good little pumpkin and mommy just loves her little angel."

"Alright. For now, we'll drop it." Clint waited a brief moment for a response that never came. Feeling shut out from the warmth and love that glimmered between Angela and Lainie, he turned away and walked out of the galley. Dammit. All he was trying to do was convince her that it wasn't because he was horny and *any* female would do... that it was *her* he wanted. He had sensed she was feeling insecure and had hoped to set her mind at ease. Instead, he'd clearly made things worse.

CHAPTER SIXTEEN

Angela watched Clint as he stood behind the command seat, studying the vidscreen. Leaning across the seat with a mug of coffee in one hand, he worked the ship's controls with the other. She loved watching him. She never grew weary of watching or thinking about him. Despite everything, all it took was a look or a touch and her insides turned to mush. However, with the exception of the wind still buffeting the ship and the sleet still peppering the hull on the outside, the next four days passed somewhat quietly on the inside. Almost too quietly. Actually, they'd hardly spoken to one another, except to complain about something. Tension ran high between them, and although it was sexually provoked, it revealed itself in an entirely different form. Clint snapped at Angela because she had managed to drink the last of the coffee and hadn't made more. She countered that he'd forgotten to take Trixie back to her spot in the cargo bay. It was his day to be responsible for her, and now there was a puddle on the floor. He complained that the stew she had made was too runny, yet neither of them had any trouble cleaning up every bite.

And beyond all the grumbling and complaining, Clint had even given her a wide berth at night as well, allowing her to have both mattresses, which she didn't need, while he slept sprawled in the Captain's chair.

By the time she had fed Lainie and tucked her into her little bed, Angela felt as though the stress of the past five days had been unbearably endless.

Admit it, Angela, a silent voice whispered. *You were glowing green jealous over the other women in his life. A stunningly virile man like Clint... what would you have expected of him? Besides, wasn't he talking about his life back when he was younger?*

With a heavy sigh, she turned and made her way from the galley to the helm where she found Clint, as usual, at the controls trying to make contact with the world beyond the storm. "Any luck?"

He turned to face her. "Well, there is some good news at least. The storm is beginning to weaken."

"It is? You were able to make contact with someone?"

"Yeah, for about thirty seconds. Then lost the connection before I could find out anything more than the fact that the storm is expected to continue weakening over the next two or three days."

"So, how long do you think before we will be able to be on our way?"

Clint huffed a soft laugh. "When it quits howling outside."

"Clint?" She couldn't help but gaze at him. And it wasn't only his dark looks, it was his unconscious grace whether he was moving or sitting at the controls. Were Acacian women completely blind, she wondered? It was hard to believe that no one had lured the notorious Clint Banner into marriage. Why hadn't one of those gorgeous females he always managed to be with captured his heart by now.

At last he turned to face her. "Yes?"

Angela swallowed hard and took a deep breath. "Clint, I want to apologize for—"

"There's no need for apologies," he replied. It's called cabin fever, Angela. It's not just you. We've been cooped up in here for a week, and we're both on edge."

It was true. The ship was far too small. There was literally nowhere to go besides the helm, the galley, or the lav. With Clint being exceptionally masculine, it seemed that whenever he came near, Angela was intensely aware of him. Everything about him shouted one hundred percent *virile male,* from his physic to his height to the way his short-sleeve shirts stretched across his bulging biceps right down to the prominent veins on his forearms. And of course, there was that unconscious yet sexy way he walked that, for as long as she could remember, had always tied her in knots. However, with only two or three places to walk to within the ship, that meant that Angela had every opportunity to watch.

But in some respects, it was a wearisome pastime. Too often their eyes would meet, and when they did, that hot ember between them would flash to life. Sheer boredom was not a good thing. There wasn't a whole lot to do that separated them from one another. Particularly when she needed help with Lainie or anything else that was hard for her to do because of her shoulder. Clint basically spent his days at the command console, which Angela suspected had more to do with avoiding her than anything. Until the storm passed, there was certainly nothing new to learn online, just repetition of the same old thing.

Angela was standing at the viewport, staring hopelessly out at the blowing sleet when she suddenly asked. "What exactly is Solarblaze?"

Clint was sitting in the command seat, nursing another mug of coffee. Her question had him pausing, his mug half-way to his mouth. "What brought that up?"

"I don't know. I was just thinking." She turned to face him. "Rae mentioned that you worked at a place called Solarblaze. I was just wondering if that's the kind of work that you went to college for?"

"Solarblaze Energy is a petroleum drilling company, and yes, that's what I went to school for."

"So, are you like a roughneck or something?"

He grinned. Amused, no doubt, at her untutored use of oilfield jargon. "Yeah, something like that. Depends on how you define the term. If you mean am I an oilfield worker who works around derricks making sure everyone's doing their job and that things are running smoothly? The answer is yes. If you mean, do I get down and dirty, actually operating and repairing equipment. Most of the time the answer is no. And yet on occasion I'll work side by side with my men on an emergency."

Finishing off his coffee, he swiveled the command seat about to face her. "Solarblaze is my company, Angela. If I'm not out on the jobsite, I'm in my office, contracting for supplies and developing new buyers. Sometimes I work with scientists, offering technical advice. Now and then it takes me off-planet, but most of the time Acacia's crude oil deposits keep me busy enough."

Not one thing he had said squelched the romantic image she had in her mind of Clint working in an oil field, in charge of the workers and their production. There was little doubt, from the dark teak of Clint's skin, that he spent a lot of time in the sun without his shirt. And in her mind's eye she could just envision him on the job. Hard hat, bronzed skin, worn Levis and work boots. He was a man's man, and she imagined he took both his position, and Solarblaze passionately.

That thought brought about another question. "So, who's taking care of things now, with you being gone and all?"

"I'm sure that between my foreman and my dad, things are being looked after." Extending his long legs, he leaned back in the chair, clasped his hands behind his head and asked. "What's with all the questions anyway?"

"I don't know." She shrugged. "It's just something I was curious about. Having worked for almost a year for a mining company, I wondered if what you did was anything similar. That's all."

"Drilling for oil and mining for ore are two completely different methods of extracting two different products."

"I see." A moment of silence passed between them before she finally asked, "So, how did you manage to have Solarblaze? Was it something you started from the ground up? Or was it already an established business?"

Clint studied her for a long stoical moment as if deciding whether he wanted to talk about it or not.

With a shrug, Angela laughed. "It beats the boredom, Clint."

"So you want to know how I acquired Solarblaze, huh? Basically, I obtained it through a bribe."

"A bribe? Well, that's certainly intriguing. What do you mean by a bribe?"

"I'll make this short. After college I worked for the previous owner of Solarblaze. I moved up the ladder within the company, almost too fast. Being young, I never gave it a thought that the owner might have an ulterior motive in mind. He eventually approached me about marrying his daughter in return for partnership in the company. Shelbi was a beautiful girl, I'll give her that, but I wasn't in love with her. I turned him down. He came back several months later with an offer I couldn't refuse."

"Solarblaze," Angela supplied.

"And I took it."

"So, you're married?"

"No longer." He flashed her an arrogant grin. "Other than mind-blowing sex, we had very little in common. Actually, it was a miracle it lasted as long as it did."

Ignoring Clint's sordid version of his failed marriage, Angela forged on. "But what about Solarblaze? Didn't her father want the company back?"

"Yeah, but Solarblaze had grown considerably by then, so I made him an offer *he* couldn't refuse. I offered to cut him in on a good percentage of the profits. Essentially, I'm buying the company with profits—up to a mutually agreed upon pay-off."

"No kidding. You made it work!"

"Damn right I made it work." Clint reveled in her smile. Angela was so pretty when she smiled. Actually, she was pretty all the time, he thought. But when she smiled, she literally lit up everything around her, including himself.

Her smile, he decided, was flirtatious and alluring, and yet completely naïve in the broadest sense of all three words.

"Okay, so now tell me about your home," she said, as if striving to keep the conversation going.

"What do you mean?"

She shrugged. "How far is it from your family home? What's it look like? Is it on acreage? Is it close to work? You know, that kind of stuff."

With a heavy sigh he dragged his fingers through his hair only to have it fall right back over his brow. "Let's see, It's about twenty miles from the folks and..." With a frown he asked skeptically, "You really want to know about the house?"

"Absolutely."

"It's a rustic one-level," he continued, "with a wrap-around covered porch on three sides. I think on Earth they'd probably call it a ranch style. It sits on about 100 acres with a barn. There's a long driveway that comes in off the main road. And before you ask whether I have animals, Rae keeps three of her horses on the property. And, let's see... what else? Oh! It's about ten miles to work. There. Is that good enough?"

Angela laughed. "Yes. It sounds wonderful, Clint. And you said once that you don't think a woman would like it there?"

"I know for a fact a woman wouldn't like it."

"Why do you say that? Have you ever invited a woman out?"

"No. And I have no intention of doing so. It's isolated out there. Too far from the city. There's no flashy night life or fancy restaurants for miles, and absolutely no social life. My mornings begin at daybreak, and when I return at the end of the day, I'm grimy and not always in the best of moods. Other than that, it's quiet and peaceful," he added as if speaking more to himself than anything.

"Then I have a funny feeling you know the wrong kind of women."

Clint didn't know what to say. Angela was poles apart from any of the women he usually sought out.

Still he wanted her, and he could tell the feeling was mutual. He could see it in her eyes every time she looked at him. He'd seen that look before, but right now it was even more evident, and it meant only one thing. Trouble.

"I need some fresh air. I'm going out," he groused.

"Out?"

"Yes. Out," he muttered, snagging his heavy jacket off a hook. "And while I'm gone, I want you to check around for a deck of cards, a puzzle, a hologram game or something, *anything* to pass the time until this damned storm finally breaks. And get something started for dinner," he snapped with the tact of a caveman. With that, he flipped up the hood on his jacket, put on his gloves, palmed the lock and strode through the main hatch without another word. Angela wrapped her sweater tighter against the blast of frigid air that blew in before the hatch cycled closed.

Glancing up at the monitor she watched as Clint, head bowed against the wind, waded through knee-deep snow. He made five determined and persevering circles around the ship. By the time he was working on the sixth and seventh trip, Angela noticed that he'd slowed down and had begun setting his sights upon the ship's hull, obviously checking for damage. Several times he bent down to wrestle with broken branches and debris that had become ensnared against the landing jacks and hydraulic stabilizing cables.

By the time he came back inside, well over a half hour had passed, and Angela was just coming in from the galley. He glanced over at her as he peeled off his coat and hung it back up on the hook. "I'm starved. Dinner ready?" His tone was still testy as he took a seat and began pulling off his boots.

His manner —that know-it-all, arrogant, condescending, brutish, masculine insolence, annoyed Angela beyond words. Sick of his sudden stone-age assertiveness, she snapped to attention. "Yes, sir. It's ready, sir," she countered with a mock salute then pivoted for the galley.

Clint sprang to his feet, and in the space of a heartbeat was standing before her, taking her face in his cold hands and covering her mouth with his. "This isn't working," he growled against her lips. "I want you too damned much, Angela. No matter what I do, nothing helps, and I am at the literal end of my endurance." He took her mouth in yet another demanding kiss, kissing her with a hunger she had hoped he had just walked off.

Although she didn't say it. Angela knew exactly what he was talking about and he was right. It seemed that no matter how hard she tried to concentrate on something else, particularly Lainie, she was constantly aware of Clint—no matter whether he was simply getting a cup of coffee or making his way to the helm. If only she hadn't injured her shoulder again. She wouldn't need his help with things she normally could handle on her own.

She met his gaze, wishing she could think of something to say. Anything. But she couldn't think at all when he was looking at her the way he was with those eyes. At last she blurted out, "Well, at least come eat something while it's still hot."

The day had worn into late afternoon. Angela stared out the viewport. Darkness was slowly creeping over the land, surrounding the ship and heralding yet another awkward night. Attempting to control the smoldering ember between them, they continued struggling with inadvertent eye contacts, accidental touches, ardent desires and secret inner thoughts.

Shortly after dinner, she had put Lainie down with the plan to finish cleaning up the kitchen and then call it a night. Besides, Clint had suddenly turned to drinking. *Great.* The only way to make herself scarce was to go to sleep. Disappearing into the lav, Angela quickly stepped out of her sweatpants and changed into a long tee shirt that Clint had dug up for her. She suspected it was one of Nick's tee shirts from the closet. It fell below her knees and served more as a nightgown than anything.

Both mattresses were nestled together on the deck beneath the heat vent. Pushing them apart, she made sure that she used only one. At last she laid down. Turning onto her side with her back to the other mattress, she pulled the blanket up to her chin and listened to the wind howl outside.

This day for some reason had been extremely tense. She suspected it had been for him as well, considering he'd capitulated tonight. For the first time that she was aware of, he had gotten into Nick's stash of liqueur.

Eyes half closed, she watched him through her lashes as he reached for the bottle that had been carefully placed on the floor beside the command seat. Trixie wandered over and flopped down on the deck next to him. Clint murmured something to Trixie and reached down to give her a scratching behind the ears. Eventually, he doused the lights over the command console and with a heavy sigh slouched down in the chair, his long legs stretched out and crossed at the ankles.

Angela didn't even realize she'd fallen asleep until her eyes suddenly popped open, her dazed brain zeroing in on low music that she just now realized had been softly playing in her sleep. Some sort of moody electronic guitar wailing out a lonely tune.

She glanced at the helm, but Clint was nowhere in sight. The captain's chair was empty. Maybe he was in the galley. But she could tell by glancing that direction that there were no lights turned on anywhere in the ship except for the tiny lights winking on the command console.

So, where was he? Rising to her feet, she shot a glance toward the main hatch and noted that all the heavy coats were accounted for. Okay, so he hadn't gone out walking again. Careful not to wake Lainie, Angela silently padded barefoot around the mattresses and headed for the helm. The minute she came around the half-wall that separated the helm from the rest of the ship, she saw him. Clint was in his stocking feet, lying on his back on the floor, one arm flung over his eyes. If he was awake, he was totally unconcerned that his belt was undone and drooping from the loops of his Levis. With one leg bent at the knee and the other stretched out, the scene was complete with Trixie curled up against his side with her chin resting on his outstretched thigh.

Angela stared at his long, sprawling length, wondering if he was awake or asleep.

"Good music, huh?" came Clint's gravelly voice as he slowly pulled his arm away from his eyes and looked up at her. "Recognize this song, Angel?"

She didn't answer, just blankly stared at him.

"No... I guess you wouldn't." With a hoot, he added, "I'll bet you were still in diapers when this one came out. Hell, I remember every song Jim Starbuck made back then." Clint sat up and scooted over to lean back against the command console.

"So, just how old were *you* at that time. Clint?" Angela asked. "You're not that much older than I am."

"Honey, that depends on whether you mean in years or experience," he drawled. "Here," he patted the floor next to him. "Have a seat. Listen to this song with me. No one ever made a guitar wail the way Starbuck could. Just makes ya' wanna' cry, doesn't it?" Angela remained standing. He was drunk. Not plastered but drunk nonetheless.

"So tell me..." he leveled his eyes on her, "once Mason quits looking for you, where do you think you'll settle? Surely not back in Aurora."

"No, not Aurora. I don't know right now, Clint."

"Ha! I can just see you heading back to Earth, living in a sleepy little burg named Happy Valley. You'll no doubt marry Dapper Dan, and Lainie will go to a private school and take ballet lessons." He threw back his head and laughed. "I'll bet she'll even learn to sip tea with her little finger curled."

"No doubt," Angela replied, her voice sounding bored.

"And you..." he continued, "you'll be baking cookies and be head of the local pool, picking up and dropping off everyone's little darlins'." He let out another raucous hoot of laughter which sounded more sad than anything.

"You're not funny, Clint."

Suddenly he sobered, and with one arm draped over his bent knee, he looked up at her with sharp eyes—eyes that appeared almost sober. Almost.

"I'm not trying to be funny, sunshine. I just don't want you to lose track of the bright future that awaits you. Dapper Dan's out there just waiting for you to find him. It's easy to get your thoughts and feelings muddled when you're stranded like this in the middle of a damned storm. But I guarantee," he continued softly, "when you get back to civilization and you find Dapper, you'll forget all about me."

At last he rose to his feet, fastened his partially opened pants and secured the buckle. Then making his way over to the controls, he shut down the music. "Go on back to bed, Angela," he said without turning to face her.

CHAPTER SEVENTEEN

Angela began to walk away then suddenly stopping, she turned to face him, hands clasped tightly together as she studied Clint's back.

"A long... time ago when I was young," she began in a soft voice, "I was racing a friend across an open field. I didn't realize that an abandoned, dried up old well-hole was in my path. It was over-grown with weeds and tall grass and I... I didn't see it until I disappeared off the face of the Earth into blackness. The well was not extremely deep, and luckily I wasn't seriously hurt, but still, the fall was deep enough that it took my stomach for a wild ride before I hit bottom. The air was knocked from me, and I struggled to drag in that first painful breath.

Slowly, Clint turned around.

Angela drew in a deep, trembling breath and continued. "It's like that when..." She twisted her fingers together. "... when you're near. My stomach feels so strange. It quivers just like it did that day I fell. You take my breath away, Clint Banner. So..." she made an awkward motion with her hand and whispered, "you see, I could never forget you."

He watched her with static blue eyes.

Angela swallowed, not knowing what to say next. She was no good at this sort of thing. It was awkward standing there wishing he would pull her into his arms and kiss her instead of making her wait for a response that obviously wasn't coming.

Between them, the air fairly sizzled with emotion and expectation. It was as if Clint was fighting an inner turmoil as she watched a conflict of emotions drift across his face.

And then suddenly as if a decision was made, Clint closed the distance between them and drew Angela into his arms. "I've been going out of my mind with wanting you." His voice was ragged, and Angela sensed that he was struggling to rein in his feelings. The very thought that she could do this to him scared her as much as thrilled her. He settled his lips against hers and breathed her name.

"I want to make love to you," he whispered.

Angela swallowed as a searing flame shot through her. She wanted him too. She, who thought she would never want a man ever again. And yet, here she was wanting Clint Banner. She wanted to know him intimately. She wanted to know what it was like to be made love to by this man, to become one with him in every sense of the word.

And she was scared to death.

Not in the way Mason scared her. In truth, it was Clint's virility that frightened her. He was so experienced, so knowledgeable in the ways of love. What did she know about pleasing a man? Mason had drilled it in over and over what a failure she was.

She felt a shock of fear as *You'll disappoint him* whispered through the back of her mind.

"Angela," Clint murmured against her ear. "Honey, don't be afraid of me," he said as though sensing her fear. "I would never hurt you. You know that, don't you?"

She nodded. "Clint... I... I" Oh Lord, it was hard to think, hard to breathe.

"What's scaring you?" he murmured as he slipped his arm about her waist, slowly drawing her close. After a moment he lowered his head and gently kissed her, and Angela felt that familiar coiling in her stomach, only it was even worse now.

"I'm not Mason, Angela."

"I know."

"And I won't hurt you. I promise I won't do anything you don't want to do."

"It's not that. It's just... I don't... I don't know how to..." she shrugged, "you know... "

"Because Mason never taught you. Right?"

She nodded.

"You let me worry about that. I'll teach you as we go."

Ever so gently Clint tipped her face up, his head descending, blocking all else from her sight. His deep blue eyes were aglow with the fires of passion. And when his mouth captured hers, she felt the flame of his kiss all the way to her toes.

Leaning into his embrace, wrapping her good arm about his waist, she burrowed her face into the hollow of his shoulder. And for several long seconds he simply held her tight, his hand moving as soft as a whisper over her back and shoulders. She could hear the faint beating of his heart beneath her ear and feel the responding thump of her own heart.

"I like your hair down best," he murmured as he ever so gently began removing the clips that held her hair in place. The heavy blond mass tumbled over her shoulders as he told her how beautiful and how sexy she was.

Relaxing under his onslaught, she whispered softly, "I don't want to meet Dapper, or anyone else." He tipped her face up and gently, slowly kissed her again, his fingers threading through her hair. This was Clint, the man she had pined for all these years. His hands, his mouth, his merest touch, easily stirred her to a fevered pitch. She drew in a breath, and the subtle scent of whiskey and leather mingled with Clint's own masculine essence.

She breathed his name, her voice trembling, her eyes clouded with desire as she glanced up at him.

"I know, Angel." he murmured as he let go of her long enough to drag one of the mattresses even farther away from Lainie's small makeshift bed.

Returning to Angela, he guided her to the mattress he had just relocated and drew her back into his arms. Ever so slowly he stretched out on the mattress, carefully easing her down with him. His hand and lips were slow and gentle, as though she were a cherished prize to be handled with caution, a fine wine to be sipped instead of guzzled.

Sensations and feelings stirred within Angela, enveloping her in a protective shelter that left her knowing only the pleasure of Clint's touch, his kisses and murmured words of passion.

Clint caressed the oversized tee shirt off of her, his mouth cherishing every inch of newly exposed flesh as he went, his deep sapphire eyes reaffirming that he found her beautiful and sexy and desirable.

Wide-eyed, Angela watched as he suddenly rose to his knees. Grabbing his own tee shirt by two fistfuls at the back of his neck, he pulled it up over his head and tossed it aside. He then returned to sink down beside her on the mattress. Angela reached for him, running her fingertips over his back, his rock-hard shoulders, his broad chest and hard flat belly.

Clint sucked in a sharp breath as she moved her hand lower. Upon encountering his Levis, she uttered a soft protest. And for a brief moment she fumbled timidly with his belt, only to sigh at her failed attempt to release the buckle.

Grinning at her boldness, he kissed her for it. "You sure you don't know what you're doing, Angel?" he murmured against her lips.

Suddenly embarrassed, Angela snatched her hand back.

Reaching down, Clint quickly released the buckle she'd been struggling with and began opening his Levis for her as well.

Angela was on fire for him. Eager for his touch, with no thought except to love and be loved. Her heart was pounding impulsively as he rained feather-light kisses upon her eyelids, her cheeks, her shoulders. Once again she slid her hand over his back, noting how smooth his flesh was. It was like warm satin over steel, and she was awed by the muscles that bunched beneath her fingertips.

And when he touched her, her breath caught in her throat. With gentle strokes, tender words and kisses, he introduced Angela to her own body, revealing secret places and shocking sensations she had never known before. Her fingers threaded through his sleek dark hair as she writhed breathlessly for release. Her skin burst into flame wherever he touched. She was driven by an inner demand that she didn't understand. Oh, but Clint understood. Yes, he knew all about that inner demand.

When he stood and removed his pants, her breath caught in her throat as she watched him. He was beautiful, a perfectly proportioned Adonis. His skin was a dusky tan to where his pants had ridden low. Again, she noted a small, but jagged scar, low on his side and wondered at the cause, but there was no time to ask, not when he was gathering her into his arms.

She moaned with unchecked pleasure as her bare skin brushed against his and breathed his name as he began kissing her again. His hand gently moved once again to her inner thighs, his breath, warm against her face as he told her how beautiful and desirable she was.

Angela welcomed his weight as his knee slid between her legs and shivered with ecstasy as he slowly and ever so tenderly entered her. Nothing else mattered, not the past and not the future, only the glorious present. Before he was fully seated he withdrew, only to ease into her again, this time deeper.

Having known only pain and discomfort from Mason, Angela hadn't expected pain-free pleasure. Clint showed her passion. He aroused sensations and burning desires she never even knew existed.

"Forgive me if I'm going too fast," he murmured. "I'm having a hard time trying to keep it slow and easy."

"It's okay. I'm not going to break."

"I've never had a virgin before," he groaned out as he lifted her hips to once again receive him.

"Ohhh!... And... and you *still* haven't had one. I... I... I'm not a virgin, Clint."

"Have you been with a man since Lainie was born?" He'd stopped moving, remaining perfectly still for her answer.

"Absolutely not."

"Then you are, in a sense, a virgin as far as I'm concerned."

With her good arm wrapped about his neck, Angela gazed up into his beautiful face as he began moving once again. She moaned as waves of pleasure continued to move over her. She just knew she was dying. No one could survive this ecstasy, this heat that flashed between them.

Suddenly time and reality faded away, leaving nothing but the two of them joined together in a euphoric embrace as they moved to the ancient rhythm of love.

"Clint! Oh Clint!" she cried as shattering waves of completion swept through her. A moment later she felt his body give up his life essence. Breathing hard, he buried his face in the hollow of her shoulder.

Angela had never felt so at peace, so content as she did at this very moment. As their breathing gradually returned to normal, she clung to him, wishing time would stand still. He had yet to withdraw from her, and she wrapped her legs about his waist to hold him in place. For the moment he was still part of her and she, part of him. Coupled together as they were, they truly were *one* in the literal sense of the word.

Clint held Angela close, his hand subtly stroking the curve of her breast. With his lips, pressed against her neck, he whispered sweet words of gentle love and praise.

After a long while, Angela shifted beneath him, an unconscious move that Clint found innocently seductive. His heart began to pound, his blood began to heat, and his body physically reacted with predictable results. He wanted her again.

"Angel?"

Angela's eyes widen. She was amazed that he would want her again and so soon. Mason never wanted her a second time. When he was finished, he immediately left her feeling painfully used and cheap.

Rising over her for the second time, his dark blue eyes aflame, Clint once again gently made sweet love to her, tenderly worshipping her with his hands and lips, coaxing her to once again let go of her fears and to ride the waves of pleasure.

His skin tasted salty, his hair damp beneath her touch. And as she approached the brink of fulfillment, she clung to his biceps, marveling at the steel she sensed lay hidden beneath her fingers. She gloried at the passion in his eyes, even as completion coiled within her, sweeping them, once again, into a *lightdance* of rapture.

CHAPTER EIGHTEEN

Angela awoke with a contented sigh the next morning. At some point through the night Clint had covered them both with a blanket. And now, as she turned to gaze tenderly at the man who had brought her such pleasure, she felt her heart skip a beat. He was so beautiful. She had never thought that a man could be called beautiful. But there was just no other word to explain him.

Unbidden, her eyes traveled over his long frame outlined beneath the blanket. Clint was devastatingly handsome all over, she reminded herself, blushing at the memory of last night. He had not only encouraged her, but had taken her hand and guided her, teaching her exactly how to explore, and pleasure him. Untutored as she had been, it had taken a lot of reassurance and coaching on Clint's part before she had been brazen enough follow through on her own. And whenever he groaned or sucked in a breath, Angela had been thrilled beyond words, surprised that her inexperience was capable of bringing him any pleasure at all.

She recalled how his hands had roamed freely and ever so easily over her body. These feelings were new to her and so unexpected. Her cheeks heated at the memory of how she had not only allowed it, but she had enjoyed it.

It was still dark out but would soon be light. Suddenly feeling embarrassed to face Clint this morning, Angela rose and checked on Lainie first. Two little eyes immediately focused on her as she cooed her joy at seeing her mommy.

"Good morning, sweet love," Angela whispered as she gently lifted the baby from her bed. The first thing Angela did was change and feed Lainie. Then once Lainie fell back to sleep, Angela made coffee and headed for the shower. Although her shoulder was still painful, the sling was helping and she was actually getting quite good at taking care of Lainie and doing other domestic things with one good arm.

All was still quiet in the ship when Angela emerged from the lav. Having showered, she immediately began frying up a mass of parsos, a root vegetable very similar to a Terran potato. She was standing at the counter, mixing pancake batter when suddenly she felt Clint's arms slip about her waist and his lips pressed to the side of her neck.

"Mornin' sunshine."

At some point while she had been busy at the stove, he'd awakened and had just now come from the shower. He smelled like heaven, a blissful combination of shower soap and shampoo. Just his nearness made her hands tremble and her voice unsteady as she replied. "Good morning."

"Angela..."

Detecting a pleading tone to his voice, she quickly piped up, "I'm making breakfast. I hope you're hungry?"

Burying his face in her freshly washed and fragrant hair, Clint's hands slid down over her belly and back up to gently cup her breasts. "I'm ravenous." But he wasn't talking about food, and they both knew it.

"The parsos are almost done, Clint. I just have to—"

"Leave 'em"

"What?"

"We'll eat later."

"Okay," she said, shutting the cooktop off. The instant she turned around to face him, however, she inhaled sharply. He was dressed simply in a towel wrapped about his lean hips.

"Clint!" Despite the crimson stain creeping into her cheeks, Angela tried for something clever to say. "Did you run out of clean clothes or something?"

"Yeah. Something like that," he replied, grinning. "Any complaints?"

"No. Yes!" she giggled then added, "You're distracting."

"We need some distraction around here." With a broad grin, he scooped her up and carried her back to bed where they missed both breakfast and lunch.

It was early evening by the time Angela was preparing Lainie for the night. Clint turned for the galley and quickly threw two commercially prepared meals into the warmer. Better that than nothing.

Through the night and over the next day, they kept each other so sated with making love that, other than Lainie, nothing else mattered. Even with her arm in a sling, Angela was adamant about seeing that Lainie's needs were met.

Early the next morning, Clint awoke. Angela was sleeping peacefully, curled against him as usual. Her head was pillowed upon his shoulder, her arm draped across his belly, her legs intwined with his. Just the awareness of her stirred his desire. And yet something was different this morning. Mentally setting sex aside for the moment, he refrained from waking Angela and lay there instead quietly listening. He heard the usual sounds of life-support blowing heat and oxygen through the vents. And every now and then a soft chime would sound from the command console designating the completion of a scheduled procedure, the usual ship sounds they'd grown accustomed to over the past week and a half. And yet something was different. As the mental fog cleared, Clint began to realize that the difference was the wind. No longer was it buffeting the ship and sleet was no longer peppering the hull.

"So, it's finally over," he whispered into the darkness. Just maybe by tomorrow they'd be able to finally make it out of here. He turned and pressed a kiss to Angela's forehead, inhaling her womanly scent. At least one more day of bliss, he thought as he closed his eyes and fell back to sleep.

BONG! BONG!

"What the hell?" Clint woke up with a jolt and scrambled to his feet. For the first time in almost two weeks bright sunshine was streaming through the port side viewport, casting an intense circle of light upon the deck near their mattress.

BONG! BONG! BONG!

By now Trixie was barking and growling furiously at the main hatch.

"What is it?" Angela asked, reaching for Lainie who had started to cry. A quick glance at the chronometer proclaimed the time as 10:00 am.

"I think we're being rescued." Reaching for his Levis and hastily pulling them on, he added. "Wait right there until I see who it is."

Quickly slipping on her sweatpants and shirt, Angela waited breathlessly in the background as Clint checked the surveillance monitor.

"Shit."

"Who is it?"

Clint groaned. "Nick, Zeke, Marc and my dad." With that he pulled a growling Trixie behind him and firmly held her in place while he palmed open the main hatch.

Instantly, Nick took in Clint's, bare chest and unfastened Levis. "We're not interrupting anything are we?" Nick asked with a knowing grin and twinkling eyes. It was obvious the Levis had been pulled on in haste and that Clint was naked beneath. A quick glance behind Clint confirmed any question there may have been. Angela had the debauched and disheveled look of a woman who had been thoroughly pleasured all night long. Her hair was mussed, and her cheeks flushed. It didn't have to be spelled out. It was easy enough for the men to sum up the situation.

"We'll uh... we'll start digging out the *Victorious* while you finish dressing," Max said, turning away from the hatch and taking the others with him. Before leaving, however, Nick turned around, raised his brows and mouthed the words, "What's with the baby?"

Clint just smiled as he closed the hatch. He could well imagine the thoughts going through Nick's fertile mind. Especially if Nick were to start counting back the months that had passed since he and Zeke had duped him into transporting Angela and her horse. Clint couldn't help grinning at that thought. *Let him stew for a while.*

CHAPTER NINETEEN

Even with Clint helping, it had taken nearly three hours for the men to dig the *Victorious* out of the deep snow drifts and debris that had piled up around it. There was some minor external damage to the ship, but Clint insisted on piloting it back when Nick mentioned he'd do it. It was late afternoon when he was able to finally lift the ship and turn it for Imperial. Despite his strong suggestion that Angela and Lainie ride back with the rescue party, she had chosen to stay onboard with Clint. She claimed that it would give her time to tidy up the ship, which he had to admit did indeed need a bit of tidying.

With Lainie in her lap, Angela was sitting up front, watching Clint pilot the ship. By now she had cleaned the cabin and galley, and despite her bad shoulder, she had even managed to strip the sheets from the two mattresses and tossed them into the washer, along with any blankets, towels and clothing they'd used. Despite all the exterior abuse the *Victorious* had weathered, the ship gave Clint very little trouble on the trip home. At last, before disembarking he hauled the two mattresses over to their rightful place on the bunks and helped Angela put the freshly washed bedding back on the beds.

"All set?" He was standing before the main hatch, shouldering Angela's travel packs.

With Lainie in the front pack, Angela was running a final critical eye over everything. "I guess as ready as I'm going to get," she said at last, and as she went through the main hatch for the last time, Angela turned to give the cabin a wistful backward glance.

"Are we going to your parent's home?" she asked as he helped her up into his Ground Runner. After transferring Lainie into her arms, he turned and lifted Trixie into the back. "No. I'll be taking you to the townhouse." Turning back to her, he began fastening her seatbelt. "Sorry, you'll have to hold Lainie. I'm afraid I don't have one of those special safety seats for her."

"It's okay."

He came around to the driver's side and slid behind the wheel. "You and Lainie will be safe at the town house until we can figure out what your options are."

"Will you be staying there too?" she asked hopefully.

The Runner roared to life, but before Clint put the vehicle in gear, he turned to face her. "No. I won't be staying there, but Edna will be there with you. She's our live-in housekeeper and I guarantee you'll like her."

"Oh."

With a slight frown he continued studying her while the vehicle idled in place. "Angela... You have to admit, we've been through one helluva lot over the last ten days and, it's been intense, particularly those last couple of days. We need some time to sort things out and get back to normal."

"Yes," she replied. So, what was normal she wondered. In truth she had no idea where she even stood with Clint, or for that matter if she stood anywhere at all. Yes, she had been through hell in the last week and a half. She'd lost her home, her job, her friends, her car... everything she owned. She'd re-damaged her shoulder, and now she had nowhere to go. Focusing her gaze straight ahead, she said nothing more as Clint backed out of the parking place. At the moment she felt very, very lost and alone.

He stopped at the spaceport terminal to make arrangements for mooring the *Victorious,* and to settle up with the parking lot for the space his Ground Runner had occupied. Then, as promised, he set off for the hospital. Occasionally Clint would glance over at her, but the darkness and soft lights from the dash only veiled his face. Only a couple of times when he reached over to touch her did she feel a hint of the warmth they had once shared.

He had told Angela earlier that no matter what time they arrived, he was taking her to the nearest hospital to have her shoulder examined. Thing was, the nearest hospital from Imperial's spaceport was an hour away. Lainie who had been sleeping ever since they'd landed, awoke half way to the hospital. By the time they were pulling in front of the emergency entrance, Angela had fed and changed her. Leaving the Runner parked directly in front of the hospital doors, Clint took charge, carrying Lainie like a pro as he ushered Angela inside. An M-scan was taken and an orthopedic physician was examining her shoulder before she'd even had a chance to fill out any forms. Clint assured her he had taken care of getting her admitted while she was getting the scan.

Lainie was quiet the entire time in Clint's gently rocking arms as he stood off to the side and watched the physician study the scan of Angela's shoulder. The doctor then proceeded to poke, press and nudge crucial points. Several times Angela stiffened and inhaled sharply.

At last the doctor looked directly at her. "You will most likely need surgery, Mrs. Banner, but let's give it a week. Along with keeping it in a sling, I'm going to tape it for reinforcement. You are not to use your left arm under any circumstances. If it continues to be too painful, or if you lose more strength, surgery will be the only recourse."

"I understand."

He handed Clint two prescriptions to have filled. One for pain and another to help with healing.

"Do not get those scripts filled," Angela said has he escorted her down the long hallway toward the exit. "As long as I'm nursing Lainie, I won't take them."

"Okay."

"And why did he call me your wife?"

"Hell if I know. Maybe because I was holding Lainie? Maybe he just assumed?"

"Then you didn't tell them in admittance that—"

"No," he lied. It had seemed expected to list her as his wife since he was paying the bill anyway.

Back in the Runner, parked beneath the intense lights of the emergency portico, Clint turned to her. "Angela, the townhouse is at least one and a half hours from here. Right now, it's going on two-thirty in the morning. If we head out now, we'd be there around four. Or... we could find an inn, spend the night and make the drive when we get up. Your call."

He watched her closely, and when she hesitated, he guardedly voiced his preference. "I say let's find a place. Get a good night's rest. Have a real breakfast in the morning and then head out. I don't know about you, but I'd sure like a nice hot shower and a comfortable bed that isn't sitting on the floor."

It was as if he'd read her mind. "I'd like that too," she said. Truth be known, Angela was mentally and physically exhausted. And oddly, leaving the shelter of the Victorious today left her once again at loose ends. And yet it was more than that. Perhaps what had really left her at loose ends was knowing that very soon Clint Banner would be walking out of her life for good. Yes, the idea of a room anywhere with him, even for one night, sounded like heaven.

It wasn't long before they came upon a large flashing road sign that directed them a mile up a winding river road where a newly constructed fishing lodge stood. From the scattering of vehicles in the parking lot, there would be lots of out-of-season vacancies.

With one arm embracing a wriggling, blanket-wrapped Lainie against his chest, Clint registered in his name for one room as though they were a family. Having paid the extra charge for Trixie, all they needed was a portable crib.

The room was warm and rustic. It was fancy with dark brown wall to wall plush carpeting and pictures of fishing scenes on the walls. But the thing that caught their attention was the large king size bed that took up half of the exterior wall.

Before long a portable crib was delivered and while Angela settled Lainie down for the night, Clint took that hot shower he'd talked about. When he finished, he emerged from the bathroom with a snowy white towel wrapped about his hips. "Your turn, Angel."

With her arm and shoulder taped up as they were, Angela opted for a bath instead of a shower. It was one of those new tubs that no matter how long you lingered, it maintained the temperature of the water until it was drained. It was heaven and all Angela could do to keep from sliding down and relaxing in its depths. She was denied that particular luxury, however, with Clint assisting her at every turn and making sure she didn't get the orthopedic tape wet.

Oh, how she longed to tell him how grateful she was for his help. And not just now but the patience and care he'd shown to both her and Lainie over the past weeks. More than anything, she wanted to tell him that she loved him, that she had always loved him, and that just being with him made her forget Mason and his abuse. But she voiced none of it.

The last thing she wanted was to go to some townhouse while he returned to his home and his life. What she wanted was to go home with him. But again, she didn't say anything that might come across as persuasive on her part. If he wanted her and Lainie, the invitation had to come from him.

Unaware of Angela's thoughts, Clint helped her soap up and rinse off. He even managed to wash her hair without getting her shoulder wet. Before she even realized it, he was lifting her out of the tub and wrapping her up in a fluffy heated towel of her own.

Still damp and smelling of clean, woodsy soap, they made passionate love in the middle of the king-size bed. For Angela it was different this time. And the difference had nothing to do with their fancy, rustic surroundings or the fact that this time their bed was not simply tossed on the floor. The difference came from inside her heart. This time as Angela gave herself to Clint, Countless stormy emotions took part in their mating—from intense need, to bliss... to desperate love. It was with silent tears that she met him on every level and surrendered everything she had to give. Deep inside, Angela knew that this would be the very last time. Tomorrow he would walk out of her life, taking her broken heart with him.

Morning came all too soon. Angela found herself waking up to

Clint leisurely threading his fingers through her hair. She'd fallen asleep on her side with her head and good arm resting upon his chest, her legs and feet entrapped with his.

They delayed leaving their room until minutes before checkout. From there they headed for the coffee shop where they lingered over breakfast.

"I need to stop at the drill site before doing anything else," he was saying. "Dad mentioned they put a crew on overtime, and I'd like to check on things."

"Of course."

"I don't know how long I'll be, Angela. Could be fifteen minutes, could be an hour. You can wait in the Runner, or I can drop you off at a mall to go shopping until I come for you."

"Thank you, but I'll just wait."

She wasn't a big shopper anyway. And besides, it would be too awkward trying to shop and hold Lainie with only one useable arm. Actually, what she really needed to do was look for a place to live, but it was mid-afternoon already, and by the time Clint returned from meeting with his foreman, it would be too late to start looking today.

The countryside had begun to turn barren as they moved farther out into the flats. They had left civilization, and the woods were beginning to thicken on both sides of the main highway. A bend in the roadway revealed a large clearing, and Angela caught her very first glimpse of a derrick off in the distance.

It was another ten minutes before Clint was turning onto a narrow, pothole-ridden passageway. Although he slowed way down, the Ground Runner still bounced over the ruts, making it next to impossible to remain seated as Angela hung onto Lainie for dear life. Thank goodness Clint had seen to it that her seatbelt was fastened. Actually, it was a miracle that Lainie wasn't screaming, although her eyes were as big as saucers. Angela turned to make sure Trixie was doing okay in the back, only to find that the dog's eyes were saucers as well. The entire scene suddenly struck Angela funny and she began laughing, until another deep rut silenced her.

"Sorry about the rough ride," he said. "Can't be helped."

At last he turned off the pathway and struck out across the large clearing that Angela had glimpsed earlier. The place was a bustle of activity, and the closer they got, the bigger the derrick seemed to become.

Several workers stopped and waved as Clint pulled the Ground Runner to a halt and hopped out. Directing Angela to wait for him, he turned and jogged toward the site's modular office building.

Angela occupied herself with Lainie, very much aware of the curious glances by the roughnecks as they continued working.

Within a half hour Clint emerged, appearing preoccupied as he made his way back to the Runner. She noticed he was wearing a leather jacket and carrying a second one, which he proceeded to help her put on when he got back. He explained with the Ground Runner being open, the jacket would help her keep warm. He reached into the back and retrieved a blanket for Lainie.

"Ready?" he asked as he slid behind the wheel.

"Yes. So how far is it to the townhouse from here?" she asked.

"Not far, but we're not going there after all."

"We aren't? Where are we going?"

Without starting the Runner, he silently sat staring straight ahead, gripping the wheel with both hands as though his life depended on it. Finally, after several long moments, he turned to meet Angela's wide, questioning eyes. "We're going shopping. How long do you think it will take you to find something real pretty to wear?"

Angela's mouth dropped open before she replied, "I don't know. Why do you ask?"

"We've got a wedding to attend in about four hours. We're getting married tonight."

CHAPTER TWENTY

Dead silence. Angela sat there staring at Clint as if he'd lost his mind. Then, "Are you crazy?"

In all seriousness Clint firmly met her shocked stare. "Yes. Without a doubt," he said glumly. "But as it stands, we don't have much choice."

Angela simply stared at the *crazy* man, who in less than two-week's time had managed to seize total control of her entire life. "Choice? What are you talking about?"

And to make matters worse, Lainie was becoming cranky.

Clint watched a couple of workers glance his way with a nod and a smile as they walked past. It was obvious he and Angela were becoming an attraction. "Angela," he began in a soft and controlled voice that she found annoying. "let's get out of here so you can feed the princess while we talk."

She gave him a dark look as he fired up the Runner. "What brought this on, this marriage thing?"

Clint feigned a look of disappointment as they bounced back across the rutted trail to the main highway. "And here I just proposed, thinking you'd happily accept."

"You're not funny, Clint, and that was no proposal. That was an order, which I have no intentions of—"

"Okay," he said, pulling to the side of the road and stopping. "Three weeks ago, before I left to come get you," he began as he turned to face her, "I contacted a friend of mine, a lawyer. I told him what I knew, how some *suit* had already been at the folk's place looking for you.

164

I asked him to keep tabs on Mason and to let me know what he finds out."

She started to comment, but Clint held up his hand. "Let me finish."

With a heavy sigh, she nodded, and he went on.

"At the time I set out to find you, I had no idea about Lainie. I thought the only thing Mason wanted was the horse. I told Tom, my friend, that I would be in touch with him every day. But as you know, two weeks have passed with zero communication. I called him late last night from the lodge, left a message saying I'd call him today."

"How do you know Mason isn't after Piper?" she asked, knowing in her heart it wasn't the horse at all.

"Angela, it's more serious than Piper. He's accusing you of kidnapping Lainie."

"Kidnapping? I didn't kidnap her. She wasn't even born yet. Besides, Mason denied her. He wanted nothing to do with the baby, saying that it wasn't even his."

"Obviously he's changed his mind and has negated all those bogus *legal* papers he filed."

"His mother is behind this. I just know it."

"It doesn't make any difference who's behind it." With a labored sigh, Clint turned to stare through the windshield at the afternoon landscape. "Besides charging you with kidnapping, his biggest argument will be the fact that you're a single parent. You'll get dragged through all kinds of legal mud. They'll bring out the fact that you have no job and no home. Compared to their wealth, Angela, you'll get eaten alive and still lose Lainie in the process."

"But—"

"Just hear me out, will you?"

Lifting the small blanket covering her shoulder and breast, she glanced down at Lainie who was growing drowsy and slowing down at nursing. Angela lovingly smoothed the down covering the baby's head.

"Anyway, I went ahead and told Tom to make the necessary arrangements for us to obtain a quickie marriage license. He has a buddy at the Court House—"

Angela was slowly shaking her head. "I am not rushing into some quickie marriage, Clint. First of all, marriage is permanent. Not some—"

"So is being charged with kidnapping, Angela. You'd better think it over. Mason is serious about taking Lainie away from you, and Tom confirmed the fact that the Cooper family has the funds to do it. I guarantee they'll fight dirty. Are you willing to chance it?"

He went on, "If we marry, we'll be a family unit. No, it's not completely fool proof, but it will definitely slow Mason down and buy us time. I could adopt Lainie immediately and seal the family image."

Angela finished nursing Lainie, whose innocent little life was hanging in the balance. She'd fallen asleep, completely unaware of the strife and contention going on around her.

Having just gotten out of one bad marriage, Angela wasn't about to jump into another. What if things weren't as bad as the picture Clint was painting? "Clint. I can't marry you," she said reasonably. "I've taken care of myself and Lainie so far and I can still do it."

Sparks of anger flashed in Clint's eyes. "Is that right? Well, pardon me for pointing out the great job you were doing taking care of yourself. If I hadn't come after you when I did, Mason's thugs eventually would have been knocking at your door, and after victimizing you, they would have taken Lainie."

"But with the storm, who's to say if they would have made it at all? But one thing's for sure," she added, "now *you're* the one victimizing me by trying to coerce me into marriage for all the wrong reasons. A marriage I want no part of."

"Oh, is that right?" He turned to face her head-on. "Well, Miss Self Sufficient, you've done one helluva job thinking of yourself. Have you, by chance, taken into consideration that I don't particularly want to sacrifice my freedom any more than you do? I sure as hell didn't make the trip up to get you, spend nearly two weeks marooned in the *Victorious,* only to rush into marriage the instant we get back. Believe me, sunshine, getting married is the furthest thing from my mind as well."

"Then why are you insisting we—"

"Because that innocent baby in your arms needs protection from Mason. That's why. She deserves to be raised in a home with people who love her, and I'm willing to marry you and see to it that it happens. I have no idea what Mason's worth is, but I'm not exactly destitute, Angela, and I would do everything in my power to care for you and Lainie, and to make both of you happy.

"There. Now you know. So, are you ready to get married?"

He'd just said all the wrong things. Where were the words of love and devotion that she so needed to hear?

"You're *willing*?" she repeated. "*You're willing* to marry me? How gallant of you."

Clint frowned. "What the hell's that supposed to mean?"

"It means that I wouldn't marry you if you were the last man alive. And furthermore, I have no intentions of staying at your townhouse. I'm going to look for a place of my own."

"Great. Where do you want me to drop you off so you can start looking? Just so you know, you'd better hurry because you haven't got more than about three hours before it begins getting dark. And this time of year, when it gets dark, it gets cold. If you don't find a place soon, you and Lainie will be out in the cold tonight."

With a lift of her chin, Angela turned away and stared outside. She loved Clint beyond words. And would have married him in a heartbeat. But not like this, not after he said that he was willing— *willing*—to marry her. Not because he loved her, but instead out of some misplaced sense of responsibility. Was she the only one in love here?

She swiped away a stubborn tear. Rational thought was impossible, especially with him sitting so close to her. He was furious, and there was no time to think. A decision had to be made, and had to be made now.

"So... what's it going to be, Angela? Time's wastin'."

How was it possible for him to remain so calm and so composed when facing a life-altering choice like this? Was he always so right about everything? So damned sure of himself? Surely there was at least one other option to consider. But Angela knew in her heart there was only one, marriage, and they both knew it.

At last she turned to face him and whispered, "Okay." If he was expecting more drama to her surrender, this was about as good as it was going to get.

Clint studied her for a long drawn out moment before finally replying softly, "All right then." His gaze fell to her lips and before she grasped his intention, he leaned over, taking her face in the V of his hands and gave her one long drugging kiss. When he let her up for air, he murmured, "There's just enough time to shop for something special for you and Lainie to wear, then we'll head out to my place to get ready." With that he fired up the Runner and pulled back out onto the road. "We've got exactly three and a half hours to do what we have to do and still get to the courthouse on time."

"But Clint, my arm's in a sling. There's no way I can hold Lainie and look for—"

"I'll be holding the princess. You just worry about shopping."

At least he wasn't reveling over her submission, and she silently thanked him for it.

By the time they left the little hole-in-the-wall specialty shop, Angela had found a delicate green dress with a cream-colored bolero shrug. It wasn't overly fancy, but then this marriage was far from a normal wedding. Clint liked the dress, saying it matched her eyes. She also found something in a similar color for Lainie. Then, at Clint's insistence, she chose a pair of soft leather dress shoes, a warm, full-length dress coat, along with whatever sleepwear and underthings she would be needing in the future.

She wanted to crawl under the counter and hide when he cleared his throat and with a knowing grin, added ever so quietly for her ears, "Be sure to choose enough underthings to last more than just one day. Okay?"

The drive to Clint's home was approximately thirty minutes from the mall. Angela was glad to leave the dress shop. She hadn't missed the double-takes aimed in Clint's direction, or the titters, sighs and whispers from the two young salesgirls who couldn't seem to keep their eyes from straying back to Clint. Whether he'd noticed or not, Angela couldn't tell. Gently bouncing Lainie in his arms, it seemed that he only had eyes for her as she quickly modeled her selections for him.

Placing her packages and hanging her dress, new coat and a casual jacket in the back of the Runner, Clint helped Angela into the vehicle. Handing Lainie over, he belted her in before coming around to hop behind the wheel. Angela subtly watched him put the Runner in gear and begin backing out of the parking space.

He'd looked so rugged with his collar flipped up against the wind, the breeze had whipped his dark hair over his brow. Did he know how utterly striking he was? It was no wonder those young salesgirls couldn't keep their eyes off of him. She couldn't blame them.

CHAPTER TWENTY-ONE

At last the Ground Runner crested a rise in the road and Angela got her first glimpse of Clint's home. Just as he had described, it was a rustic, sprawling, single story home with a wrap-around porch. Several tall trees shaded the front porch, and surprisingly, it all blended into the landscape with far more appeal than she had expected. A large barn sat off to the side, and beyond that, rambling fences sectioned off pastureland. The house was definitely Terran inspired. If she hadn't known better, she would have sworn she was somewhere rural on Earth.

"Well, we're here," Clint announced as he brought the Runner to a halt before the front steps. Trixie was the first one to jump out and quickly headed off to find the perfect spot.

"We need to be ready to leave in forty minutes," he said as he unbuckled Angela and helped her and Lainie out of the Runner. "Think you can do it?"

"I'll be ready, Clint."

"Good." He took Lainie into his arms. "Come on, I'll show you where you can change."

"Am I really the first woman you've ever brought here?" she asked as they stepped through the home's double-door entry.

"Yes, you're the first." He flashed her a brilliant smile. "Unless you want to count Rachael and Delta."

"What about your ex-wife?"

"I didn't have this place then."

Angela stepped inside the entrance hall and stopped to glance around. "Oh Clint, it's—"

"Come on, we're on a time schedule. I'll give you a tour later."

Clint was ready to go in precisely forty minutes. Angela would love to have had a quick shower, but that was out considering her taped shoulder. Instead, she quickly changed into her new things.

The trending style for Acacian men was more ultramodern. But on Clint, the retro style of buff slacks, soft blue shirt, designer tie and a navy blazer gave him an air that Angela decided would make any male model green with envy.

"What?" he asked, catching her staring at him.

"Nothing. You look nice, Clint." Actually, he looked more than just nice, he looked down right gorgeous. And Angela noted that he moved with the same ease and masculine grace in dress clothes as he did in his work Levis and leather jacket.

"Thanks." He hesitated a moment, his look serious as he gave her a narrow-eyed once over, "So do you."

"Thank you. I love the dress. And the coat is so warm and dressy, and the shoes, I love everything. Thank you again."

"Don't mention it." He sauntered forward. "Here, I'll carry Lainie. You think Trixie will be okay if we leave her here alone?"

"Yes, just put her in the same room where I changed clothes. My things are in there and she'll be fine."

Clint suggested they not take the Ground Runner this time. With them dressed up, his smaller, more enclosed and compact Land Craft would be a better choice. "I'm sorry, you'll still have to hold Lainie," he said. "The LC doesn't automatically come with safety restraints for babies. But it will have one tomorrow. I promise. We'll buy two, in fact. One for the Runner as well."

"And a crib for her to sleep in," Angela added.

"And a crib."

The one-hour trip to Imperial from Clint's home seemed like an eternity. Very little was said by either of them. Angela suspected it had to do with each being in their own thoughts. And even though she was getting married to the man she'd fallen in love with years ago, she suspected that between them, she was the only one in love. And yet, she knew that Clint was right. Getting married was the best thing for Lainie. As a family, hopefully, they could protect Lainie from Mason.

Angela slid a quick glance at Clint and wondered what was going through his mind right now. He'd accused her of thinking only of herself, giving no thought to the freedom that he might be relinquishing. Not only was he giving up his freedom, he was taking on a ready-made family. With a sigh, she silently glanced out the window and watched the scenery go by.

By the time they reached the outskirts of the city, the sky was a blazing orange as the sun was just starting to set. One of Acacia's three moons was rising on the eastern horizon. Although the courthouse was closed, Clint called his friend to let him know they were five minutes away and to asked who he was to connect with and where.

"Isn't the courthouse closed?" Angela asked when he disengaged the call. "How will we be able to get married if it's closed?"

"Tom's friend will meet us there with the license." He flashed her another one of his brilliant smiles. "All we have to do is sign it and we'll instantly be Mr. and Mrs. Clint Banner."

Still disconcerted by the idea of the sham of a marriage, she asked, "But what about blood tests and things?"

"What about them?"

"Weren't we supposed to see a doctor and have blood tests first? I mean, that's the way it's done on Earth."

"Not to worry. That's all been taken care of, Angel. Tom has a frat brother, who's a doctor here in Imperial. He filled out all the necessary forms. We're good."

Angela was horrified. More and more it was beginning to sound too much like the fraudulent methods Mason had used to deny Lainie. "In other words," she said, "what we're doing is illegal."

"Probably." He shrugged. "Quit worrying, Angela. No one's going to know how we got married. Everything will be recorded as if we stood before a preacher and you were in a snowy white gown." He took his eyes off the road long enough to look over at her and grinned—that little boy mischievous gleam in his eyes that she had seen too many times over the last two weeks. "What's *really* bothering you?" he asked still grinning. "You worried that I might have something you don't want to catch, or... is it *you* that has something?"

"Ohhh... You're horrible!"

Clint laughed. "Yeah. I know. But right now I want you to put on a pretty smile and look the part of a blushing bride. We're here."

The courthouse was the most beautiful building Angela had ever seen. From the street, the large two-story structure appeared to be made out of solid glass. If there were seams anywhere, they were invisible. A set of wide steps led up to the main entry.

Clint pulled the Land Craft up to the curb in front of the steps and killed the engine. "Wait here a second," he said as he got out and walked up to two men waiting on the steps. One of the men Angela assumed was probably the witness. After shaking hands and a brief discussion, Clint returned for her. "Ready?" Taking Lainie into his arms, he cradled the baby against his shoulder, then helped Angela from the car.

And there they stood on the steps of the courthouse saying a quick version of their vows as a breeze whipped through their hair and tossed Angela's dress and coat about. Lainie began to fuss, to which Clint skillfully switched shoulders and patted her back until she settled down.

It didn't take long—just a few minutes of I do's and signing their signatures. When it was over, Clint gave Angela a quick kiss then walked her back to the LC. After getting Angela and Lainie settled in the vehicle, he turned and headed back to where the two men waited. Reaching into his pocket, he withdrew what appeared to be a roll of credits. Upon paying the men, they quickly shook hands again then Clint hurried back to the LC.

"Are you hungry? Want to stop for something to eat before we head back?"

"No thank you. And I don't want to be dropped off at the townhouse either."

"A little late for that, Mrs. Banner. You're my wife now. You and Lainie belong with me and you'll be coming back to my place."

"Then tomorrow," she began, "I want to—"

"Tomorrow," he interrupted, "I'm taking you shopping. You need a new wardrobe and a wedding ring." He cast a glance her way, grinned and with a wink added. "Sorry, we didn't have time for you to select a ring first."

"Clint, that isn't what I was going to say. Tomorrow I want to start looking for a place of my own."

Silence. Then... "Why?" Clint slowed the vehicle down. "Angela, I can only imagine how you're feeling right now," he said turning to face her. But I don't want you living somewhere else. I want you and Lainie to live with me. You can keep that spare bedroom, if that's your preference.

"We're married, yes," she admitted, "but it's not a normal marriage. We both know that. It's a marriage of convenience and I don't expect you to take care of us. Especially out of a sense of duty. I really need to get on with my life."

"And if you make a life for yourself elsewhere, then that makes us no longer a family unit. Right? And in that case, what good did it do to get married?"

"Precisely."

The silence that followed was loud. With a puzzled frown, Clint quietly studied her before picking up speed again. The trip back to his place seemed long and wearisome. Neither Angela nor Clint had anything more to say to each other, both edgy and troubled by their new status in life. Obviously, Clint was disturbed by her inability to accept their marriage as being real. And Angela was saddened over the fact that she had once again married for something other than love. She believed in her heart that Clint would no doubt always have a roving eye and, no matter how much she loved him, would never truly love her in return. She knew from experience that being forced into a marriage would never work. It was simply another recipe for a broken heart. Hers.

Making matters worse, Lainie refused to settle and cried on and off the rest of the way back. Whether feeling the tension in the air or simply tired from such a long day, she added her own frustration to the mix.

It was fully dark by the time they arrived. By now, all three of Acacia's moons were rising on the horizon. Clint hopped out and came around to unfasten Angela's safety harness and take Lainie into his arms as she exited the vehicle.

"Angela—"

"I don't want to talk about anything right now, Clint." With a pasted-on smile for the baby, she took Lainie from his arms and turned for the house. "It's been quite an exhausting day, and I just want to go to sleep."

"Oh, all right... sure." He rushed forward to open the front door for her. "Goodnight then."

"Goodnight, Clint." She could feel his eyes watching her as she made her way down the hallway toward the spare bedroom that he'd given her earlier.

Ten minutes hadn't passed before there was a knock at the door. "Ms. Banner?"

When Angela opened the door, Trixie barged through, making a bee line for the front entry. "Trixie!" With Lainie in her arms, and looking flustered, she glanced up at Clint to find him grinning.

"I, uh... was just wondering if you would like for me to take Trixie outside while you tend to Lainie?"

"Oh, yes. I'd really appreciate that, thank you."

"No problem. But I guess I'd better hurry, huh?"

Angela chuckled as she watched Clint dash down the hall after the dog. "I'll just keep her with me for the night," he called back.

Once Angela got Lainie settled on the bed surrounded by a wall of pillows and rolled up blankets, she changed into her new nightgown and eased into bed next to Lainie.

Married... Everything had happened so fast, it was hard to believe she was married again to anyone, let alone the notorious wolf, Clint Banner.

What's with making him sleep alone on his wedding night, Angela? a silent voice admonished. *What about those last couple of days before being rescued? You didn't have any qualms about giving yourself to him then. Remember? You initiated it in fact by telling him how you fell into the well. You knew it would break his willpower, and it did. You got what you wanted.*

She assured herself that her responses to Clint back then had merely been out of boredom and restlessness—also out of gratitude for his willingness and unwavering ability to come to her rescue and keep her and Lainie both safe. Her emotions were running close to the surface and highly charged back then. And no matter what Clint wanted to read into it, there was absolutely nothing more to it than that.

CHAPTER TWENTY-TWO

Four months had passed since Angela moved into Clint's house. At his insistence, she ended up having her shoulder operated on, and by now it was as good as new. She no longer had to wear an orthopedic cast, and the pain, long forgotten.

Despite her initial mixed feelings about their unusual marriage and the resulting move into his house, it turned out to be a change she didn't regret.

Clint's home was comfortable, and in truth, she loved living here. Not to say that she loved it from the beginning. Oh, it was always beautiful, yes, but it was so big and foreign, and so very masculine. It desperately needed a woman's touch, yet she was constantly on guard at first, afraid to infringe upon his manly territory. There were only two places she had been most comfortable: in the kitchen with Lainie and at the barn with the horses. She had to admit however, she was truly most comfortable when Clint was at home with her.

Very much the city girl that he had accused all women of being, Angela had been overwhelmed in the beginning by the expanse of his home and the sprawling acreage that surrounded it, having spent the last year in Aurora, closed-in by surrounding mountains and living in a pocket-size cottage. Her neighbors, who also lived in nearby cottages, were walking distance from her. But here, there were no neighbors around for miles. Everything was so big and so different from what she had been used to. Telling Clint her hesitant feelings, however, would have been unthinkable. She didn't want him assuming she couldn't handle it, especially when she knew she could. Besides, the last thing she wanted to hear was, "I told you so."

There was one little problem, however, after two weeks of sleeping in separate rooms, Clint had drawn the line one night. Resting a shoulder against the doorjamb of her open door, he addressed her as Mrs. Banner, and in a low, husky voice said, "I'm feeling abandoned, very lonesome, and damned tired of separate bedrooms." His gaze settled on her mouth for a stretched second before meeting her eyes. He flicked a look at Trixie and then back to Angela. "Trixie can come too if you'd like, and I was thinking... hoping, maybe this room could become Lainie's room. It's really not that far down the hall from where we'd be."

Just the look on his face had all the excuses Angela had been using escaping like water through a sieve. And yet at the same time, it was all she could do to keep from laughing at his sad, puppy-dog look.

The idea of moving into his room, however, left her feeling anxious once again. Why? She didn't know. It didn't make any difference that she had already spent those last nights on the *Victorious* in shameless lovemaking. She'd told herself that back then it was spontaneous and unplanned... they were snowbound victims, marooned in tight quarters with unfulfilled desires and urges. Where now, it was expected, even if it wasn't a love match. Nevertheless, she succumbed to his wishes.

To his credit, Clint did not force himself upon her that night. Instead, he simply held her until she fell asleep in his arms. Nor did he pressure her the next three nights. It wasn't until early the fourth morning that things began to change. It was barely daybreak when Clint once again leaned against the doorjamb of what was now Lainie's nursery. Somehow, he'd managed to get up without waking Angela. But by the time he'd showered, had two cups of coffee and checked in with his foreman, Angela had been up just long enough to change and feed Lainie. She had just laid Lainie back in her crib. "There you go, sweetheart," she said as she engaged an overhead mobile of dancing horses for Lainie to reach for.

"Mornin'. How's my two favorite girls this morning?"

With a smile Angela looked up as he entered the room. "Good morning."

He was dressed in an old but clean pair of faded work Levis, a neon green tee-shirt and scuffed work boots. "Come here," he said softly, drawing her into his arms when she came forward. "I'll be heading out to the new drill site this morning. I probably won't be back until late tonight." He kissed her soundly. "Don't wait up for me, okay?"

"Alright. I take it they've started drilling?"

"Hopefully, we'll start today if everything's ready to go. The crew's been out there all night."

"Well, I'm sure your crew won't want to disappoint the boss."

"They're all good men—every single one of them." He was still holding her when he changed subjects. "I know these past weeks have difficult. You've done a beautiful job with this home."

"Clint, I—" She started to protest, but he held up a hand, silencing her.

"I want you to know I'm proud of you. He grinned. "Far as I'm concerned, I've got a wife who not only has the face but the body of an angel. And I have to admit, you've transformed this place into a piece of Heaven that is both warm and comfortable. One that I truly enjoy coming home to."

The energy between them was a palpable presence. With a low groan, Clint pulled her tighter into his embrace and kissed her. It was a burning kiss, filled with passion and desire. "I need you, Angel," he rasped as he drew her against him. "I don't know what I'd do without you. Angela released a soft gasp as he tugged her tighter.

"What? Does your shoulder still hurt?" he asked, instantly releasing her. "Should we have the doctor look at it again?"

"No, it was nothing," she rushed to assure him. "My shoulder's fine, everything's all healed now."

"Let me see."

"What? Really, Clint. I'm..."

Angela's voice trailed off as he took a step back and gently caressed her robe off of her shoulder, exposing one thin faded pink surgery line. Angry post-surgery bruises by now had basically disappeared from her honey-toned skin and eventually the scars would disappear as well.

"Yeah, I... I think you're all healed up... looks just fine." Clint's voice was beginning to sound raspy. Angela held her breath as his attention moved down from her bared shoulder, and he began deftly untying the sash at her waist and slowly parting the garment. With heavy lids his gaze took in the length of her naked body.

And when he lifted his eyes to hers, his arm slid inside her robe to encircle her waist. Although he didn't actually say the words, his look was both apologetic and imploring when his other hand cupped her breast, his touch soft and so very gentle. Afterall, he was trespassing on Lainie's sacred territory. And Angela was sure Clint was well aware of it as he bent to kiss her.

Without thought, Angela closed her eyes and parted her lips to receive his kiss. Drawing her closer, he moved his mouth over hers, giving as much as he took.

From there, he kissed his way to her neck, nuzzling the hollow of her throat. And all the while, he cupped her breast ever so lightly. With a moan, Angela arched her back and leaned into him.

It was all the encouragement he needed. From the hollow of her throat, he moved down to kiss the fullness of her breast. Angela felt his breath, warm on her skin.

The results were predictable as both Angela and Clint were aroused to heightened passion.

"Dear God... Angela," he groaned. Then before she could catch her breath, his mouth caught her aching nipple, encompassing it in sweet, moist warmth.

Silky spikes of midnight hair spilled over his forehead, tickling her heated flesh. Angela caught his head with impatient hands and held it fast. His free hand slid lower, pressing her intimately against him, challenging her to acknowledge the strength of his desire for her. Without conscious thought, Angela gradually began undulating her hips against him in a rhythmic cadence. It was a little something he'd taught her during those last couple of days on the *Victorious*.

Clint allowed it for only so long then suddenly he grabbed ahold of her arms and without warning, abruptly pushed her away.

The robe she'd been wearing dropped, pooling at her feet and she stood there in all of her naked glory, staring at him. "Did I do something wrong?" she asked.

His face was flushed as he bent at the waist and inhaled deeply. "No, baby, you did nothing wrong." His breathing was ragged.

Angela shuddered, afraid she had somehow done something terrible. "Clint. Are you sure you're okay?"

He huffed a soft laugh, "No. But I'll live if that's what you mean." With another deep breath he straightened. "Baby, if you keep doing—"

"But Clint, you taught me how to do that. I thought..."

He grinned. "I know I did, Angel. It's just that you're a quick study, and if we take it any further, I'll be here all day."

"I'm sorry..." And she was.

"Nothing to be sorry for." He picked her robe up off the floor and held it for her while she slipped it on. "Angel," he added as he closed the robe and tied the sash with reluctant determination, "the only thing I'm sorry about is that I have to be on the job today." With the tip of one gentle finger, he lifted her chin as his head descended, blocking everything else from sight. His eyes were like a deep blue flame, and when his mouth closed over hers, Angela felt it clear to her toes.

"I just hope to hell I can keep my mind on business today," he said with a wink and a chuck under her chin.

CHAPTER TWENTY-THREE

Angela no longer regretted her decision to marry Clint, despite the fact that life was so different from what she had been used to. Back in Aurora, everything had been predictable. She could count on what was going to happen each day. But then suddenly one day the very self-motivated and compelling Clint Banner showed up at her door on a rescue mission, and nothing had been the same since.

As the days and weeks passed Angela had adjusted to being married and living in Clint's home. She got used to the bigness of everything and had begun to realize that no matter how vast his property, she would not get lost taking Lainie and Trixie for walks or going to visit the horses in the barn. She was even able to see Piper again. Clint mentioned that Rae had moved Piper to his place for safety in case Mason was looking for the mare.

A couple of days a week, Delta and Rachael would stop by to visit and play with Lainie. Angela would always have lunch ready with something freshly baked for dessert.

Clint's ranch house itself was feeling very much like a home instead of a man's hunting lodge. She had managed to soften each room with things such as plants, woven baskets and wall hangings. And she spent her days taking care of Lainie, polishing the furniture and baking everything from cookies to pies. She discovered that one of Clint's favorite desserts was kelpie pie made from kelpies, Acacia's version of an apple. But the frosting on the cake, her very favorite time, were the nights filled with Clint. It frightened her to think what might have happened had she not been home when Clint showed up unannounced to rescue her that day. What if he had been caught in the worst of it while on his way to get her? Or, what if he hadn't come after her at all? As doubtful as it had been back then that there could ever be a relationship between them, Angela couldn't imagine now what life would be like without him. And even after four months of being together, her heart danced whenever he came near. Not only did he make her feel safe and protected, he met her every need.

Lainie was a strong bond between them. Watching Clint develop a relationship with his newly adopted daughter was heartwarming. And as the weeks passed, both Angela and Lainie flourished. She had found a pediatrician that both she and Clint liked and it seemed that each well-baby visit ended with a good report. Lainie was still a baby, yes, but each day she was losing more and more of her baby features and looking more like a little girl.

Clint was completely enamored by Lainie's cheery personality. He didn't make a big issue of it in front of Angela, and yet she would often catch him off in a quiet spot playing with Lainie. Clint would always double check on her before going to bed and again when he awoke at dawn. It was obvious Lainie loved her *daddy*. She knew him the instant he entered her room, eventually raising her arms and babbling, begging to be picked up. Their relationship was so innocent and so loving that it often brought tears to Angela's eyes just watching them.

Clint had pre-programed the Land Craft's navigator so Angela could drive to the drill site any time. Today was a beautiful early summer day, and Angela decided she and Lainie would surprise Clint with a picnic lunch. Having carefully packed a lunch for two, complete with fresh fruit and cookies, she then loaded the lunches and Lainie into the Land Craft and headed off to the drill site to have lunch with the boss. It was a beautiful warm day and she had chosen to wear jeans and a mint green tee-shirt. Her hair was loose and softly curled about her shoulders, just the way Clint liked it.

By now she had gotten to know most of the workers by name, and whenever they would see her, they'd always look up and greet her with friendly smiles and a wave. Today was no exception, except for Dan,

Clint's foreman. Angela had no sooner parked the LC and was out and reaching for Lainie when Dan approached her. "Honey, I don't think you want to go in there right now."

"What do you mean?" By now she had Lainie positioned on one hip and was reaching for the picnic basket. "Why?"

The frown on Dan's face didn't tell her much as he all but snarled, "He's got company."

"Oh." Angela glanced at the unfamiliar vehicle parked near the modular office. It looked sporty and expensive, and she assumed it belonged to the person with Clint. "They're talking business?"

"They damn well better be," Dan muttered.

"Oh..."

Dan's attention turned to Lainie and with a broad smile he quickly changed subjects, "Damn, if you aren't growin' bigger every time I see you. If I wasn't covered in grime, I'd ask your beautiful mommy if could hold you."

Just then, the door to the site office flew open and a tall woman stormed out onto the porch. She was stunningly beautiful with shoulder-length auburn hair and long shapely legs encased in tight black leggings. Before slamming the door, she turned and shouted something inside that Angela didn't catch over the noise of the derrick. Still muttering as she stalked toward her vehicle, the woman then noticed Dan and Angela and purposefully began making her way over to them.

Dan took a step closer to Angela. "I *was* going to get back to work," he mumbled, "but on second thought, I think I'll stick around for a bit."

"Why hello, Dan," the woman said in a sugary sweet voice as she drew to a halt before them.

"Shelbi..." Dan replied in a bored tone.

So... this was Shelbi, Angela thought. The woman was gorgeous in her designer clothes and every hair in place. The only thing out of place was the fact that her eyes were bloodshot. Obviously, she'd been crying.

"Sooo, you must be the little wife," Shelbi said, directing her attention to Angela. "You know, I was married to Clint before you." Her smile was dazzling as she went on. "Isn't he a magnificent lover though?"

"Shelbi!"

Ignoring Dan's censure, she continued, "Well, it's the truth." Turning her attention back to Angela, she pointedly nodded to the picnic basket still sitting on the passenger's seat. "You know... I used to meet him for lunch too." She laughed and with a wink added, "Only what I brought him for lunch, didn't come in a picnic basket. Don't you just love how he takes total control when it comes to sex?"

"Dear god, that's enough!" Dan shouted, as he glanced anxiously toward the modular, willing Clint to come out.

Still ignoring Dan's disapproval, Shelbi released a theatrical sigh and studied her manicured fingertips with avid concentration before going on. "Clint always managed to turn our little *lunch* trysts into smoldering marathons."

Quivering with jealousy, Angela tried not to stare at Shelbi. She had to admit, albeit grudgingly, that Shelbi was exquisite. Her hair was a glorious shade of dark auburn, her eyes, snappy brown. Her smooth skin was flawless, and her figure could not be faulted.

"Tell me, does he get-it-on with you like that too?" Shelbi asked in a teasing voice. "Especially at night? Or... was it just with me?"

"I said, that's enough, dammit!" Dan angrily stepped around Angela and took ahold of Shelbi's elbow to lead her away. "I think you've said quite enough."

"Wait!" she said, jerking her arm free of his grasp, her attention suddenly now on Lainie. "And this... why this must be... *the child*. How very charming. Clint always did want kids. Not me. I didn't want kids, didn't want to share him with anyone. In fact, that's the only reason we divorced." Her smile was not kind. "How very clever of him to find a ready-made family." Shelbi slowly raked Angela from head to toe before releasing her final bombshell, "Although he's got a mousey wife, at least he's got a cute kid." As if it was so unbelievable, Shelbi slowly shook her head and released a dramatic sigh. "But then," she added sweetly, "Clint always was a sucker for a sad cause." With that she turned and with hips swaying, sashayed her way over to her vehicle.

Watching in stunned silence, Angela remained where she was.

"Don't you go payin' any attention to her, honey," Dan offered as Shelbi's fancy vehicle screamed out of the drill site. "It's been a long while since she last came around. You never should have been subjected to her."

"It's okay, Dan."

"No. It's not okay, and I'm sure the boss has no idea you're here, or he would have been out here to run interference, instead of me."

"Where *is* Clint?" Angela asked, her voice sounding weak and barely audible over the noise of the machinery.

"I'll get him for you, darlin'."

"No. It's alright," she said, blinking back tears. "I think maybe I'll just... I'll just go home."

"Wait. Let me get him for you, honey. I swear he doesn't know you're here."

"Oh, I'm sure he doesn't."

Angela was just securing Lainie in the safety seat when Clint arrived.

"Angela."

Ignoring him, she handed Lainie a soft toy to hold and then closed the door to the Land Craft.

"Angela," he repeated, moving to stand between her and the driver's door. When she made to go around him, he grabbed her arm. "Dammit, just hear me out, will you?"

"Let go of me, Clint. I'm not interested in any of your explanations. Had I only realized you were entertaining your ex-wife, I would have stayed home."

He blew out a compressed breath and lifted his sights to look out over the peaceful landscape beyond the drill site. "I was *not* entertaining her."

"Yeah, well that's what *you* say. According to her, the two of you enjoy—" Her words were cut off when he eased her back against the side of the LC. His arms were outstretched, his palms anchored against the vehicle, effectively trapping her between the LC and his hard, unyielding body.

"I don't give a flying... I don't care what Shelbi told you. Whatever she said, was purposefully said to hurt you."

"Well, she did a good job," Angela replied, tears on the brink of her lids.

Catching sight of the picnic basket sitting untouched in the passenger seat, Clint instantly calmed, lowered his voice and with the edge of one finger, gently lifted her chin. "Angel," he said softly, "you and Lainie came all the way out here to have lunch with me, didn't you?"

Still trapped against the LC, Angela wordlessly turned her head and stared off into the distance beyond.

"I would have liked very much having lunch with my two favorite girls." Coaxing her head back to face him, he found her mouth. His kiss was incredibly tender. He passionately sipped at her lips until she began to relax her steely tautness. Angela felt her body begin to betray her as she slipped into submission. Despite the fact that her mind was screaming, "Nooo," her resolve always seemed to melt under his caresses and flagrant virility.

But not this time she vowed. She refused to be drawn-in by him. As far as she was concerned, none of his kisses and caresses meant anything. He simply used them as a means of breaking her will and self-control.

With every ounce of strength she could muster, she pushed Clint away from her. "Goodbye, Clint." And with that, she got in the LC, slammed the door and lowered the window part way. "You can call *Shoobi* now," she said, "Let her know I'm gone and that she can come back. I'm sure she will be more than happy to satisfy your baser needs."

Clint put a restraining hand on the open window as she turned on the engine. "I'll be home at the usual time tonight."

"Don't come home hungry."

At that, he had the audacity to laugh. "Okay,"

CHAPTER TWENTY-FOUR

Never had she felt so betrayed, so hurt. Clint was her first real love, and now it was as if he had thrown it in her face.

"Smoldering sex marathon, indeed." Talking to the windshield the entire trip home, Angela recounted every one of Shelbi's cruel allegations in a sing-song tone. She couldn't help but wonder how often Shelbi visited Clint. Dan had mentioned that it had been a while since she last came by, but was Dan just being kind? It was obvious the woman was still in love with Clint. But the real question running through Angela's mind right now, is Clint still in love with Shelbi?

She was still talking to herself when she pulled up in front of their home. Calling both Clint and Shelbi every horrible name she could think of, she reached over, removed the picnic basket and set it on the steps. Lainie had fallen asleep on the ride home, and as she lifted her out of the safety seat, Billy, their young ranch hand came running up.

"Here, let me help you, Mrs. Banner."

"Thanks, Billy, I got it. But I'll tell you what, if you're hungry I have a picnic basket sitting right there on the steps with two complete lunches in it, including dessert. It's yours if you want it."

"Oh yes, I sure do. Thank you," he said, rushing to open the door to the house for her.

Thankfully, Lainie was still asleep and Angela quickly settled her in her crib then tiptoed out of the nursery and headed down to the room that she and Clint shared. It was not like her to throw herself across their bed and surrender to a deluge of tears. No matter how bad things were, she was always one to remain cool and in control of her emotions. But, then again, never had she been so let down, so deceived. Not even Mason had betrayed her on this level. However, she never completely trusted or loved Mason in the first place. But Clint... she had let her guard down with him. She had permitted herself to love him, allowed her heart to open wide and bask in the hope that he would love her. Even worse, she had trusted him with Lainie's heart as well.

So, she wondered, how long was he married to Shelbi? And when? Clint had briefly mentioned Shelbi but explained very little about their marriage other than it didn't last long. Shelbi, on the other hand, mentioned that the only real reason for their divorce was his desire for a family.

That brought up another question that Angela couldn't ignore. Was Clint so despicable that he would marry her to gain a ready-made family, and at the same time get revenge on Shelbi for her refusal to give him a child? Angela wondered if all along that had been the driving force behind their sham of a marriage? Her thoughts going from bad to worse, Angela moaned his name, buried her face in the pillow that held his scent, and wept her heart out. She should never have let her guard down. She had no one to blame but herself. She knew what he was like, was well aware of his character. Even back when she was a teen, the three of them, Clint, Nick and Zeke were known for their reputations as wolves, heartbreakers. So, what did she expect? Did she think she would be treated any different?

Once the tears subsided, Angela put the bed back in order and headed for the kitchen. Despite the fact that she had told him not to come home hungry, she knew she wouldn't—couldn't follow through with nothing for him to eat. That is of course, providing he came home at all tonight.

With reluctant determination she began preparing an easy Terran recipe for oven lasagna, her mind in a whirl as she rehearsed how she would act and what she would say when and if he walked through the door.

Once she placed the lasagna in the oven, Angela headed for the shower. The last thing she wanted was to look sad and miserable. Now that she knew his game, she could play too, and she would match him with her own cool composure. Ha! How would he like it if she found herself someone else too? Not that it was a likely option. She'd tried that approach once with Mason and paid dearly for it.

Despite all the self-talk to convince herself that she didn't care if he came home tonight or not, Angela's heart did a flipflop when she heard his Ground Runner pull to a stop in front, and his footsteps on the porch.

She had no sooner laid a blanket on the floor in the living room for Lainie to sit on when he came through the door. "Hmmm, smells good."

Without even so much as looking at him, Angela continued settling Lainie on the blanket with a couple of her favorite toys within easy reach. It would have been nice if Lainie could have cooperated and not be so happy to see him. Instead, the instant she saw her *daddy,* she began babbling, and waving her arms and kicking her pudgy little legs in excitement.

Jaw set with annoyance, Angela wordlessly turned and headed for the kitchen.

The thing that was driving her over the edge was that Clint was behaving as if nothing was wrong. Just as always, after cleaning up he played with Lainie before dinner. And despite her plan to also act normal, unlike Clint, she failed miserably at disguising her feelings.

In fact, the longer she worked, the louder she got, banging lids on pans and even slamming a cupboard door once. It was exactly what she said she would *not* do—wear her feelings for him to see. And that, alone, made her all the madder.

Carrying Lainie, Clint wandered into the kitchen. "Need any help?"

"No," she snapped. "I'm doing just fine without you."

"Okay..." He was the personification of composure as he strolled back out of the kitchen with Lainie, talking to her as if she knew exactly what he was saying. Ohhh, he was *so* annoying.

Clint eventually changed Lainie and had her settled in her crib for the night. When he returned to the kitchen, Angela had dinner on the table and they ate in silence. That is, Angela picked at her food in stony silence while Clint ate with gusto, complimenting her epicurean talents as he piled on a second plateful of everything.

At last, after helping her with the dishes, they left the kitchen. "Angela, I want to talk to you," he said softly as he settled himself on the edge of the couch.

She took a seat in the chair across from him. "Good, because I have something I want to say too."

For several silent moments he sat there staring at his arms draped over his open knees. At last, he glanced up at her. "Dan told me what all Shelbi had to say. I'm sorry you had to hear it."

"Oh, I'm sure you are," she snapped. "Embarrassing, huh?"

"Dammit, Angela. Can't you even give me a chance to explain?"

"Are you going to deny it, Clint?"

"Would you believe me if I did?"

"No, I wouldn't. Lainie and I came to have lunch with you, only to find a gorgeous, voluptuous redhead in tight designer clothes coming out of your office." Angela looked away long enough to blink back tears. "You know, I might have bought your excuses, Clint, had that floozie not marched directly over to me to make sure I knew exactly who she was, what the two of you were doing in there, and what a great lover you are."

Angela rose to her feet and crossed the room to stand before one of the windows. "And as far as our marriage is concerned, I think we each need to go our own way and do our own thing," she said with more conviction than she felt.

"Is that what you want, Angela?" His voice was barely audible.

"Yes," she said rebelliously. She didn't dare back down now. She had just given him her blessing to see Shelbi as often as he wanted. But, was it really what *she* wanted? Would she be able to withstand it if he took her up on it?

"For Lainie's sake," she struggled on, "we probably should go on pretending to be a family unit. That is, of course, if you agree." She paused, giving him time to respond. When he didn't, she turned her back and stared out the window. "I... I also think that we should... should be able to do whatever we want to do. And... I feel it best if we no longer share a bedroom. From now on, I will sleep in Lainie's room."

There. Her well-rehearsed ultimatum was delivered, but where was the gratification she had hoped for? Where was the feeling of compensation? Instead, she felt empty and most of all, scared.

Wordlessly Clint stood up and made his way toward her. "Angela," he began. "I think you might be right."

Lifting her chin, she looked away, denying the agony his declaration was causing. Even after her brave speech, still she hoped he would try to explain Shelbi's visit and beg her forgiveness. And yet, she had set the rules and he had accepted them... almost too readily.

And now, he was standing directly behind her. "Yes, I agree. Each of us should do whatever we want to do," he said as he gently turned her to face him. "And right now, kissing my wife is what I want to do."

Powerless to resist him, Angela stood as though hypnotized as Clint reached out to caress the curve of her cheek. Ever so gently he tilted her face up as he bent down to cover her mouth with his own. Time seemed to stand still, and Angela secretly wished that her world had not come crashing down today and that she could stay in his arms forever.

But then he released her and turned for his bedroom. "Good night, Angela."

Damn Clint Banner. Why was he the only one who could stir the passion in her soul? And why was it that he had only to look at her to make her blood sing and her heart beat like a butterfly caught in a trap?

CHAPTER TWENTY-FIVE

The next two weeks passed agonizingly slow with Clint acting annoyingly normal, as if all was well and nothing was wrong. He'd carry on conversations with Lainie—which usually had to do with how pretty her mommy looked today or whether Lainie wanted him to ask mommy about going for a drive in the country. And when he got home from work, he'd also inform Angela how his day went at the drill site, or complimented her on her cooking, or any number of small talk subjects to which she didn't often respond. Unable to forget her encounter with Shelbi, Clint's easy chatter, *as if nothing was wrong*, was annoying.

Summer was just beginning to arrive in a panorama of color and warm, sun-kissed days. In an effort to escape the apathy that gripped her, Angela threw herself into a surge of house cleaning. It was as if her very life depended on shiny waxed tables, sparkling windows, and glistening floors.

It was early one breezy afternoon when Clint received a call at work from Billy, his hired ranch hand.

"Mr. Banner, I think something's wrong at the house." Billy went on to explain how he'd been hearing the baby crying and the dog barking furiously for well over a half hour. "And when I rapped on the door, no one answered."

"I'm on my way. Go ahead and enter the house. Call me when you get inside and let me know what you find."

Within a few short minutes, Billy was calling again. "I found Mrs. Banner on the kitchen floor. She's unconscious."

"Oh my God... What happened?"

"I don't know, but the dog won't let me near her."

"Shoot the damn dog if you have to," Clint roared.

"Plus," Billy added, "I don't know what to do for the baby. I'm no good with babies."

"Where *is* Lainie," Clint asked.

"She's in her crib."

"Good, she's safe then. Let her cry. Crying won't hurt her. Call Delta to come help. I'm calling Doc Adams. I'll get there as soon as I can."

"Yes sir."

A moment passed before realization turned to gut-cold fear. Clint struggled for composure—his thoughts scrambling for some logical reason why Angela would be lying unconscious on the kitchen floor. Never in all of his life had he known such fear. Pushing the Runner to its very limit, the afternoon landscape flew by in a blur, so calm and serene while Clint's mind raced with a thousand unanswered questions.

His Ground Runner skidded to a halt in front of the house exactly thirteen minutes from when he'd last talked to Billy. Hitting the ground running, he took the steps in one leap and burst through the front door. "Where is she?" he hollered as he raced toward the kitchen. Not finding her there, he yelled even louder "Where in the hell *is* she?"

"Quit hollering, Clint." Quietly closing the bedroom door behind her, with Lainie in her arms, Delta came down the hall.

"What's wrong with her," he asked in a slightly softer voice, as he stalked toward the bedroom.

"Wait." Delta said, extending a restraining hand. "She's not conscious. And you need to calm down before going in there."

"I want to see her, dammit."

"Clint! Listen to me. You're not going to do her any good rushing in there like a wild man. For all you know she might be able to sense those around her."

"What the devil happened to her anyway?" he asked.

"We don't know. I was on my way over with a pie when Billy called. He got her up off the floor and moved her into the bedroom."

CHAPTER TWENTY-SIX

"So, where's Grant?"

"Doctor Adams is on his way," Delta said calmly. "He should be here any time now."

"Yeah, well he'd better."

"Calm down and take a seat. Let me get you some coffee."

"I don't want coffee. I want to see Angela."

"Well, have it anyway," she said as she headed for the kitchen. Within moments, she returned with a steaming mug of black coffee. "Here," she said thrusting it into his hands. "You need a moment to calm down, Clint. You're no help to any of us like this."

Clint wordlessly took a seat on the arm of the couch and stared down at the mug of coffee he loosely held between his parted knees. Suddenly setting his coffee down on a nearby table, he rose to his feet and started purposefully down the hall toward the bedrooms. "I want to see her. Now."

Then he saw Billy and stopped. "She's going to wonder where her dog is. Did you end up having to shoot Trixie?"

"No. When Mrs. Banner, your mom, arrived, Trixie calmed down, and Mrs. Banner put her outside."

"Thank God."

"I don't think I could have shot her anyway."

"I hear someone coming up the steps now," Delta said as she headed for the door.

"Doctor Adams, thank you for coming so quickly," Delta said as he entered the house. "This way, please." Carrying Lainie on one hip,

Delta led the way.

"So, what's going on," he asked as he followed Delta and Clint down the hall to where they'd taken Angela.

"We're not sure. Billy's, the one who found her. He was outside by the barn and could hear the baby crying and the dog barking." Delta explained how Billy had called Clint at work... "After that's when he found Angela lying on the floor, unconscious."

"I see." He turned to Clint, "Will you help me get her undressed."

Clint stepped forward and between the two of them they removed Angela's boots first. They were just starting to work on her jeans when Doctor Adams said, "Well, I see right now what the problem is."

"You do?" both Clint and Delta asked in unison.

Doctor Adams looked up at Clint. "You got snakes around here?"

"Every now and then I'll see one, but nothing harmful. Why?"

Grant lifted the leg of Angela's jeans and pointed to her swollen foot and ankle. Two inflamed bite marks were located just above her ankle. The surrounding area was purple. "Snake bite," he said. "My guess is she was probably bitten outside and made it into the house before collapsing."

Clint remained speechless as he stared down at Angela's swollen leg.

"We need to know what bit her, Clint. I can't give her just any antivenom until we know."

A moment passed before disbelief and confusion turned to panic. Struggling for composure, Clint whirled about and left the room. "Billy!" he bellowed, "are you aware of any snakes around here? Angela's been bitten, and doc needs to know what kind?"

"Nothing out of the ordinary," Billy replied.

"Do you know if she was outside this morning? Maybe at the barn, or in the garden?"

"Yes, I saw her in the barn brushing Piper."

"I need you to come with me to help track down a snake."

"Yes sir."

The search didn't last long before they found the culprit. Trixie was more than happy to tag along and once in the barn, she proudly led them to Piper's stall where a large snake lay dead in the corner. It didn't take a genius to recognize the combination of dog bites and circular hoof marks flattening parts of the snake's fat body.

"What the hell kind of snake is that?" Billy asked, frowning as he stared at the mutilated body of a very large snake scrunched into the back corner or the stall.

"Beats me. But it looks like some kind of rattlesnake."

"Rattlesnake? What's a rattlesnake?"

"They're not from around here. I used to see them every now and then on the drill sites when I was in Texas. Although not quite this big."

"Texas! So how the devil did it get here?"

"That's a good question. Offhand I'd say it was brought here." Clint stepped into the stall and picked up the mangled snake by its tail and dragged it out of the barn. "We've got to get back and let Grant know what bit her."

As they raced back to the house with the snake in tow, Trixie followed along, growling and barking furiously at the snake's lifeless head bouncing along in the dirt behind Clint.

"Rattlesnake?" With a frown of concentration, Doctor Adams began searching his portable medical workstation for information on the rattlesnake and what antivenom might be needed to counteract the effects. "Aren't they native to Earth?" he asked as he anxiously continued searching.

"Yes." Clint pulled up a chair beside the bed and reached for Angela's limp hand.

Adams released a compressed sigh. "Well, we don't have anything that specifically says rattlesnake. I transmitted a message to Earth, but it could be hours before we hear back. We don't have that kind of time, and I think this one will do it."

"What do you mean, *you think*?"

"It means, I don't know for sure. It's not like it's a snake native to our area. I know nothing about a rattlesnake, Clint. Therefore, I have to rely not only on the VDU but also on my own gut as well. It's the best

I can do right now. Plus, there's another factor involved."

"What's that?"

"According to what I'm reading here, if, and I emphasize the word *if*, Angela received a full bite, she should be dead by now and not still struggling for her life." He looked up at Clint and asked. "Have you ever heard of a dry bite or a metered bite?"

Clint nodded. "I've heard the terms."

"A dry bite," Doctor Adams explained, "is when no venom is released with the bite."

"So, are you saying that this snake is possibly not venomous?" Delta asked.

"No. That's not what I'm saying. Number one, a nonvenomous snake wouldn't leave puncture wounds. However, sometimes a venomous snake will choose to conserve venom and bite to scare off their victim without wasting venom.

"And a metered bite," he continued, "is when the snake injects less venom with the bite, probably for the same purpose. To conserve venom.

Delta stepped closer. "Doctor, shouldn't she be in the hospital?"

"Yes. Absolutely she should, but we need to stabilize her first. We can only assume how long ago she was bitten and the length of time that has passed." Adams went on, "Given the fact that she is still fighting for her life, I believe she must have received a metered bite. Just enough to stop her but not kill her outright.

"There's one other thing, and it makes it complicated. If it was indeed a metered bite, then I must also meter the antivenom to the best of my ability... but there again, it's guesswork."

"Dammit, Grant. I don't like guesswork. I—"

"And neither do I," Adams interrupted, "but we have no choice but to sit tight and wait. If the antivenom is going to work, we'll see some improvement soon."

"And if not?" Clint growled.

Grant ignored him. There was no need to respond. The answer was obvious.

A full bite from a rattlesnake, if untreated, could be deadly enough to kill an adult male, but to a child, or to someone Angela's size, even a metered bite, if left untreated, could very well mean her life.

Angela drifted in a bright liquid-like void, floating between the worlds of consciousness and nothingness. She could see the snake in the void with her, its body twisting and gyrating as it floated about in the abyss to eventually disappear in the distance beyond. She recalled its bite, as though it were a lightning bolt striking her leg. And although she could still feel it, somehow, it was growing less and less painful until suddenly it no longer seemed important. Nothing seemed important. She was warm and comfortable and very, very sleepy.

From somewhere outside the void, she could hear voices, echoey sounding. She recognized Clint's voice, imploring, begging her to come back to him. But she didn't want to go back. It was so peaceful here. Nothing mattered anymore.

Then she heard her mother's voice coming at her from a long way off. *"Angela, you do not belong here. It is not your time yet. You need to go back. You have a husband who needs you, a baby to raise with more children yet to come. You have your life ahead of you."*

"But momma, I don't want to leave. It's so peaceful, and I'm so tired, so very tired. I want to stay."

"Yet, you must return. Follow the path, Angela. It will take you back."

Her mother's words began to fade as Angela slowly began clawing, fighting her way upward, inch by perilous inch. And just when she thought she could go no farther, a golden softness surrounded her with such an overpowering feeling of love that her heart seemed to burst with it.

Ever so slowly she opened her eyes to discover she was lying in a dim room on a big bed and covered by a soft blanket. As her head began to clear, she found herself staring up at a dark paneled ceiling and realized she was in their bedroom. She shifted her gaze and there was Clint, slouched in a stiff chair that had been pulled up next to the bed. He was asleep, his eyes closed, his chin dropped down to his chest. He looked careworn, his upper lip and jawline unshaven, his dark hair in shaggy disarray, and yet to Angela he had never looked more wonderful than he did right now.

"Clint," she murmured, barely finding the strength to do more than whisper his name.

He glanced up with a start. "Angela! Oh god... baby, I thought I'd lost you."

She strained to sit up then fell back on the pillow.

"Don't try to sit up, honey," he said as he leaned forward and took her hand in his.

"A snake... Clint, there's a snake... in the barn."

"Yes. It's dead now. Piper and Trixie took care of it."

"It bit me, Clint."

He drew her palm to his lips. "I know, honey. Doctor Adams saved your life."

There was a long moment of silence. Then suddenly, "Lainie! Where's Lainie?"

"She's here, Angel. Mom has her, and she's sleeping right now."

"How long have I—"

"Shhh. Just lie still," he said, his eyes glowing with love. "You've been unconscious and fighting a fever all day and half the night. Doctor left strict orders for you to rest and remain in bed at the very least for two more days."

Angela eventually fell asleep and Clint eased out of the room to join the others in the parlor. By now, Nick, Zeke and Max had arrived.

"How is she?" Delta asked.

"She woke up for a few minutes. We talked for a bit then she fell back to sleep. Grant says he wants her to stay in bed for at least two more days and to drink plenty of fluids. If there's any complications we're to call him immediately and in that case she would no doubt have to be hospitalized."

"That's quite a snake," Max said. "I've never seen one like that. It's not native, is it?"

Clint took a seat. "No. We don't have rattlesnakes."

"Then where do you suppose it came from?"

"Earth." Clint said."

"Earth?" Nick piped up. "How? As a stowaway?"

Clint huffed a cynical laugh. "I doubt it. If my hunch is correct, it was transported here and deliberately planted on the property. Hell, there could be more than one for all we know." He looked pointedly at Billy. "So, be careful and stay on the lookout around here until we know for sure."

Max cleared his throat. "So, do you think Angela's ex is behind this?"

"That's *exactly* who I figure did this. The problem is, I can't prove it."

"Who would he be trying to kill?" Zeke asked. "And why?"

If he kills either me or Angela, then he has broken the family unit and Mason and his parents would use that as leverage to get Lainie."

Zeke crossed the room to stand in front of the large window. "None of this makes any sense," he said, looking out over the tree-shaded yard. "Having adopted Lainie, wouldn't that make you the surviving parent?" He turned to face Clint. "And you're not exactly flat broke, so he can't accuse you of being unable to care for her. Plus, I thought he didn't want the baby. I mean, didn't you say he went to a helluva lot of work denying her?

"That's right," Clint said.

Nick spoke up. "Then why would he—"

"Apparently, his mother wants to raise her. Angela feels that she's the one behind getting custody of Lainie."

"Well, they almost got their wish," Max said. "Thank God she's going to be okay."

CHAPTER TWENTY-SEVEN

Three months had passed without any more snakes materializing. Angela was thankful that Clint had finally begun to loosen up and was allowing her to venture outside without an armed guard at her side—preferably him.

It was mid-morning. Angela was in the kitchen putting together a pie for Clint, when Trixie started barking at the front door. Quickly grabbing a kitchen towel to wipe flour from her hands, she cast a hasty glance at Lainie who had fallen asleep in her baby swing and made her way down the hall to answer the front door. A quick peek out of the side window gave her a glimpse of an unfamiliar vehicle. Cautiously approaching the front entry. Angela slowly opened the door but only part way to keep Trixie from lunging out.

"Well, Angela, I was beginning to think you weren't going to answer the door."

"Mason," she said and was about to close the door on him, when he stuck his foot in the way.

Angela frantically looked beyond Mason to see if Billy was anywhere around only to find that he wasn't. For now, she held her ground. As always, Mason was impeccably dressed in the latest Terran fashion, right down to his polished retro loafers. His light brown hair was fashionably sun-streaked and flawlessly combed. To Angela's way of thinking, he looked completely out of place with the surroundings.

"What are you doing here? What do you want, Mason?"

"Aren't you going to invite me in?"

"No."

He grinned. "Afraid?" His smile faded. "I came to see our baby."

"She's not yours to see. Besides, since you adamantly denied her, I can only assume your mother is the one who put you up to this."

Without invitation, he pushed the door open and stepped over the threshold into the house. Showing her teeth, Trixie growled as Angela quickly sidestepped him, escaping outside onto the porch he had just vacated.

"Billy!" she called at the top of her lungs. "Billy!"

"Really, Angela? There's no need for that."

"I think there is."

She glanced toward the barn to see Billy tenaciously making his way toward the house. "Billy, may I have your help for a bit?" she asked as he advanced. "This man is my ex-husband and I don't want to be alone with him."

"You've *got* to be kidding," Mason groaned as he quickly leapt back out onto the porch, barely escaping Trixie's threatening teeth.

"Certainly." Billy said, taking the two front steps in one stride, he folded his arms, leaned back against the balustrade and proceeded to insolently study Mason. Although Billy was young, he made up for his youth in both size and muscle. Even in his seemingly relaxed pose, it was obvious that the two men were not evenly matched.

"Feeling brave now, are you, Angela?" Mason asked snidely.

"You need to leave, Mason."

"Not until I see my daughter. What's her name... Lainie?"

Angela remained stone-faced. "She's doing just fine. And she's not *your* daughter. Remember?"

"Can't I at least see her?"

"No. Besides, she's sleeping."

Mason turned to stare brazenly at Billy for a long moment before finally turning back to Angela. "I won't wake her. I just want to see her."

"No. You will never see her. I have all the papers you ever signed waiving any claim you and your family think you still have on her. Regardless, she's been adopted. Her last name is no longer Cooper. And now that you know we're doing just fine, and that you can't see her, you might as well turn around and leave."

Mason didn't budge, instead he cast a quick glance over the surrounding landscape. "Surely you don't intend to raise her *here*, do you?"

"We're done, Mason. Leave." His very presence was sullying the happiness that had enfolded her over the last six months—something that was decent and good and wholesome.

Ignoring her, he continued. "What are you doing here on this God-forsaken planet anyway? Not to mention clear out here in the middle of nowhere. Animals live in places like this, Angela. Not people." He specifically cast his glance Billy's way and repeated, "Animals."

Despite the personal insult, Billy remained where he was, sprawled negligently against the porch railing, his eyes promising retribution at the slightest incentive.

"It's none of your business, Mason."

"What the hell kind of life is this?" he continued. With a wave of his hand he shot a disparaging glance about then turning back to Angela he said, "I ask you, what kind of life is this to raise our daughter in."

"Again, she's not your daughter. Never was. Never will be. Lainie and I are happy here, and now that you know that, you need to leave."

"Happy with your flyboy are you, Angela?" Mason laughed, "Wait, he's more than just your flyboy, isn't he? What is he, your rancher or your roughneck? No matter. I bet at the end of the day he comes home stinkin' dirty."

Angela drilled him with a stoic look.

"You can't be serious wanting to live like this. How can you even consider raising our child in this... this hovel? This isn't life. If you want to live like this, that's one thing, but to bring a child up in it... It's merely existence. There's nowhere to go shopping around here? Where do you eat out? You're miles away from civilization. Where's the culture? Oh, that's right, Acacia has no culture. Plus, you're denying Lainie the chance to play and see other children instead of... of living with animals and *people* who I bet never even went to school." He cast another mocking glance Billy's direction.

Angela was livid. "What an asinine thing to say."

"Oh come on, Angela. You know exactly what I'm saying."

"Actually, Mason, I don't. I'll have you know that the people I've met since leaving you are honest and intelligent. And they're head and shoulders above you and your family when it comes to kindness and good judgment. I'm sorry, but you're a product of an environment that Lainie and I want nothing to do with."

Mason laughed. "Don't tell me I hit a nerve," he said, flicking another scathing glance at Billy. "What? Don't tell me you're puttin' out for him too?"

Angela's mouth dropped.

Billy bolted from his slouched position against the rail, but Angela halted him with a raised hand. "You get the hell out of here, Mason!"

"I told you, not until I see my daughter."

Angela was thankful she hadn't answered the door with Lainie in her arms. Instead, Lainie was tucked safely away in the kitchen, fast asleep in her swing. "Well, that's not going to happen, sooo..."

But Mason wasn't listening at the moment. He was watching a fast approaching ribbon of dust about a mile out. Reflecting off of the advancing vehicle's windshield, sunlight glittered in and out of the trees lining the drive. Mason turned to face Angela and grinned. "That your roughneck coming to your rescue?"

Angela looked beyond Mason and was relieved to know that indeed, it was. She silently thanked Billy for having let Clint know she had unwanted company.

"Where's Lainie?"

"Forget it." Angela was thankful that between Billy on the outside and Trixie on the inside, Mason would not be barging in to search the house.

"She's my daughter, dammit, and I have a right to at least see her."

"You gave up that right."

"And if I had it to do all over again—"

"You would," she said, remaining stone-faced.

"No, I wouldn't, Angela." He flicked an awkward look at Billy then back to Angela. "I'm trying to tell you I've changed."

Angela cast a glance at the impending Ground Runner. "You'd better leave. Now. While you still can."

But instead of leaving, Mason held his ground. "Think about it, Angela. That's all I ask. I love you, and I made a horrible mistake letting you go."

"You certainly did."

"Please," he went on, "bring Lainie and come back to Earth with me."

He turned and darted a quick glance at the Runner which, by now, had reached the beginning of the long driveway leading to the house.

With a quick move, he snatched Angela's left hand, ignoring Billy who immediately uncurled from his slouched position once again. "Well, at least he married you," he said, seeing her wedding band. "Why just a band? Where's the diamonds?"

Angela yanked her hand back. No diamonds, Mason. My idea."

"You sure he loves you, Angela? Bet he hasn't told you that he loves you, has he? He married you to gain a cook, a laundress, a housekeeper... and a lover all under the guise of marriage." Mason shook his head sadly. "Plus," he added, "he didn't just marry you, he took on a child too, one he didn't make.

"You know, wedding bands mean nothing, Angela," he said. "Marriages can be undone as easily as they are initiated."

"Believe me, Mason, I'm well aware of how *nothing* a wedding band can mean."

In a cloud of dust, the Runner came to a sliding halt at the base of the steps.

"I don't care if he has adopted Lainie," Mason said, "she's not his blood. You think he's still going to want the two of you when she becomes a teenager and wants things her way?"

"What the hell's going on here?" Clint asked, his voice rough and threatening as he took the steps in one agile leap. With his eyes narrowed on Mason, Clint put a possessive arm about Angela's shoulder. "Who the devil are you?"

"This..." Angela said unsteadily, "This is Mason, my ex-husband."

"What's he doing here?" Clint asked, his eyes stony with unbridled fury.

"He came to see how... I was." Angela lied, deciding to not to bring Lainie into it. Clint was angered enough as it was. "But he's just leaving. Aren't you, Mason?"

Although Mason didn't respond, the look on his flawlessly tanned face left no doubt but that he was pissed. It was easy to see why he chose not to argue with her. Mason was tall, yes, but Clint was taller. More than that, Mason was no match as far as brawn was concerned. The difference between them was laughable. Clint was not only broader shouldered, but he was by far more heavily muscled. There was no doubt but that Mason recognized a menacing adversary when he saw one. Without a word, he sent a disdainful look at Angela then squaring his shoulders, he walked with dignity past her and Clint, with his perfect tan, his perfect hair and his perfect clothes, down the steps and across to his perfect sport vehicle. He'd barely opened the door and was getting in, when Clint bolted off the porch after him.

"Clint, please. Just let him go."

Without looking back, Clint lifted a hand in response. Angela watched anxiously as Clint, with lightning speed, reached through the open window, grabbed a fist full of Mason's designer shirt and yanked him halfway out of the vehicle. Without releasing him, Clint leaned low and was in Mason's face, but between the rustle of the breeze, Clint's low voice, and the distance Mason had parked from the porch, Angela was unable to hear what Clint was saying. His body language, however, was saying plenty.

At last, Clint straightened, drew back his fist and popped three vicious and brutal blows into Mason's face. From the resulting cry and the copious amount of blood spurting from Mason's nose and mouth,

Angela seriously suspected that Clint had just permanently rearranged Mason's perfect looks. Without a doubt, he was not only missing teeth, his nose was severely broken.

He was bloody and half-conscious when Clint finally released him and with a hard shove stuffed Mason's sagging body back through the window into the driver's seat. "Now, get the *hell* out of here. Next time I see you or your men, I'm coming after you."

That much Angela did hear, and it took a moment or two after Clint stepped back before Mason's vehicle finally started up and slowly began to move away.

"Well, I suppose I'd better get back to work," Billy said as though nothing unusual had just happened.

"Oh! Yes, of course." She'd forgotten about Billy being there. "Thank you, Billy, for staying here with me until Clint arrived. I appreciate it."

"No problem, Mrs. Banner."

"And..." she added in a whispered voice, "I apologize for the insulting things he said."

"No apologies necessary."

"Billy, please just forget everything between Mason and myself. What's done is done. No need to upset Clint any further."

"I understand."

"Thank you, Billy."

"Certainly." With that he hopped down off the deck and headed back toward the barn.

Heart pounding, Angela was already inside and hurrying for the kitchen as Clint returned to the porch.

Lainie was awake and happily entertaining herself with a small toy that Angela had hung from the swing. At seeing her mother, she began waiving her arms and kicking her feet. "Hi, sweetheart," Angela whispered as she lifted Lainie from the swing. Closing her eyes, she gently swayed back and forth while protectively hugging Lainie.

Clint entered the kitchen. "What the *devil* was he doing here?" he asked as he made his way to the sink and began washing the blood from his hands. "You're white as a sheet, Angela. What did he say? Did he threaten you?"

"No," she replied softly, still swaying back and forth with Lainie in her arms, "It was just horrible seeing him again. That's all."

"Well, I guarantee he won't be back."

Angela stopped swaying, and opened her eyes. "What all did you say to him?"

"Let's just say I told him in crude detail what I'd do to him if he or any of his goons ever come near you again."

"Oh."

Having dried his hands, he tossed the towel into a nearby bin. "Hi princess," he said softly when Lainie reached-out to him. Ever so gently he lifted her from Angela's embrace. "So... was he here long?"

"Only a short time before you showed up."

"What about Lainie? Did he want to see her?"

"No," she lied. "He just asked about her." Lying was not in Angela's nature, and she hated having to lie to him, but the last thing she wanted was to have Clint angered further. Besides, the bottom line was, Mason was denied seeing Lainie, and after all, that's what really counted.

CHAPTER TWENTY-EIGHT

As time passed, Clint wanted to ask Angela what all Mason had said to her, but he didn't ask. It would look insecure, and that wasn't exactly the image he wanted to reveal. Besides, he trusted Angela. It was just a matter of time, and she'd tell him what Mason had to say. And if not, well, he guessed that would be okay too, as long as life went back to the way it was before that bastard showed up.

But as the days marched on, Angela had changed somehow—not overnight, and not all the time. But in many ways she was no longer that happy, carefree person she had come to be. Clint was profoundly aware of her quiet moods, despite the fact that it was obvious she was trying to hide it from him.

And when he was at work, he couldn't help wondering how often and how long she spent thinking about whatever was heavy on her mind. He couldn't help worrying about it, especially given the fact that he was having to work longer hours lately at the new drill site.

He'd love to talk to Billy. But there again, he wasn't about to press Billy for answers when it was obvious he wasn't getting the answers from Angela.

Had Mason made some sort of an offer, he wondered, and she has been quietly mulling it over? Surely not. She hated Mason. Didn't she? A wave of panic ripped through him. What would he do if she were to pack up and leave? What would he do if he lost her?

Nah... she wouldn't. Or would she?

Hadn't he married her, and hadn't he adopted Lainie to keep them both safe from Mason? All this time, he thought she was happy.

No, it didn't start out that way, as he recalled how upset she was the day they were married. She had hated their so-called wedding, called it a sham. But before Mason had shown up, she seemed happy, or at least he thought she was happy. But what if she isn't? What more could he do? Especially if she wouldn't tell him what was bothering her?

Like it or not, there was only one way to put an end to this charade, and it came to him later that afternoon. "Angela, how'd you and Lainie like to go for a little ride," he asked. It was a beautiful summer afternoon and they'd just finished an early dinner.

"I'd love it. Let me get Lainie."

His gaze followed her as she headed down the hall to Lainie's room. "Oh! And grab a blanket to sit on," he called. Before long she was back with a blanket and a packed bag. She'd dressed Lainie in a jumpsuit with a matching light weight jacket.

"Hey, pumpkin," Clint said softly to Lainie as he took the blanket and bag from Angela and headed for the Ground Runner.

"So where are we going?" she asked while securing Lainie in the safety seat.

"Not too far. I thought we'd follow the stream to a small lake. It's a nice drive this time of the day, and the scenery's great."

They had been driving for about a half an hour before coming to the lake. "It's beautiful here," Angela said, glancing around as Clint pulled to a stop and killed the engine.

"Yeah, it's a nice getaway." He reached into the back to get the blanket and bag that Angela had packed. They were in a secluded valley. Tall trees surrounded the area, their branches covered in bright shades of summer foliage. A nearby lake sparkled in the sunlight. Multi-colored flowers bloomed on the surrounding hills and along the shoreline. Angela thought it looked like a scene out of a Terran fairy tale, as though it had been plucked from the pages of a book she remembered from her childhood.

"Pretty, huh?" he said as he spread the blanket out on the grass.

Angela sat down and positioned Lainie on her lap. "It's so peaceful. Do you come here often?"

"I used to. Not so much anymore.," he said, as he settled beside her and leaned back on his elbows. "The pond is one of the main reasons I bought the property."

Angela handed Lainie a teething ring to chew on. "So, how's the new well doing?" she asked. "It seems you're gone so much of the time lately we never get to talk anymore."

"It's coming along just fine."

"Good. Good."

"Angela, there's something—"

"Clint, would you like a cup of coffee? I managed to sneak in a small canteen of coffee and some fresh baked cookies in the bag."

"Not right now, thanks. Listen, Angela—"

"Did I tell you that Lainie is starting to cut her very first tooth? When your mom and Rae stopped by today, we—"

"Angela. Would you please just be quiet for a minute and give me a chance to say what I have to say?"

Biting down on her lip, Angel hugged Lainie and waited apprehensively for Clint to go on. She'd been rambling on about mundane things, mainly to keep from shouting out that she loved him, that she and Lainie missed him when he worked late, and more than anything, she feared she was losing him. Was Shelbi the reason Clint worked late? Had he brought her and Lainie out here to this beautiful place to let her down easy, to tell her that it was over between them?

Clint recalled Angela saying that Mason had only been there a short while before he arrived. Yet, in that short time, Mason had said something that lingered. He was sure of it, and the longer he had wondered about it, the more insecure he had become. Once again, he asked himself what the hell would he do if he were to lose her and Lainie?

Angela was quietly staring at him, her expression tense.

Clint took a deep breath and jumped head-long into the heart of things. "Look, I've been doing a lot of thinking. I know you said Mason was there only a short time before I arrived."

"That's right."

"And I also know that he said something you've been stewing

over ever since."

"I don't know what you're talking about?"

"Yes, you do. You've changed ever since Mason showed up, Angela. And I want to know why. What did he say?"

"Well, you've changed too," Angela shot back, "ever since that floozy showed up at your work. Tell me, Clint, does Shelbi come by very often? Is she the reason you work late?

"What? No! And that's no to both questions."

She went into great detail, you know, explaining what a great lover you are."

With a heavy sigh, Clint looked away and muttered. "And you believed her of course."

"What choice did I have? You've never denied it. You never even tried to explain her presence that day, Clint."

"Would you have believed me if I had?"

"No."

"Wow... She must have been pretty convincing."

"She was detailed. She made sure I knew she met you for lunch, only it wasn't lunch the two of you shared. Ha! Even you said yourself, back on the ship, that the only thing the two of you had in common was... let's see... how did you put it? Mind-blowing. That was it. Mind-blowing sex. Those were your very words and she pretty much said the same thing."

Clint's mind floundered. Had he actually said that to her? Was it the night when he'd been drinking, he wondered? His memory was a bit sketchy regarding their talk that night. "Angela... Shelbi means nothing to me. Never did."

"Just as I mean nothing to you?" she shot back. "And you know what? I don't care anymore. I'm—"

"That's not true! You and Lainie are my life." He raised his hand when she started to interrupt. "Please, just give me a moment. I know I'm not wording this very well, but... I never loved Shelbi."

"Well, that's certainly reassuring. Then why did you marry her, Clint?"

He fell silent.

"Oh, wait. I remember now. You said that you married her in order to gain Solarblaze. Right?"

"But Angela, I had also just learned that you had gotten married, and—"

"Ahh... So, in other words," she cut in, "it's okay to marry someone for personal gain? Particularly if you're on the rebound? Is that what you're saying, a marriage of convenience?"

"Hell no, that's not at all what I'm saying."

"Sure sounds like it to me. And now that I think about it, isn't it pretty much what you and I have? A marriage of convenience?"

"Angela—"

"I'd say you've got it pretty good. A cook, a laundress, a housekeeper... and a lover. All for the price of a quickie marriage license. Not a bad deal, Clint." Lainie had fallen asleep in her arms. Rising to her feet, Angela carried her back to the Ground Runner with Clint following on her heels. Reclining the car seat, she gently laid Lainie down and secured her. "I don't know about you, but I'm ready to go back home." She reached for the passenger door only to have Clint place the flat of his palm against the door.

"Is that what you think, Angela? That I bought myself a built-in maid and lover for the price of a marriage license?" This wasn't going at all as he had hoped. He had a pretty good idea now what Mason had said to her. "Look, I've made my share of mistakes, but marrying you isn't one of them."

"And why is that, Clint?"

"What do you mean?"

"What makes you say that marrying me is not a mistake?"

"Because I'm happy with the life we have together. I like coming home to you, Angela—you and Lainie."

"But why?" she asked again. "With your good looks and charming charisma, you could easily find yourself someone else to play house with. Why me?"

He stared at her in astonishment. "I'm not looking for a

housemaid, and I don't want just anyone in my life. I want you, Angela. And I *need* to know that you won't pack up and leave."

"And how do I know you aren't simply saying a bunch of pretty words just to keep me from leaving... all because you *like* your life the way it is?"

Wordlessly he stared at her. "*Are* you planning on leaving?"

She didn't answer.

"What is it you want to hear, Angela? What's going through that head of yours?"

Angela studied his handsome face, studied the firm set of his jaw, the straight line of his mouth, those troubled sapphire eyes searching for reassurance. And even though she wanted so badly to throw herself into his arms and tell him that she wouldn't leave him, to tell him that she loved him, that she wanted to make him happy and wipe that worried look from his face, she knew that she needed to know more. She couldn't go through life wondering if Mason's visit had prompted his insecurities and desire to hang on to her. But more than anything, she needed to know that Shelbi was not a threat. "Why now are you so concerned that I will leave you. Why now, Clint? Surely I'm not the only housemaid you can scrape up."

"Because I..." He frowned. "I don't think of you as a housemaid, dammit." Taking her face in both hands, he said. "I've tried to make you a good husband. I've tried to make Lainie a good father. I want to have more kids... Oh hell, I'm no good at saying this... I'm in love with you, Angel. And that's the reason I don't want you to leave. I love you."

Huge tears welled in Angela's eyes as she melted into his arms. "Oh, Clint! If you only knew how long I have waited to hear those words. Tell me again."

"I love you. I never stopped loving you. You have no idea how many times I tried to connect with you before you married Mason," he said, nuzzling her cheek.

"And I you," she whispered.

"I lost count of the trips I made to Earth, only to be turned away."

"It doesn't matter now," she said, blinking away tears of love and happiness, only to have them trail down her cheeks. "None of that matters anymore."

He kissed her then, one hand tangling in the golden mass of her hair, the other pressing against her back, holding her close. It was a long, lingering kiss, full of passion and promise.

"Marry me, Angela. And I mean, a real wedding this time?"

"I can't."

He pulled back to look down at her. "Why not?" he asked, frowning.

"Because we're already married, Mr. Banner. Remember?"

"But you hated that marriage."

"Yes, I have to admit, I did. It was crazy, and outrageous. I'll never forget that windy afternoon we were married... on the steps of the court house of all places. But I wouldn't trade that memory for anything. And someday we'll be able to share that story with Lainie and our other children yet to come."

"I love you, Angela Banner."

"Oh Clint, and I love you too," she whispered as she lifted her face for his kiss, shivering with delight when his lips covered hers.

Resting her head against his shoulder, she trembled as he lifted her into his arms and carried her to the blanket that was still spread upon the grass.

"I love you, Angel," he murmured again, as he followed her down onto the blanket.

Closing her eyes and basking in the music of his words, Angela sighed as he worshipfully removed her clothing, caressing her with his hands and lips as each article fell away. "Say it again," she begged.

"I love you."

"Again..." she moaned as he quickly opened and pushed his Levis down no farther than necessary.

"I love you. Dear God, I love you," he whispered as their bodies, ever so tenderly merged to become one.

At last Angela was home. Home where she belonged, in the safety of Clint Banner's arms.

EPILOGUE

Five years later

Angela released an exhausted sigh as she eased herself into a rocking chair on the back deck. She was beyond ready for this child to be born. It seemed, she thought wearily, as if she'd been pregnant forever.

Not only had she and Clint expanded the size of the Banner Clan, Nick and Tressa had added another boy to the lot as well. Plus, Tressa had just recently learned that she, too, was pregnant again.

Angela's musings and weariness evaporated the instant she glanced up and saw Clint striding toward her with Jonathan, their youngest son, perched upon his shoulders. The twins, Dane and Scott, were excitedly running circles around their father as the throng advanced toward the house.

All of the adult Banner males were notoriously handsome men, including their father, Max. But for Angela, Clint was by far the most handsome of them all. At least that's how she saw him.

"We thought we'd bring Piper's new foal up to the house so you could see him," Clint said, unconsciously blessing her with one of his heart-stopping smiles.

Billy was leading Piper with the colt loose and trailing close behind. Lainie was helping Billy hold onto Piper's lead rope. She looked so proud and so grown up, Angela thought, blinking back tears. Six years old already. Where had time gone?

"Isn't he a beauty, momma?" Scott called out.

"He certainly is."

"And daddy said it's my turn to name him," Dane piped up.

"So, what do you think?" Clint asked, grinning.

"He's gorgeous, Clint. And he's a Medicine Hat too. Just like his sire."

"Yep," he said as he lifted Jonathan from his shoulders and set him down on the porch. He then sat down on the steps not far from Angela. Trixie ambled over and plopped down next to him, resting her gray muzzle on his thigh. With a nod, Clint indicated that Billy could take Piper and her foal back to the barn.

Life was good. Solarblaze was flourishing. They had enlarged the house, having added two more bedrooms. The barn had also been expanded, along with a bunkhouse for the hired help. Billy had since married, and Clint had promoted him to foreman.

Angela lovingly gazed at her three sons, each a small replica of their handsome father with their dark hair and those trademark Banner blue eyes. Without a doubt, they would all grow up to be future heartbreakers.

"Oh Clint, we have so much to be thankful for," she said, glancing over at the corrals where eleven young fillies milled about—all of which had been sired by Rachael's beautiful Thor. Four, however, were born to Piper, and were, in her opinion, the best fillies out of the bunch. "And they all have top bloodlines," she added.

"I agree." Clint's heated gaze smoldered with tenderness and unspoken love as he glanced pointedly at Angela's swollen belly. "And not just the horses."

Despite Angela's insistence that she wanted nothing to do with Southern Charm Development, Clint had made sure that her father's forty percent was transferred into her name. As a result, with the added income, the breeding of horses had become Angela and Rae's dream partnership. They had even hired a native American horse trainer who came highly recommended by Nora, the woman who had taken such good care of Angela's injuries. As it turned out, Nora had been right about the trainer. His reputation had followed him all the way from Earth. Besides local sales, people from all parts of the United States were inquiring about horses that not only had top bloodlines but had been gentled by Jake Prowling Wolf.

Just then Dane and Scott scrambled up onto Clint's lap. "Daddy, tell us again about the huge snowstorm."

"Yeah. We want to hear how mommy's LC blew away."

"And I want to hear," Lainie piped up, "how you and mommy got married outside on the steps to the church."

Clint laughed. "Tell ya what. Today it's the snowstorm because Dane and Scott asked first. Then tomorrow, I'll tell you all about how mommy and I got married."

With a deep breath, Clint began telling a story the kids all knew by heart. "It all began with your mommy, Lainie and Trixie living waaay up in the mountains." He turned to look at Lainie. "You were just a tiny baby at the time, princess. And when I found out there was a great big snowstorm coming, I borrowed Uncle Nick's ship and hurried just as fast as I could to the rescue."

"The *Victorious*," Scott supplied.

"That's right, The *Victorious*. And I had to park it in a valley at the bottom of the mountains because there was just no room to land it in mommy's front yard." That brought forth a soft muffle of snickers from the boys.

"So, we had to pack everyone into mommy's little Land Craft. Whewww..." Releasing a long breathy whistle for added drama, Clint continued. "So, here we are... me, mommy, Lainie and Trixie, all racing as fast as we can out of the mountains, trying to beat that ol' storm, when all of a sudden..."

With a soft smile on her face, her arms enfolding two-year old Jonathan on what little was left of her lap, Angela leaned back and quietly listened as Clint retold the story of the snowstorm rescue.

It was a story that Angela knew first hand had a very happy ending.

About the Author

Carole Ann Lee is a Pacific Northwest Native. Having grown up in Oregon, she presently lives in Washington State with her own special hero who shares her crazy sense of humor and love of animals. They have two grown children and two grandchildren.

The Lees live on fifteen acres, and are owned by Lancer, a German Shepherd, a Medicine Hat Paint Horse named Nacoma, and River, a buckskin-dun Quarter Horse.

A hopeless romantic at heart, Carole discovered writing by accident as a stay-at-home mom with two young children. A devoted Star Trekkie, Carole has always been fascinated by the thought of space travel, yet equally captivated by the romance of the tall sailing ships of the past. Carole's goal has been to integrate both worlds into a futuristic romance.

First and foremost, her stories are geared for the romance reader, and thus they lack those hard to pronounced scifi words and names. Just for fun, she even incorporated an off-planet Marriott in one of the stories.

Banner's Bonus is the first book in the Banner series. *Solar Wind* is second, and now *Banner's Renegade* is third. And Marc Banner, the youngest brother, is presently sitting hip-shot on the edge of her desk, staring at her.

Carole loves hearing from her readers and answers every letter. You may email her at caroleannlee3@gmail.com

Banner's Bonus
Banner's Series Book One

INNOCENCE MEETS HEDONISM: He's a father's worst nightmare. Yet cargo pilot Nick Banner is Jonathan Loring's only hope of getting his daughter, Tressa, safely off-planet and out of harm's way.

Within the tight confines of Banner's ship, Tressa battles a girlhood crush gone dangerous. As a sheltered teen, she secretly worshipped the hotshot cargo pilot from afar. Even his carnal reputation seemed romantic. But now, those old feelings are unsettling.

Banner misses nothing, particularly her coy glances. Yeah, he's noticed, and sexual tension smolders. Danger stalks them across the galaxy and when Tressa is captured by pirates, Banner finds himself willing to sell his soul to free her.

CHAPTER ONE

Earth Date: 2105 Port Ireland
Terra Four 70 A.C. (After Colonization):

"Listen, Garrett, I don't give a rebel's damn what game or whose bed you have to drag him out of, *just get Banner.* You hear me?"

Standing behind his massive desk and bracing his weight upon the knuckles of firmly planted fists, Jonathan Loring's voice could be heard into the main hallway of LorTech's Central Control.

Lending him distinction, Loring's dark hair was dusted with gray at the temples. Though generally good-natured and quick to find humor, a frown now creased his brow.

"According to his itinerary," Loring continued with less volume, "he should have arrived in port sometime this afternoon."

Dan Garrett's shoulders slumped. "He's here all right, Mr. Loring, but it's been over two hours since I last saw him. He had just finished unloading a large shipment and said something about heading to the Star Cruiser. Sir, I'll never find him in that place...providing he's even still there."

"Look, I don't give a damn where he--"

"I'll get him," Garrett quickly cut in. "I'll find him for you, Mr. Loring."

The Star Cruiser was noisy and crowded. The atmosphere was a mixture of music, loud voices, laughter and a heavy blanket of smoke.

A wide variety of people mingled together. Some were off long-haul freighters, eagerly celebrating the end of an eighteen-month run. Then there were the miners--*diggers,* as they were called--just in from the asteroids and anxious to set their fantasies into motion, most of which had been months in the making. Still others, like Nick Banner, were there merely to celebrate the payout of a six-week cargo run.

Like so many other freelance cargo pilots, Banner was the owner and sole operator of a small cargo ship. With cargo runs being long and lonely, it was common for some pilots to take a woman aboard. In essence, she needed a lift to his destination, and in exchange she offered her companionship with all its connotations. Nick Banner wasn't interested in that kind of arrangement. Six weeks in space can be a big mistake when stuck with someone you don't happen to get along with. He'd tried it once--shortly after he'd acquired the *Victorious.* It turned into a catastrophe and from then on he resolved to limit his women to port only.

Terra Four's port taverns, and the love-starved crewmen who frequented them, were no different now than they were on Earth a little over two centuries ago when the tall sailing ships would come to port.

Just as it was then, an easy lay could always be found hanging around the port bars. Banner, however, had never known a time when he wasn't surrounded by women vying for his attention. He had never once paid for a woman's favors, and being with the same one for more than a couple of days didn't happen to be his idea of a good time.

He was barely twenty-one when he fell hopelessly in love with Linnae. So crazy in love, he turned his back on all the others, even walked away from the gaming tables and asked her to marry him. Blind to everything, he closed his mind to the ugly rumors going around about her.

"She's a whore, Nick. Dammit man, open your eyes; she's using you. Why can't you see that?"

More than once Nick's fist had split his older brother's lip for those very words. Even his friend, Zeke, had tried to dissuade him, but to no avail. Stubborn and hardheaded as they come, he had defended Linnae's honor right down to the bitter end, when he'd shown up unannounced one evening. As the door opened, Nick simply stood there watching in mute shock while another man in the background scrambled about for his clothing.

Drunk and giggling, Linnae tried to coax Nick to join the fun, but he turned away without a backward glance. And in many ways was still on the run.

He left home shortly thereafter. Setting out for a small, untamed world called Echo, he spent the better part of two years burying his heartache and anger in hard labor and life-threatening assignments. If nothing else, those years had taught him the meaning of being tough and living hard. He also earned damned good credits for his endeavors, and when he returned to civilization it was with a determination to live again.

The first thing he had done was place a hefty down payment on a small cargo ship, already christened the *Victorious*. Not long after that he formed a partnership with a drinking companion, Quint Kendyl. It was a business venture that entailed using Quint's connections and Nick's ship to make short runs for a local courier. Eventually, however, the partnership failed due to conflict of interests between the two men.

Looking for bigger and better brought Nick to Terra Four when, operating under the name of Banner Enterprises, he picked up a variety of freight and mail runs within the sector. By now he was over Linnae, though the scar of her betrayal ran deep. Vowing no one would ever own his heart again, he regarded women as nothing more than playthings-- entertaining diversions to be enjoyed and left behind.

Nick Banner had been branded a hard case back then. Come payday he could usually be found bucking roulette at one of the local port dives, where he drank everyone under the table, fought half the security force with his bare fists, and generally wound up passed out in some woman's bed.

But that was *then*. Miraculously recognizing Nick's ingrained honesty and reputation as a hard worker, a man named Linc Sheldon took Nick under his wing. It was Sheldon who, in time, introduced Nick to Jonathan Loring.

~ * ~

Dan Garrett entered the doors of the dimly lit Star Cruiser. To his left, a brawl had broken out in the corner, and two men seated at a nearby table were taking bets on the winner. To Garrett's right, a group of inebriated coworkers were starting the next game of *"Bounty"*.

"Hey, Garret, come on over. You wanna get in on this? We've got room for one more." James Cleary had a stupid grin plastered on his face and eyes at half-mast. Four others in the same condition were poured into their chairs around the game table--full mugs of ale within easy reach. One of them absently shuffled a deck of cards while the others had already positioned their pawns on the holograph game board.

"Not tonight, Cleary. I'm looking for Banner. Have you seen him around?"

"Not more than thirty minutes ago," Cleary answered.

"'Ee's 'ere...somewhere," one of the other men spoke up. "Lucky devil had two blondes hangin' on 'im." The man grinned then added, "Both of 'em clinging to 'im like *shateries.*" With that, the men at the table burst into a round of raucous laughter. It seemed the *shateri* was always the brunt of someone's joke. The small fur-bearing animal, found along the southern coastline of Terra Four's main continent, was not only known for its luxurious fur but was also notorious for its enthusiasm for procreation.

Garrett couldn't help but grin; their laughter was contagious. "Thanks, fellas. If you happen to see him again, tell him I'm looking for him."

Dan Garrett continued making his way through the crowd, his eyes intently sifting through a murky sea of smoke and faces. Finally, he climbed a set of wide stairs that led to a mezzanine from which he could survey the entire main floor. The mezzanine was an extension of the bar, a balcony furnished with tables and chairs that completely encircled the room.

Finding an empty table near the balustrade, Garrett claimed it, and from his perch began methodically scanning the entire main level. Behind him several drunk and boisterous crewmen were engaged in singing a bawdy song. All around, people were drinking and laughing, either burying their fears and troubles or celebrating their good fortune.

Banner, who seemed to rarely have fears or troubles to bury, was drinking to his luck when Garrett's eyes finally locked onto him. Seated at a game table on the opposite side of the room and true to form, Nick Banner was casually sprawled in his chair--all six-foot-four of him. From the smug grin tugging at the corners of his mouth and the stack of game chips at his elbow, there was little doubt who was winning.

There was an unconscious grace about Nick Banner. He always seemed to turn heads. In all honesty, Garrett was secretly envious of Banner's magnetism and innate ability to attract women. Though they were traits he yearned to possess himself, he had resigned long ago to the fact that he simply didn't have it and never would.

Even the faded, scarred leathers that Banner wore would have looked shoddy on anyone else. But with his dark hair and hard, lean body, the well-worn attire lent a primitively appealing air of danger.

~ * ~

Reaching for his mug of ale, Nick laid the winning cards on the table. He liked winning, but cleaning up on a table of drunken comrades wasn't much of a challenge, not to mention that it grated on his sense of fair play. It was time to call it quits. "Gentlemen, I believe this completes the game, and it looks like I win." He grinned and added, "Again."

A stunning brunette now stood at his back, both hands draped possessively over his shoulders as though she might lose him to another should she dare to let go. Leaning down, she whispered something in his ear that brought forth a crooked grin as he downed his last swallow of brew.

"Fellas, what can I say? I hate to win and run, but worse yet, I hate keeping a lady waiting. Here," he said, separating half of his winnings and tossing the coins back onto the table. "The drinks are on me." With that, the table burst into a round of boisterous cheers and Nick rose to escort his luscious companion to the nearest exit.

He no sooner began guiding her, his hand at the small of her back when, "Hey, Nick! Wait up!"

Banner turned to see Dan Garrett elbowing his way through the crowd.

"Garrett. What's up?"

"Loring wants to see you."

"Tell him I'll drop by first thing in the morning." He turned and resumed guiding his companion toward the exit.

"Nick. He means to see you. *Now.*"

Groaning inwardly, Nick stopped short, turning to Garrett in exasperation. "And it just *can't* wait until tomorrow."

It was clear from the look on Garrett's face, that he was painfully aware of his ill-timing. "Sorry, Nick, but no it can't. I wish I could tell you what it's all about, but I'm sure it's important."

With a heavy sigh of regret, Nick turned to the girl. Tightening his hold on her, he drew her near. "Baby..." he began, capturing her chin in a hold that was both gentle and possessive at the same time.

"Gina," she corrected. "My name's Gina."

Nick grinned. "Gina, honey..." Nuzzling against her ear he murmured something that made the woman glow, then punctuated it with a lusty kiss.

At last he turned to Garrett. "Let's get out of here 'fore I change my mind."

A landcraft waited outside the Star Cruiser for the 30-minute ride from Port Ireland to the headquarters of LorTech Equipment. The sleek, low-slung vehicle was a sporty two-seater model. Her shiny black exterior said she was new; the logo on her doors said she belonged to

LorTech.

"Well, I see Jonathan finally broke down and replaced one of those tired vehicles. How long have you had this?" Nick asked, running an appreciative eye over the smart new rig.

"About three months now," Garrett answered, fishing a remote from his pocket and entering a code. In response, both doors disengaged and slid silently backward to disappear into the rear quarter panel on each side.

With a low whistle, Nick climbed in and continued his appraisal from the inside. The complex dash was a mini cockpit, loaded with options ranging from a host of digital readouts to a small rear display monitor. "N i c e," he drawled approvingly as the control console snapped to life the instant Garrett's weight settled into the driver's seat.

Owned by Jonathan Loring, LorTech was a fast-growing research equipment company presently booming with a recent contract to supply equipment to Echo, a small and relatively unexplored rim world.

It was nighttime, and traffic was heavy at first but thinned progressively the farther they traveled from the city. Soon, the landcraft picked up speed and the landscape began whisking by in a blur. Both men remained silent, each deep in his own thoughts.

The environment was particularly dreary, consisting mainly of processing plants and warehouses. Then the scenery gradually changed. The buildings became taller and seemed to stretch farther apart. Some had tanks attached to them. Others had pipes that ran from one building to the next. Eerie puffs of vapor rose from their stacks, illuminated by the surrounding floodlights.

Terra Four was a Class E planet, located within the Sector Five System. Its distance from Earth measured in time was roughly six weeks. Before *Stellar drive,* it had taken years to reach the Sector Five System.

First discovered around the turn of the century by an unmanned probe during Earth's so called "Race for Space" era, Terra Four was the fourth of five planets that were named for their likeness to Earth. Colonization didn't occur, however, until almost thirty-five years later.

The first settlement formed was a tiny mining colony, Port New America, nestled high in the Cascades, Terra Four's northernmost mountains. Eventually more colonists arrived; more settlements sprouted up, and with them various forms of livelihood developed. Ultimately, through economic evolution many small mining towns combined to create thriving cities. Port Ireland grew to become the largest and most advanced city on Terra Four.

Pulling up to LorTech's outside gates, Garrett flashed the required credentials to the guard and they were waived on through.

As Nick palmed the security lock at the main entrance to the massive complex, a hidden scanner began crosschecking his palm print, retinal and voice patterns with his stated identity. "Come on...*come on,*" he muttered, releasing an impatient sigh as they waited. As if prompted by his frustration, a green light snapped to life on a small panel and the lock on the door clicked open. Nick wasted no time barging through. Garrett followed at his heels, trying to keep up with Banner's lengthy stride.

Taking the steps three at a time, Nick hastily made his way up a flight of stairs and down a long carpeted hallway until they finally came to a door with "Jonathan T. Loring, President" inscribed on it.

"Hi, Lizzy," he muttered, striding through the reception area toward the inner office.

"Nick. Wait! Let me tell him you're--"

"It's okay darlin', I know my way in."

"Yes, but--"

Skipping formalities, Nick hit the pressure-plate and barged in as the door opened into Jonathan's spacious office. Loring's back was turned as he stood before a floor to ceiling glass wall overlooking the compound.

"Ah, Nick!" he said, whirling around. "Thank God he found you."

"Yeah. Your timing's impeccable, Jon."

"Have a seat. *Please,*" Jonathan said, indicating one of two leather chairs in front of his desk. At the same time he turned to Garrett, thanking and perfunctorily dismissing him.

Nick sank into a comfortable chair, planting one booted foot across the opposite thigh. "So, what's going on?"

Taking his seat, Jonathan lifted an envelope off his desk and wordlessly handed it to Nick.

Accepting the note, Nick held eye contact with his friend, assessing the indisputable mixture of terror and anger in the man's eyes. At last he withdrew the note from its envelope and began reading.

Mr. Loring, I overheard part of a conversation that could cost my life as well as those in my family. For that reason, I choose not to reveal myself, but I want you to know that your daughter's life may be in danger. I wish I had heard more, but I strongly suspect "The Leader" is behind this.

Without comment, Nick patted his pockets, found a cigarette, lit it, and blew a lazy stream of smoke toward the ceiling where it was instantly ushered into the nearest vent. "I seem to be missing a few lines here, Jon. Maybe you'd better take this from the top. And who the devil's *The Leader?*"

Staring at Nick with blank eyes, Loring began. "That's just it; I'm not sure. There are several possibilities. Rumor has it there are at least two mega-corps that want total possession of Echo."

Maintaining eye contact with Loring, Nick took a slow drag from his cigarette. "Just exactly who are these two corporations?"

Loring hesitated. "Hell, it's a rumor, Nick. Your guess is as good as mine."

"Then *guess,* dammit!"

A long moment of silence passed before Loring reluctantly offered a name. "Frontier Enterprises could be one."

"And?"

"These are just guesses, Nick. There's no way of--"

"And?" he persisted.

"Possibly...Chase Explorations."

Nick examined his cigarette intently, deep in thought as he watched smoke curl off the tip. "Chase Explorations," he mused. "Aren't they based out of Paragon? What the devil are they doing clear out here, messin' around with a small rim world like Echo?"

"Howard Chase has become greedy over the years," Loring explained, dragging his hand through his thick hair. "His company has grown, but at the expense of others."

"So you figure Chase is *The Leader?*"

Loring shrugged. "It's possible. They've certainly managed to cut down most everyone in their way. It's known they want control of Echo, and LorTech is one of the few left in their path."

"Making *you* their target now. Right?" Not waiting for an answer, Nick lifted the note for emphasis. "Does *she* know about this?"

"Hell no. And that's the way it stays...at least until I can get her out of here. Knowing Tressa, she would refuse to leave."

Reading the note over again, Nick winced against up-trailing smoke as the cigarette dangled from his mouth. "So, what is it you want from me?"

Jonathan dragged in a deep breath, letting it out slowly. "Nick," he began, "I need you to take Tressa off-planet for me. Surely you know of some place where she will be safe until we find out what the hell this is all about."

One dark brow arched. "Me? I appreciate your confidence, but it's a bit out of my line, wouldn't you say? Sounds like you need a hired gun. Not some randy cargo pilot traipsing all over the galaxy trying to find a safe place to stash--"

"Dammit, Nick, you're a hell of a lot more than just a cargo pilot and we both know it. Besides," he added, "I don't need a hired gun. I'm not asking you to assassinate anyone. All I'm asking is that you get my daughter out of here until I can get to the bottom of this." Loring's voice eased off, betraying the depth of his feelings. "Believe me, if I thought there was anyone else..." He left the sentence hanging.

Nick calmly leaned forward, depositing a lump of ash into the ashtray on Loring's desk. "I'm not sure I'm your man for this, Jon," he said quietly. "Besides, I still have two deliveries yet to make. I can't just take off."

"I understand your position, Nick. Go ahead and make those deliveries. She wouldn't be a problem. I just need her out of here, that's all."

Nick tensed, shifting uncomfortably in the chair. Glancing away, he smiled in polite restraint. "We're talking about a chunk of time here," he said, his eyes cutting back to Loring. "You aware of that?"

Three hellishly long weeks at the least, a silent voice echoed.

A frown creased Loring's brow and his gaze darkened as he slowly rose and moved from behind his desk. There was no misreading the grim look on his face as he came around to settle hip-shot upon the front corner of his desk. "Make no mistake," he began slowly, his tone laden with warning. "I know full well what I'm asking of you. Just as you do."

Loring's grave expression eased. "Besides, you seem to forget, I've always seen more in you than you see in yourself. If I didn't, believe me, I'd never entrust Tressie into your care for a single minute."

Deep in thought for a long span of silence Nick stared at the smoke curling up from his cigarette.

"Dammit, Nick, this is my daughter!"

"And I'm telling you, you've got the wrong man." With his beautiful daughter, Loring didn't know how wrong.

"But you're the only one I trust. I know what you're thinking," he added, "and it might help to know that she's already spoken for."

Nick's eyes lifted to meet Loring's. "Oh yeah? Anyone I know?"

"He's new around here. Name's Sinclair. Look, I'm not saying it would be easy. You'll need to let her know who's boss right from the start. After that, she'll settle right in for you.

"Oh, and those rumors you may have heard," he added, "Tressa has not inherited her mother's gift. Thank God."

Nick shot him a puzzled look but said nothing. It had been eight years since he had first walked through the doors of LorTech Equipment. Tressa was just a kid then. With her off to boarding school most of the time, their initial introduction had never progressed much beyond a nodding acquaintance. It had only been in the last six months that he remembered seeing more of her around the complex. She had definitely grown up. And along with it, her personality had changed from giggly to politely aloof.

He had heard of Jonathan's desire for Tressa to work at his side, so whether her aloof indifference was due to shyness, conceit or professionalism, it was hard to tell. At any rate, he had never lost any sleep over it. Spoken for or not, she was *Loring's daughter* and *that* made her off limits under all circumstances--even if he was interested. Which he wasn't.

Now here he was, doomed to baby-sit this spoiled, liberated woman/child for however long it took. Worse yet, he would have to still be on speaking terms with her by the time they arrived at their destination--wherever the hell that was.

"Well?" Jonathan asked with an edge of desperation.

Doubt laced with irritation coursed through Nick. Leaning back, he unconsciously studied Loring, wishing like hell he could come up with some alternative. At last he released a compressed sigh. "So, when do we leave?"

Relief flooded Loring's face. "You'll do it then?"

"Under the circumstances I don't have a hell of a choice. I'll take her to Acacia. It's roughly a three-week flight from here. That should buy you a little time. Delta will enjoy the company, and after I see Tressa safe, I'll do what I can to help."

"I'm thinking that it might not hurt for you to stay off-planet for a while yourself. If that electro blade had gone much deeper..."

Nick's entire left side still ached, a pain he had successfully been ignoring until Jon brought up the subject. For a brief moment he reflected on the night he'd been attacked. *He had just finished loading a shipment into the hold. Turning to key-in the security, he had detected movement in the shadows and a glint off something metallic. He vaguely remembered whirling to ward off the attack, but too late to evade the thrust. Gut-wrenching pain began in his lower back and ripped up his side as he went down.* In that clouded moment, he had recognized one man: his ex-partner, Quint Kendyl.

The pain kept him semiconscious as he lay face down on the scarred surface of the landing zone. And although he had been unable to distinguish little more than the grating edge of voices, there was no doubting the distinctive boots of the man who stood before him. "Kendyl" was the last thought that registered as he slipped into unconsciousness.

"Are you listening to what I'm saying?" Loring broke in.

Without comment Nick leaned forward to deposit another lump of ash into the ashtray.

"I was saying...that if--"

"Yeah, I heard you," Nick mumbled. "I'll deal with it in my own way, Jon. I won't hide, if that's what you're suggesting."

Silence passed as Nick contemplated the plan. "I'm going to be up-front with you. No matter how careful we are, there's no guarantee that Acacia's going to be a safe haven. It's not common knowledge I'm from Acacia, but if someone gets to nosing around, it's on the security records. You have no way of knowing how big this operation is."

"I'm aware of that." Jonathan relaxed. "Look, I know this won't be easy, but I'll see to it you won't regret it. I assure you there will be a double bonus in it for you." A smile tipped the corners of his mouth. "I'll even double your high-risk credits on this one."

"I'm not doing it for the bonus, Jon. Besides, you couldn't afford me even if I were. And as far as regret is concerned," he grimly added, "I started *regretting,* the instant I heard Garrett's voice." He fought down the mental image of Gina.

Ignoring Nick's cynicism, Jonathan continued, "Now I figure if you come back to the place with me, we can work out the details on the way. Then we can bring Tressie on back with us. Besides, I know Mary's going to want to meet you. Hell, she'll probably want to speak privately with you."

Great. Nick nearly groaned aloud "That ought to be real interesting. I just got into port, Jon. Look at me. I'm not only beat, I'm half-crocked."

Questioning his own sanity, Nick rubbed the back of his neck and tried to sort through his feelings. Having hit port three hours ago from a five-week run, he had spent the first hour and a half overseeing, as well as assisting in the unloading of cargo off his ship. He was tired, and the way he figured it, by now he should have been well on his way to getting drunk, counting his winnings and getting laid, in roughly that order.

Though past experience had taught Loring that Nick Banner was a man of his word, he looked at him for the first time since Nick had entered his office. Unshaven; worn leathers; his hair in serious need of a cut; he grimly admitted that Nick Banner looked every bit the rogue. Jonathan was certain Mary would not approve of Tressa leaving with him. In fact, he was tempted to question the wisdom of the plan himself.

Nick's eyebrow arched knowingly. "Second thoughts, Jon?"

"I haven't got time for second thoughts! I'll go on back and square things away at home. You, on the other hand, have exactly two hours to make yourself presentable. We'll meet you back at the *Victorious* at that time."

Swinging his feet down, Nick stood, crushed out his cigarette and turned for the door. "You're the *only* one I'd do this for," he said, pausing briefly at the threshold.

"Yes, I realize I've called in my markers on this one, Nick."

"Damn right you have."

Also by the author
at
Rogue Phoenix Press

Solar Wind
Banner's Series Book Two

In this sequel to *Banner's Bonus*, Zeke Slater poses as an average cargo pilot, yet in reality he's a privateer for a secret alliance of merchants turned vigilante. He captains a cargo ship that is covertly super-charged, heavily armed and anything but harmless beneath its benign guise. The mission is to seek and destroy pirate ships marauding the trade routes.

Four years have passed since Zeke worked for Kira's father. Zeke has changed, and Kira, knowing no more than he allows, senses he's up to no good.

Despite the fact that Kira too has changed, Zeke refuses to see her as anything other than his past employer's unruly daughter.

While sexual tension smolders on board ship, the bad guys lay in wait at the next port.

CHAPTER ONE

Port Chance, Quade's World:
20 A.C. (After Colonization) Earth Date: 2106

Slater rolled to his side, bringing Celeste with him. "Thank you," he breathed, pressing a kiss to her damp forehead.

A slow smile tugged the corners of her mouth. "My pleasure, Captain." Stroking the tightly corded muscles banding his ribs, she felt his heart kicking her palm. "Rest assured there's more where that came from."

"There is, huh?" His voice was husky from the passion they'd just shared. He squeezed her gently. "Ahh, Celeste...if only I could stick around long enough to take advantage of your sweet offer."

Even now as she watched all six-foot-three of him rise languidly from the bunk, Celeste easily read the male power he emanated, the heady virile control he unconsciously held over women. Zeke Slater was a magnificent lover--merciless in his demands, yet at the same time always carefully attentive to his companion's responses. And it was this potent combination of opposites that women found irresistible.

Rising upon her elbows, she watched him cross the room, tawny, sun-streaked hair spilling across his brow as he gathered his clothes off the floor. "Take me with you," she said, her voice a soft pleading purr as he began dressing. Celeste's hopes rose a notch when his hand stilled on the fly of his pants and he smiled as if weighing her words.

"Take you with me where?" He studied her with an intensity that totally addled her brain.

"Come on, Slater," she pleaded. Celeste was stunningly gorgeous, and she knew it as she armed herself with the perfected pout that always got her what she wanted.

Zeke returned to her side, the mattress dipping beneath his weight as he sat down to pull on his boots. "Celeste, we've been all through this before."

Tossing the cover aside, she scrambled to her knees and moved up behind him. "I guarantee you wouldn't be sorry," she whispered, wrapping her scented arms about him, her deep russet hair draping about his shoulders.

Slater's laugh filled the small cabin. "Sorry? Hell, I'd never survive."

"Sure you would." Dipping her head, she gently kissed the jagged scar marring the burnished flesh just below his right shoulder blade. If asked, Zeke would simply laugh and say it was a souvenir. Rumor said it was a grim reminder of a place called Steel and a rescue mission he'd been involved in.

Celeste tasted her way back to his ear. "I'd go easy on you," she cooed. "I promise."

Slater grinned. "You would, huh?"

"Will you at least think about letting me keep a dwelling for you here in port?"

Celeste felt Zeke's body stiffen, and with practiced ease she pressed her firm breasts against the hard-muscled contours of his back. "I know we've been through this before," she purred, pressing her lips to the outer shell of his ear, "but lots of other captains do it."

"I'm not other captains." Gently peeling her arms from about his neck, he rose to his feet. "Come on, Celeste, get dressed. *Solar Wind's* scheduled to lift in two and a half hours, and I still have a slew of things yet to do."

A rush of heat surged through her as she climbed off the bunk, her lower lip pouting in a display of pique. "This arrangement of ours is getting embarrassing."

"Oh, yeah?" He turned to face her. "How's that?"

"All of my friends are aware that I'm the only one you seek when you come to port, and--"

"You'd rather I see someone else?" he interrupted with endearing puzzlement.

"Of course not. It's just that it's becoming noticeable that this is a nowhere arrangement for me."

A muscle clenched along his jaw as he retrieved her fluidly soft dress off the floor and handed it to her. "Don't spoil the evening, Celeste. I've never led you to believe there could be anything more. Besides, we set the rules ourselves. Remember?"

Oh, yes, she knew the damnable rules. And it was true; to remain uninvolved was as much her idea as his. However, between her desire to move up in social rank along with his prowess as a lover, Celeste found herself willing to bend a rule or two.

She dressed quickly, soft fabric hugging every curve as it settled into place. "But what if I want more?" As soon as the words were out, Celeste knew she had just made an irrevocable mistake.

He glanced up, studying her a moment. "Then I'd say it's time to move on."

She came forward. "Look..." she whispered, drawing herself up against him, "We're good together, Slater."

With a soft chuckle he tweaked her nose. "Yeah, I have to agree with you there."

Rising up on her tiptoes, she cupped his face. "So what do you say?"

Second after second ticked by before he finally answered, "You'll have no trouble finding some eager pilot willing to accommodate you."

It wasn't the first time she'd badgered him about keeping a port-side dwelling. But this time she'd crossed the line, and it was obvious her arsenal of beauty and feminine charm held no weapon powerful enough to repair the damage.

"Captain?"

With an air of dismissal, he moved to the wall and pressed a small intercom pad. "Slater here."

"They're preparing to load up, Boss."

"On my way."

Damn him. As easy as that, it was over. Celeste's gaze dropped to the sexy black lace teddy lying rumpled at her feet, and with a rush of indignation she swiftly kicked the fragrant item beneath the foot of his bunk. She'd not be so easily forgotten. Finally, with a sigh of resignation, she stepped into one sandal then the other and came forward.

"Hey..." Placing an arm about her, he drew her near. "I understand they're opening a new 'Made On Earth' shop in the spaceport mall," he said good-naturedly. "Eight weeks ago half my hold was filled with their inventory." Reaching for her hand, he pressed a sizeable cluster of credits into her palm. "Check the place out."

"I don't want your credits, Zeke. There's never been credits between us, and I don't want it now."

"I know," he said, gently cupping his hand over hers. "But I want you to buy yourself something pretty."

"But--"

"Besides, you're going to have a new condo to decorate before you know it."

Pulling out of his embrace, she faced him toe to toe. "But I don't want a condo with anyone else."

Celeste knew instinctively as he quietly escorted her off ship, she would not be invited back.

~ * ~

Running an experienced eye over the belly of his ship, Slater always insisted on performing his own pre-flight check. The way he saw it, there were four things you just never turned over to someone else's care: Your ship. Your gun. Your credits. Or your woman--in roughly that order. It was a rule that had been firmly ingrained over the years.

Finally making his way up the ramp, he entered the main hatch of the *Solar Wind*. No high security consignments this trip. No customs, and no time-consuming red tape to go through at the drop. With a little luck this would be a slide-in-slide-out run.

Easing into the command seat, he watched the U-shaped screen snap to life as he entered destination coordinates into the NAVCOMP. With a final pause he swept the perimeter vid-cams across the surrounding landing zone. To starboard, a private yacht was just lifting. To port, several nearby freighters were taking on freight, and the biker he'd noticed earlier was still circling the LZ. No one seemed particularly interested in the *Solar Wind*, and that was just fine with him.

"I said I'm not moving until I see Captain Slater."

Slater's pre-flight preparations were suddenly shattered by a familiar voice coming from the open hatch.

"And I already told y' the captain's busy," came an equally disgruntled reply from *Solar Wind's* First Officer, Frank Reno.

"Look, just because I'm homeless doesn't mean--"

"Thaaat's right. It don't mean a thang. It ain't got nothin' to do with how y' live. It has to do with the fact ee's busy."

"Then I'll just wait right here until he's not."

"Frank--" Slater called without taking his eyes off the console.

But Frank wasn't listening. He was too preoccupied addressing the shoddy young man standing just outside the main entry. "The captain can't be bothered right--"

"Frank," Slater tried again, this time with a little more volume. "It's okay. Let him come in."

"But, Boss--"

"It's all right. I've got a few moments."

"I need to talk to you, Captain," the young man broke in. "Gibby asked me to give you something important."

"I tried tellin' him yer busy," Frank interrupted, "but he don't seem t'--"

"Its okay, Frank." Stifling a sigh, Slater finished entering the final sequence into the onboard computer before swiveling about. "Come on in, Leon. I have a few minutes."

"I won't take long, Captain." Spearing Frank with a scowl, the rangy youth took off his hat and stepped inside the ship's main hatch to wait. "And just to let you know, sir, my name's Wolf today," he said proudly.

"Then, Wolf, it is." Grabbing what he figured to be his last breath of fresh air, Slater rose to his feet and bounded down a short flight of metal stairs to the entry. "Come on back, while I get us both some coffee."

Ignoring his First Officer's set features and fixed stare, Slater led the way down the corridor and into the galley. "Have a seat, Wolf," he said, motioning toward a built-in booth and hoping that whatever the kid had to say, he'd make it quick. Zeke suspected it had been a long while since Leon had considered any personal hygiene. Without a doubt his unique essence would take a serious toll on the ship's atmosphere.

Leon eased into the booth, clearly making a point of ignoring the canister of biscuits sitting in the middle of the table--a point that didn't escape Slater's notice.

"You hungry?"

"Nah, I just ate. But thanks."

Slater nodded. Truth was he probably hadn't seen a decent meal in weeks. But unless it was handled just so, a simple offer could backfire into an insulting handout. Slater knew the ritual. "Well, in case you change your mind," he said, shoving the container toward Leon. "I'll get us some coffee then you can tell me what's going on."

Had the biscuits not been offered, Leon would never have touched them. But since they were, Slater figured several would be stuffed into a pocket by the time he returned with the coffee.

"Here you go, man," he said, handing the young man a steaming mug.

"Thanks."

"On the house." Zeke settled into the booth across from Leon. "So what's up?"

Wrapping both hands about the warmth of his mug, Leon leveled his gaze. "Gibby wants you to know that there's trouble about to go down."

Slater halted his mug half way to his mouth. "What sort of trouble?"

"Some guy on a jet bike is out there on a serious manhunt. And he's got a T-30 stashed beneath his jacket." Leon shrugged. "Anyway, Gibby figured you might want to put in for an early departure before all hell breaks loose around here."

Slater's eyes narrowed. "Yeah, I noticed the biker," he said, setting his coffee back down. "But I didn't notice the weapon."

"It's concealed. The only reason we noticed it is because we've been watching him for a while. I doubt he's going to give up until he finds who he's looking for.

"Oh, and there's one more thing..." Leon paused to dig into a pocket. "Gibby found this lying out on the landing zone not far from here." Sitting in the center of his outstretched palm was a woman's delicate hair comb adorned with five sparkling jewels.

There was little doubt of the comb's value as Slater reverently lifted it from Leon's grubby hand. "Where did you get--"

"Gibby found it laying out on the LZ."

Slowly turning the comb over in his hand, Slater leaned back in the chair and thoughtfully lifted his gaze. "Somebody's got to be missing this. I suspect the authorities should be notified."

The kid huffed a laugh. "I'm sure they should, but you're the only one Gibby trusts with it."

"Me?"

"Said he wants you to hang on to it until the owner's found."

"But I have no idea when I'll be back this way."

"Just the same, he wants you to hang onto it." Leon took another sip of his coffee then rose from the chair. "Well, I'd better be on my way."

"Wolf, wait a minute." Rising to his feet, Slater reached into his hip pocket and fingered out a credit clip.

Leon held up his hand. "Look, Gibby and I--we don't want money for doing the right thing."

"If you or Gibby should find the owner or need to get a hold of me," Slater said, withdrawing a small card from the clip, "contact this sector. They'll know how to reach me."

Wolf accepted the card. "Okay," he said studying the contact information.

"And...as for both you and Gibby," Slater added, withdrawing a folded credit, "I appreciate the forewarning about the trouble." Laying the credit on the table, he slid it toward the young man. "Consider this a reward."

Leon started to protest when Zeke withdrew another credit from the clip. "Plus," Zeke continued, "eventually somebody's going to be happy to see this comb again and will also want you to have a reward. I can collect from them later."

Several pondering moments passed before Leon finally glanced up. "I suppose there's nothing wrong with accepting a reward."

"I'm telling you, man, people do it all the time."

"Okay," he muttered, snatching up the tender and stuffing it into a pocket. "But Gibby isn't going to be happy about this."

"Well then, Wolf, you just tell Gibby it's the only way I'll hang on to this comb for him."

A wide, toothless grin spread across Leon's young face as he rose from the booth. "I'll tell him, Captain--and thanks."

It was with mixed emotions that Leon made his way back down the boarding ramp. Technically, everything he had said was true. But it was what he hadn't said that was eating at him--the minor little detail he had deliberately left out of the telling.

He liked and respected Captain Slater. In truth, Slater was one of very few who treated him and Gibby with genuine kindness. He just hoped he wouldn't be too angry when he discovered the girl.

And he would discover her. There was little doubt of that.

~ * ~

"Good heavens! Why in lasers did y' have t' invite 'im in?" Frank asked, furiously fanning the air. "Whew-eee!" Striding to the nearby controls, he switched the air filter on high.

Zeke laughed.

"And then," Frank went on, "when y' invited 'im to sit down fer coffee and a friendly little chat...hell, I was beginnin' to think y' were gonna ask 'im t' stay fer breakfast too." Snatching the canister of biscuits off the table, Frank stomped directly to the trash.

"Frank, I need you to put in a request for an immediate lift," Zeke said, ignoring his First Officer's on-going tirade.

"Already in the works, Boss. Clearance should be comin' through any moment."

"Good." Slater's attention was riveted on the comb as he turned it over in his hand once again. "You know what this is, don't you?"

"Yeah, a woman's hair bauble."

"It's a little more than that." On a hunch, Slater carefully pressed what looked to be a touch point along the top ridge of the comb. Immediately a miniature compartment snapped open revealing a tiny hidden micro disc no larger than one of the jewels decorating its surface.

"I'll...be...damned," Frank murmured.

www.ingramcontent.com/pod-product-compliance
Lightning Source LLC
Chambersburg PA
CBHW051428170626
46809CB00006B/2365